SUSAN IN
AMERICA

*Recent Titles by Jane Aiken Hodge
from Severn House*

BRIDE OF DREAMS
UNSAFE HANDS

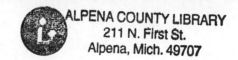
SUSAN IN AMERICA

Jane Aiken Hodge

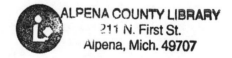

This first world edition published in Great Britain 1998 by
SEVERN HOUSE PUBLISHERS LTD of
9–15 High Street, Sutton, Surrey SM1 1DF.
This title first published in the USA 1998 by
SEVERN HOUSE PUBLISHERS INC., of
595 Madison Avenue, New York, NY 10022.

British Library Cataloguing in Publication Data

Hodge,   Jane Aiken,   1917-
        Susan in America
        1.   English - Massachusetts - Boston - Fiction
        2.   Boston (Mass.) - Social life and customs - 20th century - Fiction
        3.   Love stories
        1. Title
        823.9'14 [F]

        ISBN 0-7278-5353-8

Typeset by Hewer Text Ltd,
Edinburgh, Scotland.
Printed and bound in Great Britain by
MPG Books Ltd, Bodmin, Cornwall.

Author's Note

This is my first book, written long ago, in New York, after the war. Set in New England in 1938–9 it is a period piece now, and my heroine an old-fashioned girl. Like my Susan, I went to Radcliffe College for a graduate year and her impressions of America are mine, but her story is not. The only character drawn from life is Irish Mary, whose name was Annie. Aside from her, plot and characters are fictions, though full of memories for me. Did we really drink all that sherry? But I am not going to change that, or anything else, except literal errors.

Jane Aiken Hodge, 1998

Chapter One

Susan was alone again. Ensconced in the corner by the grand piano, she sipped her tasteless American tea and watched the still-fluid party jell around her. Kaleidoscopic, its groups shifted this way and that; patterns formed and re-formed, avenues opened here and there through the gathering crowd, and friends, suddenly catching sight of each other across the room, made vague, enthusiastic gestures, or, more definite, plunged to meet each other and start at once a new nucleus for a pattern of their own.

Only Susan was alone. But why not join one of the groups? On her right, conversation about Munich. Stray phrases reached her: "poor old Chamberlain . . .", "hopelessly unprepared", "umbrella . . ." On her left, an incomprehensible exchange of technical terms. Football, probably: "Dartmouth's forwards stink . . .", "If it rains on Saturday . . ." But why not join the Munich group? One moved in, casually, of course, the self-possessed international: "I was in England at the time . . ." Then the impressed pause, the questions. It was so easy.

It would be so easy. She took another bitter sip. They could not even make tea in this country. Why on earth had she come? Idiocy. Gloomily, she stared over her cup at the crowd. The dormitory drawing room was filling up. Young men in alarming ties and jackets that studiously failed to match their trousers gesticulated at girls in smooth black

1

(basic, Grace would call it – where had she got to?) or the inevitable bright mismated sweaters and skirts that seemed almost to be the college uniform. Their voices grated on Susan's ear, the men's harsh, the women's shrill; the accents all strange and all ugly. And why did the men have their hair cut like that: short and brutally standing on end? It reminded one of a storm-trooper in a film, though a storm-trooper would be more tidy, would hardly wear a plaid shirt and sloppy shoes. At the thought, her pausing eye caught that of the fair young man in question and she turned, confused, to look out of the window.

It was golden autumn still. The campus (silly word), stretched green and placid between the undistinguished brick dormitories. Here and there a group of girls (what bright colours they wore), or a tree scattering its scarlet leaves accentuated the brilliant green of the grass. The autumn colours were striking enough, it was quite true, if only people didn't expect constant admiration of them: "Isn't our fall gorgeous?" The question was inevitable in a country where so little distinction was made between conversation and cross-examination. The opening shots: "You're English?" "Your first visit?" led up relentlessly to the predictable, the embarrassing, "How do you like America?" and its easier companion query about their extravagant autumn.

No use to tell them that it was the quietness of England, the deeper notes of its autumn that one missed; brown chestnuts shining under the stream in the Magdalen water walk; Christ Church quad a new and brilliant green after September rain; savage beech leaves in an equinoctial wind. There would be the usual note of patronage ("Such a pretty little country", as Mrs Morton would say) and the usual change of the subject. It was not England these people wanted to hear about, but one's impressions of America. And of course the impressions had better be good . . .

If only . . . but what was the use of wishing it? She might be walking the green road from Woodeaton to Elsfield with a prospect of tea in Hall before her tutorial, or, at home, taking her favourite walk by Dead Man's Lane to Icklesham. Instead (for God's sake, why had she come?), she was drinking bitter tea in Cambridge, Mass.

It had seemed such a good idea when she made the plans at Oxford in the spring. It was all to have been so different here. Angrily, she remembered walks under the budding trees on Port Meadow when she had let herself riot in dreams of a new life. At last she was to escape from the magic circle of loneliness that had imprisoned her since those first agonised days when she had been plunged, a solitary country child, into the maelstrom of boarding school. Had it been then that it started? Or had it been a few weeks later, with the news of Father's death? Poor Father. If Mother had been at home they might have operated in time. But Mother had seldom been at home. That time she had been at Brighton (*Brighton*, of all places, Susan could still blush at it), with another man. No wonder Miss Turnbull, breaking the news to Susan, had seemed embarrassed. Remembering, Susan felt again the cold assault of Miss Turnbull's buttons as she tried to draw her sympathetically to her: "We must be a brave girl for mother's sake." She had escaped into the garden and hidden, all the endless afternoon, among the rhododendrons. Had she been escaping ever since?

No getting away from it, coming to America looked like another attempt. And another failure. As she planned it there in Port Meadow, she was to have been the heroine, the belle of parties, the wit in conversation, suffering perpetually from an overdose of champagne and orchids. Instead, here she was, outside again, her nose still pressed against other people's window panes.

There was not even Donald. Or had she been trying to

3

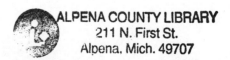

escape from him too? It had certainly been satisfactory to announce, casually, over tea and crumpets, that she was coming to America. His cup had rattled in its saucer: "*America*?" How he had taken her for granted. And why not? "The trouble about you and Donald," Mother had said in one of her frequent bouts of criticism, "is that you don't see any other boys." What one was supposed to do about it was another question, and one which Mother had never attempted to answer.

Well, she had done something all right. Fool and idiot to think crossing the sea would make any difference. This beginning had been incalculably worse than the one at Oxford. The long corridors of her private hell were now peopled, not by detached erudition in academic dress or casual, hawk nosed young Englishmen, but by brisk Radcliffe competence and the overwhelming tribe of Morton.

If she had only been put in a dormitory . . . They said she was lucky to be living with Mrs Morton ("One of the best Boston families," the Dean had said). Lucky? To be out of it again; condemned again to live differently from everyone else. ("Be nice to poor Susan, her father's just died . . ." *Poor Susan*). How could she be expected to make friends here when she was perpetually in a hurry, trying not to be late back and cause a crisis on Brimmer Street? Mrs Morton's head ached if meals were late. The other graduates lived together; gossiped, no doubt, in the bathroom, in the corridors, doing their hair, over meals. They all knew each other well by now; used Christian names, borrowed books, shared incomprehensible jokes before class.

In a whole month, Susan had made only one friend. Still, Grace was a host in herself. She had taken Susan under her wing from the moment they met, both homesick and both lonely, on the library steps that first chaotic day of term. Grace was from the Midwest, "And how I wish I was back there."

4

The daughter of a Psychology Professor, she did everything extravagantly. Her despair that first day of term had made Susan's own misery seem the poor ghost of an emotion. It was equalled only by the gusto with which she had since thrown herself into life at Radcliffe. There was no mean between her extremes, or rather, as Susan had gradually realised, the very extremes provided their own balance. Behind her flamboyant masks of tragedy and comedy, Grace lived placidly, steadily from day to day. If a late composition was a major crisis, a broken heart could hardly be more serious. "But then," she had explained to Susan, "having five brothers is very toughening."

"Having a good time?" As if the thought had been her cue, Grace appeared, followed by a pale, fair haired, bespectacled young man. "This is Merton Dennison," she went on. "Susan Monkton."

His wide, white smile showed one gold tooth. "Merton K Dennison," he corrected. "Call me Bud. We don't go in for surnames much down in Texas where I come from. You're from England, I hear? Quite a little country, that is. I was over there this summer myself."

"Oh, really?" Impossible not to watch the gleaming tooth.

"Yes, ma'am. Worked my way over as a deck steward and spent the summer biking round the country: the Lake District, Dove Cottage, Stratford-on-Avon, the Hardy country – I reckon I didn't miss much. And a very successful trip, too, though I do say so. You must come round for a drink some time and see my collection. It's worth it, I can tell you: I've got postcards of all the places I've been and autographs from everyone I met. I never cheat, mind you; there isn't a card from anywhere I haven't been."

"How about autographs?" Grace's face was guileless as a child's. "Do you have to meet the person for it to count?"

5

When he giggled, pink spots appeared in his pale cheeks. "I'm not quite so hard on myself as that. Of course letters count: I've got a beauty from Masefield explaining why he couldn't see me. And then I've got a lot of autographed letters from people who are dead: Hardy, and so on. It wouldn't be much use insisting on meeting their ghosts; not even in England, would it?" He giggled more than ever and turned to Susan. "How do you like our little old country, Susan? What made you come over here, I wonder? It's not many of the English have the sense. Cambridge isn't a bad little place, is it? Of course it all seems kind of small scale after the University of Texas, but I reckon I can stand it for a year. I'm only going out for an MA, personally. None of that PhD stuff for yours truly. How about you?"

He paused to nibble fruit cake and Susan realised that this question actually required an answer. "I'm just taking an MA too," she said.

"Sensible girl. No use wearing yourself out studying and then ending up teaching in a one-room school the rest of your life. I'm going to be a reporter. I did some stuff for the Texas *Evening Journal* when I was on the other side and they liked it fine. Remind me to show you. I'm to be their Boston correspondent this winter, so I hope plenty goes on up here. I don't expect it will, though. How about some more tea?"

"I'd love some." Anything for a respite from this flow of talk.

He took her cup and vanished into the crowd. Fortissimo now, its pressure on Susan was almost physical. She shrank into herself and looked desperately around for Grace, who had vanished. Why on earth had she let herself be persuaded to come to this thing? Of course it was nice of Grace ("High time you got to know some people, Susan; you never will, living in that morgue on Brimmer Street"), but it was no use. The morgue was all she was fit for. At least she could talk to Mrs Morton, or rather Mrs Morton could talk to her.

At first, as she had listened to Mrs Morton's endless stories about her grandchildren, she had had visions of making friends with them, of going dancing with George, the favourite grandson who was in his last year at Harvard, and spending weekends in New York with his sister, Olga. Or perhaps it would be the twins, Ralph and Randall, described by their grandmother as 'such dear boys', but shy. After she had met George and Olga (if they had been enough aware of her for it to count as meeting them), she had been sure it would be the twins. Fun to have two of them, too.

Fun, however, had not turned out to be exactly the word. The twins were as frightened of her as she was of George and Olga. Their advantage was that there were two of them, so that even their silences were sociable and somehow exclusive. Nice to be a twin. Though their grandmother did not seem to think so. Sitting across the polished dining table from Susan, she held forth tirelessly about the children. George and Olga had always been perfect, but about the twins there were some reservations: "Of course I never dream of criticising my daughters-in-law, but I do sometimes wonder . . ."

For one who would never dream of it, Mrs Morton had a genius for criticising. Not explicitly, of course; it was all done by the most delicate of indirections. She would pause in the middle of reporting Olga's latest dance, sigh, and wish that poor Susan had a gayer time. "We must arrange something for you, Susan." The threat had never been carried out, but constantly recurred, with its latent suggestion that, as a young companion, Susan was something of a disappointment.

Mary, the Irish maid, did not bother with subtleties. From the moment Susan had entered the house she had been talking, first hopefully, then wistfully, now almost obstinately about

7

possible 'beaus' for her. Donald's picture had helped, of course, and she now treated Susan as a miracle of constancy. A doubtful compliment enough from her, it was made all the more embarrassing by the increasing infrequency of Donald's letters. Poor Mary, it was a shame to disappoint her; forty years of waiting on Mrs Morton must have been a dull enough business. "She's quite a member of the family," said Mrs Morton, and it meant that she was free to work for them seven days a week, trotting mop in hand about the old house on feet that more and more unashamedly ached and burst their shoes. Her own life had stopped forty years before when she kissed her boyfriend a last goodbye in Queenstown and set sail for Boston. Since then, the Mortons' life had been hers, her reminiscences undercut Mrs Morton's.

It was she who had told Susan about Mr Morton's death thirty years earlier. "A mild and gentle man, he was", she had pronounced a belated epitaph for Susan's benefit. He had died, apparently, of an overdose of Boston. "Of course, Mrs Morton, she never could abide New York," Mary explained. So the mild and gentle man had finally given in, given up his job in New York and moved back to his wife's old home and his father-in-law's Boston firm to die, quietly and without fuss, within a year. "But then, Mrs Morton was always the man of the family," Mary summed it up.

Her methods, however, did not seem to be altogether masculine. It had been, apparently, to expedite the move back to Boston that her weak heart had first declared itself. "Blue in the face I've seen her," Mary took it all quite seriously, "and breathless. I remember the time Miss Gertrude got engaged to that Italian . . . but it all blew over. Mrs Morton always says she chose Mr Horwood herself, and see how well it worked out? Just look at George and Olga." Like Mrs Morton, Mary idolised them.

Queer, Susan thought, to have left home because she did

8

not get on with her own family and to find herself landed into so much of somebody else's. At least Mother's criticisms had been outspoken, not roundabout like Mrs Morton's: "Susan, can't you remember to put a towel round your shoulders when you brush your hair?", "Susan, your petticoat again", "Susan . . ." Thoughts of the querulous, familiar voice brought a picture of Mother in crimson slacks waving goodbye from the garden gate. She had not come to the boat with Susan. "Peter thinks it would be extravagant," she had explained, and Susan knew that whatever treatment her father had received, her step-father's word was law.

It was Peter who had decided that however inadequate the fellowship at Radcliffe might seem, Susan should take it. *Glad to be rid of me*, Susan thought, not for the first time. "It would do her good to economise," he had said. As if she had ever done anything else.

She looked up. What on earth had happened to Merton Dennison ('Call Me Bud', she reminded herself)? Even in this crowd it should not have taken him as long as this to get her a cup of tea. But of course it had merely been a pretext to abandon her. Ridiculous not to have realised sooner. It was the American way: they made a great fuss of you, said you must come and see them; acted altogether as if you were dearest friends at once, and then, quite simply, vanished. It was high time, after a whole month here, that she stopped letting them make a fool of her.

A whole month. In some ways it seemed far longer than that since she had landed, dizzy and exhausted from eight days of storm and sea-sickness into the aftermath of the New England hurricane. There had certainly been time for several years' worth of disillusionment. First, there had been the discovery that she was not to live in a dormitory but had been boarded out at Mrs Morton's, then, close on its heels

at the same brisk interview with the Dean, the destruction
of all her plans for the year's work.

The best laid plans of mice and men . . . It had been fun
laying them, too. Remembering, Susan heard again the spatter
of April raindrops against Miss Marchant's high window, and
saw her tutor's delicate, determined profile as they talked. The
conversation had hesitated, almost stammered: the romantics,
perhaps? . . . philology? . . . Here, Susan had become suddenly
definite. It was settled: the Elizabethans. She was to do a thesis
on an Elizabethan dramatist so minor as to be unknown to
literary historians. The sidelights to be gleaned on his greater
contemporaries were, said Miss Marchant, most illuminating.
It was to be a genuine piece of scholarship and, again under the
trees on Port Meadow, Susan had imagined it published – by
the Modern Language Association, perhaps – and her future
as a scholar assured: *Some Minor Elizabethan Dramatists*, by
Susan Monkton, Fellow and Tutor of St Rosamund's.

Well, that dream had vanished like the others. The Dean
had wasted little time on it. In the residue of the rapid, ten
minute interview she had pointed out that the requirements for
an MA left no room for a thesis, produced a catalogue, tossed
the names of a few courses into the air – Old High German, The
Elizabethan Prose Romances, Eighteenth Century Poetry –
and dismissed Susan to take further counsel with her tutor.

How nice Professor Winter had been, she thought, staring
vaguely across the room at a tall gesticulating girl with purple
lips and a red sweater. She had been furious and incoherent
when she got to his office, and dangerously near to tears.
Surprisingly, when she left a few minutes later, she had been
almost cheerful about the whole business. Sympathetic, he
had managed to make it all seem faintly comic. The Dean
was a dragon, but must be humoured. He and Susan were
immediately in collusion; what sop for this Cerberus? It was
settled that Susan should be excused one course and do her

thesis instead (miraculously, Professor Winter's subject was the Elizabethan period). As for the other courses, he had laughed: "I don't think they'll give you much trouble."

Of course, in the compromise a good deal had been lost. The learned treatise on John Fuller's plays had turned into a more general work on the Elizabethan dramatists; but after all, she told herself, it had not really been for love of scholarship that she had come. There had been enough of that at Oxford to last a lifetime. It was all very well to dream ("Miss Monkton, well-known authority on the Elizabethan drama"), but was she really a scholar?

What was she anyway? *What is this life?* she asked herself, *what asketh man to have?* An orange leaf drifted slowly past the window and settled on the lawn. Close beside her, a tall, stooped young man with a spotty face (what bad complexions American men had), was lecturing three girls, "Half an hour before breakfast," he said, "and you're all right." They listened admiringly, lips apart and eyes shining with interest. *They can't help but be bored*, Susan thought, *how do they do it?* "If you can't talk, Susan," Mother said, "surely you can look interested?"

If Father had been alive it would all have been different. He and Mother would have got divorced and Susan would have lived with him. Susie, he used to call her. He had taken her to school that first time, and, looking down at her frightened face, had promised, "If you really hate it, Susie, I'll come and take you away." Was she imagining memories, or had he looked ill even then? Anyway, he had never answered her letter asking him to come for her; three weeks later had come that interview with Miss Turnbull; he had been dead. The corridor had been long and silent as she ran from Miss Turnbull's office. Maybe she would never find the way out . . .

*   *   *

11

The crowd was growing restless. Teacups were balanced on chair-arms, people moved vaguely here and there, conversations flagged. Soon it would be decent to leave. What a fool she must look, standing alone all this time. Thank God no one but Grace knew her. Through a gap in the shifting crowd she caught sight of Merton Dennison talking intensely to a small, fascinated girl with blonde curls and glasses. So much for that. So much, in fact, for the whole idea of coming here. "How I wish you had a gayer time," Mrs Morton said. "What, still no letter from the boyfriend?" said Mary. "What do you expect, living in that morgue?" said Grace. Well, what *did* she expect?

Not this, at any rate. Not this loneliness in the midst of a talking crowd. Not this feeling of strangeness, of hostility all around her. "The Americans are such friendly people." Who had said that? It was not true, anyway. To each other, perhaps, or to strangers who were prepared to be perpetually enthusiastic: "Don't you love our fall tints?" "How do you like this little old country?" "You don't have anything like this at home, I expect?"

How tired she was of all the voices, all the ugly, strident, repetitive voices. In the drugstore where she and Grace had lunch they gave her a hamburger when she asked for a ham sandwich and then laughed across the counter at her for being strange. At Radcliffe, the freshmen (bright little things of seventeen with permanent curls) made a game of imitating her accent to her face. And of course at Brimmer Street Mrs Morton's evening-long, droning reminiscences (the summer on Long Island, the year abroad, Olga's first party), were in themselves an implicit criticism of her.

If Father had been alive she would be running his flat for him in London. Donald would come to see them and sit silently listening to Father talk. It was an effort to imagine

12

Donald sitting silently listening to anyone, but never mind. Would Father have liked him? Thinking of the cocked head, the faintly supercilious smile, Susan was compelled to admit a doubt. But then, if Father had been alive she would have known so many people. Donald would have been unimportant. He was anyway, for that matter.

The crowd was really thinning. She could see Grace on the other side of the room; small and animated, she was laying down the law while a square brown hand pushed back the curls from her forehead. Why not go over and join her? As easily cross the Sahara as this room full of cold and voluble strangers.

Across the room, Grace looked up, caught her eye, and smiled. Too many teeth in that smile for beauty, Susan thought, but how it warmed the freckled, irregular face. Grace said something to the man she had, apparently, just convinced (*telling him she's got to do some rescue work*, Susan thought), put down her cup and came over.

"Well," she said, "had enough?"

"Just about." Susan switched long, fair hair back from her face. "How do you do it, Grace?"

"Do what?"

"Oh, talk to people . . . get on. You know."

Grace laughed. "Easy as rolling off a log. You just let yourself go. What a God-awful dull party, though. I can't say I blame you for being bored. But we can do better, we really can. You wait till I get you to a real party. Good lord," she was looking past Susan, "there's Professor Winter. I wonder how they managed to drag him here?"

"Where?" Susan turned as he came up to them. Out of his office, with its dark and bookish background, he looked thinner and uglier than ever; his dark hair, as always, untidy on his forehead, his brown face almost louring until he smiled.

13

Then, miraculously, he was a delighted twenty. And yet, he must be nearly thirty Susan thought. How could he be? How could so much have happened to him?

"Well," his smile worked its miracle, "how's my prize student? Are you liking our poor United States any better these days?"

No, I hate and detest it. She said nothing, but stood – what was Grace's phrase? – with egg on her face.

As usual, Grace came to the rescue. "She grumbles like anything," she said. "I'm afraid she thinks we're a bunch of barbarians."

"Oh, no," she must defend herself. How *could* Grace . . . "It's all so big and untidy . . . and noisy. I don't know." She trailed off into helpless silence. She managed to talk to him all right in tutorials. Why was it so much more difficult here?

"I'm afraid it's partly the hurricane," Grace came to the rescue again. "I keep trying to explain we don't usually have trees down all over the place and no electric lights the way it was when she arrived."

He considered it. "I suppose it must make us seem rather violent. But then," he appealed directly to Susan, "don't you think there might sometimes be something to be said for violence? What about your Elizabethans? They went in for it all right."

"Yes, I suppose they did. But it was all so different somehow." Impossible to make herself clear.

"Why? Because Tamburlaine and Co are safe in books?" He was laughing at her.

Why did she always have to blush? "Oh, no. But theirs was a more romantic kind of violence, wasn't it? I mean, not just gangsters and machine-guns and – oh, I don't know – hurricanes and things."

"Oh, if it's romance you're after . . ." He smiled down at her. What a fool he must think she was. "Seriously, though,"

14

he went on, "I do think you'll find there's something to be said for our extremes: not the gangsters perhaps – don't you think you've been going to too many movies? – but at least we do go about things with gusto. Maybe we haven't got any manners, but give us time; we're a young country, we'll learn."

"It's not exactly manners," she began, but was interrupted by the high, unmistakable voice of Merton Dennison: "Why, *there* you are," he came up from behind her and jogged her elbow, "I've been looking all over for you." The lie was patent. "I don't expect you remember me, Professor Winter," he went on, "but I took your Elizabethan drama course last year and very inspiring I found it."

"Thank you very much." Faintly quizzical, Professor Winter looked at his watch. "Good lord, I must be going. I'll leave you to convert Miss Monkton to America."

"Do you need converting?" He leaned hungrily at her, the gold tooth agleam. "We'll take care of that in no time . . ." His voice trailed on. Half-listening, Susan followed Professor Winter with her eyes. Why did he have to go? She had just been beginning to enjoy herself. It was always fun talking to Professor Winter. He made it easy, somehow. But he had vanished. The crowd was dissolving; only a few persistent conversationalists were at it still. On her right, the party's ebb revealed the group she had first noticed. They were still discussing Munich. Stray phrases reached her: "hopelessly unprepared", "umbrella", "poor old Chamberlain". *Everything goes on for ever*, she thought, suddenly desperate, *and this is hell*.

But Merton Dennison had stopped talking. She looked up. "Of course," she said vaguely, and then noticed that he had turned half-away from her and was staring across the room at the small, curly-haired girl he had been talking to earlier. She looked at her watch. "I really must be going," she caught Grace's eye. "Goodbye." Should she say goodbye

15

to Merton Dennison? She did not know what to say, and anyway he was looking in the other direction. What did one do? She smiled helplessly at Grace, made a little, unobserved movement toward him, gave it up, and left.

Outside, a slight vagueness of outline in the distance, a general greyness of things nearer to, marked the autumnal waning of the day. In the half-light even the violent scarlets, to which so much of her attention had been called, were muted and subdued. Shivering as a chilly Atlantic wind caught her, she turned right on Shepherd Street. It was over, anyway.

The wind hit her afresh as she turned on to Garden Street, and she walked faster, the sidewalk deceptive under her high heels. Pity that her only pair of decent-looking shoes were so uncomfortable. But Grace had insisted that she wear them to the party: "Not those respectable English ones, for heaven's sake." Her clothes were frightful, of course, even she realised that. There had been no need for Olga's one devastating glance to pick out the weak points of her best blue suit: the limp pleats, the dragging hem, the shoulders that would never accommodate themselves to her own. At least Grace had fixed the hem for her, but with no money what could one do? It was all very well for Olga in her fur coat and surplus orchids . . . silly how that casual offer of the smaller of her two orchids had rankled. But then, if one had never had an orchid of one's own . . .

The houses along Garden Street showed here and there a lighted window. Sounds of radio music came out and, from one window, a burst of laughter. At home they would be sitting around the fire after tea. Mother would be long and elegant on the floor: "But don't you do it, Susan, you'd never get away with it."

At the corner by the Continental a young man and a girl were arguing. Her plaid jacket was thrown casually over her

16

shoulders, her moccasined feet set wide and firmly apart. "You can go wherever you damn well please," she said, "I'm going home." Passing them, Susan stifled a qualm of jealousy – or was it homesickness? Impossible to tell. She hurried on.

The Continental and the Commodore Hotels were in a Thursday lull, resting in preparation for the weekend influx of parents and friends. Here, tomorrow night, fathers would be reunited with their daughters; advice would be given, and cheques: "I'd stick to it, if I were you . . .", "Your mother and I think . . ."

Father would have thought coming to America was a good idea. Perhaps he would have come too. They would be living together on one of the little twisting English streets on Beacon Hill. They would ask Professor Winter to Sunday tea; George and Olga would drop in, and perhaps the twins and Roger, Olga's friend that Mrs Morton disapproved of. Nice to think that Olga wasn't perfect after all. Nice name, Roger Merryweather. Susan looked at her watch. Mrs Morton's Thursday bridge party would still be going on. Old Mrs Merryweather was a dear: "How she does overbid her hands," Mrs Morton said, and it was just like her, she did everything lavishly to match her opulent figure.

Fay House looked deserted. What a crowd, and what a coming-and-going there had been that first day. The taxi from the dock had cost two dollars and the driver had sneered at her tip (they were so rude, the Americans), and all the time she was talking to the Dean she had been terrified she was going to be sick. At least nothing could ever be as bad as that again. Or could it? Her arrival at Mrs Morton's house had run it fairly close. That had been a Thursday, too, and the witches' sabbath had been in full swing over the bridge table, the house a nightmare place of shadows and stale memories. No wonder Mr Morton had died of it. Or had it died with him? At any rate it had stopped thirty years ago. It was like living

17

in a historical monument: "This is where the beautiful Miss Thorpe made her début. The portrait over the mantelpiece shows her in her bridal gown (note the Valenciennes lace)."

Walking through the dark house, one almost expected to open a door and see the blonde, beribboned girl of the portrait bending again over her bridal bouquet with that strange, faintly triumphant, faintly disappointed expression. And in the long evenings when Susan played double dummy with Mrs Morton and listened to her stories of her girlhood, it was sometimes hard to be sure which figure was the reality, which the ghost. It was a relief when Mrs Morton emerged from the tide of reminiscence to complain about the way Roger Merryweather wasted Olga's time when she came to Boston: "She has such a brilliant future ahead of her."

The path across Cambridge Common was beaten hard by the constant tread of academic feet. Professor Winter hurried across it three mornings a week to repeat, at Radcliffe, the lecture he had just given at Harvard. "Oh, he takes out the jokes," Grace had explained to Susan. Pleased with herself, Susan had retaliated with the story of the Oxford misogynist who spent the first few lectures of every term telling stories of increasingly riotous impropriety in the vain hope that they would weed out the women from his audience. Warned in advance, Susan said, they stayed there doggedly and blushed.

"But what were the stories?" Beneath her extravagance Grace was always practical, and Susan, blushing herself, had said she could not remember. That was the day Grace told her about Professor Winter. Susan dodged to avoid a football. Poor Professor Winter. She looked to right and left at the crossing into the Square. American traffic was as wild and uncontrolled as everything else. Was there really anything to be said for violence? Professor Winter's own life had been violent in a way. His wife had left him for a man

18

who sold vacuum cleaners in Minnesota. She had taken their three children and vanished one summer afternoon. "At least she must have been fond of them," Grace said. And he still believed in violence. It was very strange.

"I beg your pardon." Susan had bumped into an amorphous Cambridge lady in tweeds.

Outside the Co-op she paused. She needed a fountain pen that worked for taking lecture notes. *"Do her good to economise,"* she heard Peter's voice. If she spent any more money this month she would have nothing at all extra for Christmas. Economise. If she spent less on lunch, she would starve; even Peter would hardly call soup and a sandwich extravagant. But the subway cost twenty cents a day; six days a week, a dollar-twenty. Say nine months; eleven dollars. It was no joke.

Anyway, no fountain pen. She dodged out among the traffic. It was much worse than Piccadilly Circus. You wouldn't think anything could be. The policeman on duty was standing in his box above the mêlée, ignoring it blandly as usual. "You want to keep out of their way," Grace had told her, "they don't like the British much."

But she was safe on the island. Professor Winter's wife used to work in Schrafft's in the Square. She'd had lunch there with Grace one day before she'd had the courage to explain about her twenty-five cent maximum and Grace told her the whole story. "Of course, the Harvard Dames snooted the hell out of her," Grace had said, "you can't really blame her for getting sick of it."

The stale smell of summer still lingered on the subway steps. Susan felt in her purse. As usual, she had no dime and had to get change. Wearily, the man in the booth took her dollar and pushed the little pile of silver towards her. As usual, she did not have the courage to count it. "Don't you find our decimal system wonderfully simple?"

What must Professor Winter have felt like? Had his wife told him she was going? Or had he just got home from class and found her gone and a note in an old milk bottle? But of course it was the summer; he wouldn't have been at class. No wonder his face had that dark, closed look. It all changed when he smiled. Did he smile more when they were first married? For one can smile, and smile . . .

A train sidled into the station. It had been ages before she understood about the station's two levels – one for arrival and one for departure – and why you never saw anyone getting out. That was the kind of thing that made one feel alien: it was not understanding the little things. As she moved forward, a man pushed her aside and got in ahead of her. Professor Winter was right, they had no manners at all here. It wasn't even as if there was a crowd. But of course, if she did have to stand, it would never occur to anyone to offer her a seat. *I could be dying*, she thought. But after all, as Grace said, why should they?

Why indeed? What am I worth anyway? She stared at the advertisements: "Let up, light up." A young woman in a scarlet bathing-suit; gardenias, "P.M." Did they do nothing but enjoy themselves, these people? When you looked at the glum, pale faces in the subway it seemed unlikely. They all looked so unhealthy; the women thin as rakes, with tense, hungry faces, the men sloppy-looking and running to pimples. At home, she had always been considered pale and rather delicate-looking; here, she felt positively rubicund. 'The English miss', Professor Winter called her when he was pleased with her work.

He was nice to work for. He made everything so easy. Father would have liked him, no question about that. Poor Father. Had he known where Mother was, that weekend he went into hospital? Was it because he knew what was going on that he had insisted that Susan go to boarding school? "*If you really hate it, Susie, I'll come and take you away.*" Had

he known even then that he never would? No, he had never
lied to her. If Mother hadn't been at Brighton (thank God it
had not been Peter she was with) . . . maybe they would have
operated in time? No good going through all that again. He
was dead. What would it feel like? He hadn't even left her
a message; there should have been a note; the feeble voice,
"Paper, please, I want to write to my daughter." But there
had been nothing.

The train was gathering speed after Kendall Station. Mrs
Winter must have left a note. If she had told Professor
Winter he would never have let her go. He was far too
determined a person. He looked quite savage, sometimes,
but that was probably his wife's fault. She even refused to
give him a divorce, Grace said, because she was a Catholic.
"She just wanders round the West from Confessional to
Confessional."

"But how on earth do you *know?*" Susan had asked, and
Grace, already the old inhabitant, explained, "Everyone
knows everything in Cambridge." Poor Professor Winter.
She had heard the girls talking about him before class and
it was obvious that anything they did not know they invented
lavishly. When he came in, tall and thin and potentially savage,
a sudden hush would fall, punctuated, perhaps, by a quickly
suppressed giggle. They might gossip behind his back, Susan
thought, but there was no question that they were afraid
of him.

The train grumbled its way up to the surface. It was almost
dark, and the lights were lit on the bridge and along the great
curve of Memorial Drive. They sparkled back at themselves
from the water, suddenly magic under a scattering of stars.
"*Would I were heaven that I might gaze with all those eyes
on thee.*" Gilbert Murray? Very likely. She'd written a poem
herself about a falling star she had seen with Donald, but
she had never had the courage to show it to him. Just as

21

well, too. Poetry was hardly his line. Anyway, it was lost now. "You write poetry?" Professor Winter had said at her last tutorial. It had been more statement than question. "Of course you do. Well, take my advice, and keep it ten years before you show it to anyone." Had he shown some to his wife? Josephine, her name was. What could she be like? He must have been tremendously in love with her; the marriage had nearly ruined his career, Grace said.

The train was slowing down. She stood up, swayed on her unwontedly high heels and caught a strap to steady herself. The doors opened (what happened if you caught your heel?), and she stepped on to the platform. Only two other people got out: a young man and a girl. As Susan watched, he put a protective arm over her shoulder and urged her towards the exit. Susan stood for a moment in the lonely darkness as the train gathered momentum, snarled, and was away. In the gap of silence it left, the river looked more peaceful than ever. If only she was going home to quietness . . . But Mrs Morton's Thursday bridge would still be going on; cigarettes still smouldering in ashtrays, fleshless old hands keeping score, brittle nails tapping against the cards they dealt.

Still, it would mean fewer questions about the party. It seemed ages ago already. It was just another failure anyway, why think about it? There was nothing to be done about any of it. She pushed through the turnstile and went slowly down the dirty stairs. She might as well make up her mind to another dull, studious winter. She would go to lectures, go to tutorials (they were fun, at least), eat her soup and sandwich with Grace and come home to listen interminably to Mrs Morton's stories. That was all, and it might be worse. At least the loneliness would not be acute and public as it had been this afternoon.

The subway under Charles Street smelt sour and airless. Everything was stuffy. Or is it me? she wondered. "*Where'e're*

I go is Hell, myself am Hell." She passed the garage and
the silent, unlit windows of her favourite antique shop and
turned down Pinckney Street. Mother had taken to buying
antiques for people on commission after Father died. That
was how she had met Peter. Anyway, it had not been Peter
at Brighton.

Brimmer Street was quiet, as usual. Only the street lamps
and one excluded cat washing itself on a step showed that
here, too, life went relentlessly on. Susan climbed the steps
of No. 35, fumbled for her key and fitted it into the reluctant
lock. The door swung back into the dark hall and a faint,
sweet smell of decay came out to her. It was the smell of
old dresses in wardrobes, the smell, she had finally realised,
of the perfume Mrs Morton always wore, but stale now and
suggestive of mummies and great lengths of faintly yellow
linen. No wonder Grace called the house a morgue.

Chapter Two

Susan tiptoed up the shadowy stairs. If she could only get past the drawing room door without Mrs Morton seeing her . . . She knew by experience that it was no use taking the elevator that had been installed because of Mrs Morton's heart. Its creaking and laborious progress would betray her at once.

She paused on the first floor landing. As usual, the heavy velvet curtain was drawn only halfway across the drawing room door. Mrs Morton liked to know what was going on in her house. She would have to risk it. Mrs Morton's voice came out to her: "Of course, if I hadn't trumped Eliza's ace they'd have got them all." The postmortem was in progress. Oh, that Thursday bridge . . .

Mrs Morton had instituted it the year she moved back to Boston, the year Mr Morton died. She had hardly missed a winter Thursday since. For thirty years the four of them had sat, week after week, around the card table in the high drawing room, while dust settled thick on the picture frames and heavy on the everlastings, and the blue loose-covers faded to lavender. Only in the portrait over the mantelpiece they still showed brilliant peacock behind the bride's train.

Mrs Merryweather's voice joined Mrs Morton's in a low murmur of assent. *Now.* Her bag tucked casually under her arm, Susan walked quickly past the door without looking in. The thing was to look as if she had forgotten all about them.

"Why, Susan," Mrs Morton's voice told her it was no use. "There you are at last. Come and tell us all about your party."

Trying to look surprised, she turned back into the room. "Hullo," she said. "How are you, Mrs Merryweather? I thought you'd still be hard at it."

Mrs Morton and Mrs Merryweather were alone. As usual, Mrs Morton was sitting, wrapped in her taffeta quilts, on the old blue sofa. Submerged in the gently rustling folds, she looked young and frail, the thin face curiously unlined, the long hands soft and white. It was not for nothing that she spent every Thursday morning at Elizabeth Arden, coming home smooth-skinned and azure-curled in time for chicken-à-la-king and the Thursday bridge. Looking at her, Susan remembered her original shock of surprise when the neat ankles had swung to the floor and Mrs Morton stood up, revealing the stocky little figure the quilts so successfully camouflaged. No wonder she only moved from her sofa for serious occasions and meals. Sitting there, the fragile invalid, she had her world at her feet.

"You must have had a good time," the sweet voice was reproachful. "You're late. Eliza Larraby's giving a party for Betty Jane so she had to leave early. We hoped you'd get here in time to take her hand, but now Lavender's gone too, so it's no use."

"That's too bad." Susan thanked God for an agony missed. She was no match for the Thursday bridge club and could never decide whether she minded the open or the implied criticism more. The nightly sessions of double dummy with Mrs Morton were bad enough. Under that sweet and piercing eye she became paralysed, her natural casualness degenerating into something that amounted, in Mrs Morton's view, almost to insanity. Too bad she had never paid attention when Mother tried to teach her bridge. But it was like dancing; she had felt so

26

sure she would make a fool of herself that she could never do anything right. "You certainly don't take after your mother," Peter had said on the only occasion they had taken her dancing. No doubt he'd refused to take her again: "*I won't be made a public fool of.*"

"So, it was a good party?" Mrs Merryweather got up from the bridge table and moved heavily over to an easy chair. "That's better!" She settled her vast, satin-clad bulk into the chair with a sigh of relief, her grey lisle knees mountainous in the low chair. "Really, Emmeline, you're going to have to get me a bigger chair to play in one of these days," her smile shone across the flat, red face. "It's all right for Lavender and Eliza, they're young, they can stand it; but we're not getting any younger, you and I."

"Is it getting any better out, Susan?" Mrs Morton did not like to be reminded of her age. If she had not known Mrs Merryweather for the kindest of seventy-year-old sentimentalists, Susan would have suspected her of doing it on purpose. But it was pure innocence, she was sure. Mrs Merryweather hardly seemed to remember, let alone regret, the far off days when she and Mrs Morton had been débutantes together. Living, as she did, contented and platitudinous in a present full of grandchildren, it never occurred to her that, however she might talk about being a frail old invalid, Mrs Morton still lived in that remote past. She might call herself a poor old lady, but she did not want other people vulgarising her fragility by talk of her seventy-eight years.

"I'm so glad you had a good time," she went on. And then, to Mrs Merryweather, "Poor Susan has such a dull life of it with an old thing like me."

"Oh, no." Susan provided the required response.

"Did you meet anyone interesting?" Mrs Morton's voice betrayed the age-old, inevitable curiosity. She was just as bad as Mary; it was just that she was a shade less obvious about it.

"Not really. Grace was there, of course." She must make it sound reasonably interesting for them. "There was a queer man from Texas called Merton Dennison. He collects autographs." The announcement fell flat. They were not interested in queer people from Texas. "Oh, and Professor Winter was there."

The afterthought was more successful. "Oh, yes, David Winter," Mrs Morton took it up. "You knew him didn't you, Martha? The New Bedford Winters. His elder sister was quite a friend of Gertrude's for a while; an odd girl, I thought. But then they're a queer family; Gertrude says David could have done anything, but he would go into teaching. And then he married that dreadful girl; out of a soda fountain, or something. But of course Gertrude stopped seeing Julia Winter long before that. What was it she said about her? Really, my poor old memory . . ." She trailed helplessly off into silence.

She wants it both ways, Susan thought, to be frail and helpless and yet not to be old. How like her; the world on a silver salver. Anyway, she had missed the latest story about Professor Winter's wife.

Mrs Merryweather had been heavily restless in her chair. "I don't know why you have such a prejudice against teaching, Emmeline. It's a very fine profession, after all. To teach the young ideas . . ."

"Oh, yes," Mrs Morton was sweet and deadly. "It's very high-minded, of course. I'm afraid I'm just a practical old woman, Martha, and I don't like to see young men going into something with so little future."

They were launched on a discussion Susan had heard time and time again. It was comic, she thought, how they argued in abstractions about what was actually such a personal matter. Mrs Merryweather's grandson, Roger, and Mrs Morton's granddaughter, Olga, had been friends, as Mrs Merryweather said, from the cradle. Now, Roger insisted that he wanted to teach. Without saying anything definite (she seldom did if she could help it), Mrs Morton was busy making it clear that she did not think a schoolmaster would be a suitable husband for Olga.

There was more to it than that, though, and Susan had heard all about it over the nightly double dummy. She was becoming an expert on the family history. *I ought to write it up some time*, she thought, settling more comfortably in her chair by the window as Mrs Merryweather played a familiar gambit, "After all, think of dear President Eliot . . ." They were safe for half an hour at least. Susan stared out at the dark river, her thoughts contrapuntal to the discussion that was taking its familiar course behind her.

The trouble really lay in the diverging histories of the two families since those remembered days when Martha Tilsit had been Mrs Morton's bridesmaid (in pink satin and roses; "It didn't suit her very well, she was too fat, even then"), and Mrs Morton had come up from New York to return the compliment as matron of honour a year later when Martha surprised everyone by marring Roger Merryweather the First.

The Merryweathers had stayed in Chestnut Hill, while their old house crumbled around them and two successive Rogers fumbled disastrously with the family business, gave it up, and died. Now, Mrs Merryweather's younger son was doing his charming best to pull things together, but Mrs Morton, who never actually talked about money, managed to imply that the prospects were not encouraging. And his nephew, Roger the Third who admittedly had the brains of the family, refused to go near the business. Now in his last year at Harvard, he divided his time between trips to New York to see Olga, and visits to one New England school after another. There were few that did not boast their historical Merryweather

29

and his chances looked good, "But schoolmastering," said Mrs Morton. "Really!"

While the Merryweather fortunes had dwindled, the Mortons' had flourished. Mr Morton's death had merely meant that the family affairs passed into the capable hands of his wife and his son, Donald. The Depression, which gave the quietus to the Merryweathers' prosperity, had been merely a parenthesis, a momentary breathing space, in the Morton story. Now, with Donald in command in Boston, Gertrude treading a safe and social path in New York, and William (the father of the twins), satisfactory, if not outstanding, in Chicago, Mrs Morton did not need to explain that her own quiet mode of life was from choice, not necessity. While the old house grew dustier and dustier, and Mary less and less able to cope with it, Mrs Morton lived happily in her own memories, and her plans for her grandchildren's marriages. *She has no present*, Susan thought, *only a past and a future*.

In that future, Olga's marriage loomed large. She was the oldest and the favourite grandchild, and her grandmother's strongest hopes centred around her. An ambassador, perhaps, or a Lowell; nothing less. No wonder she did her best to discourage the inconvenient childhood friendship with Roger Merryweather. In the old days Mortons and Merryweathers had had adjoining summer homes in Vermont; the habit of summers together had held through the changes in the Merryweather fortunes, and Roger and Olga had shared too much poison ivy and too many childhood diseases for Mrs Morton's present comfort.

A silence made Susan look up. The two old ladies had reached the usual deadlock, and as usual it was Mrs Merryweather who finally changed the subject. "Is George going to the Larrabys' tonight?" She was still eating cake.

"Yes, indeed." The subject was a happy one. Mrs Morton was prepared to talk for hours about the possibilities in

George's friendship with Betty Jane Larraby. "And he's taking Betty Jane to the game on Saturday," she went on, then paused. A momentary cloud of discomfort shadowed the smooth face, then vanished as quickly as it had come.

Mrs Merryweather noticed nothing. "That's very nice," she said. "I do like to see the young people enjoying themselves. Are you going, Susan?"

"No, I'm not." Who would ask her? Merton Dennison? Ridiculous. He had obviously not meant the invitation for a drink. He probably said it to every girl he met. It was just the American line.

"That's too bad. All work and no play, you know, Susan . . . What a pity Olga's not coming up for the game, Emmeline. Roger's longing to see her, I know. He can't afford to keep running down to New York, poor boy." Mrs Merryweather was cheerfully frank about the family's restricted finances.

"I'm thinking of going to New York for Christmas," Mrs Morton went off at a vague tangent. "Gertrude's been begging me to come . . . Dear, how my head does ache. Susan, dear child, would you fetch me my medicine?"

When Susan returned with the familiar bottle and spoon, Mrs Merryweather had gone. Mrs Morton took the bottle from her, poured herself a lavish spoonful, and swallowed it. "Such an exhausting day. I thought Martha would never go. She does talk so. I think I'll just rest for a little while before supper, Susan. Would you be a dear child and tell Mary not to have it till half past?"

Mary was making pastry. "Not till half past?" She pushed her hair back from her forehead with the back of a floury hand. "Well, that's a comfort. With Olga coming Saturday and all, I'm sure I don't know which way to turn."

"Olga coming?" Susan was surprised.

"Didn't Mrs Morton tell you? She had a special delivery from her this morning. She's coming for the game, of course.

31

You would think she could have let us know a little earlier, but not our Olga. Too busy going to parties to write, I expect. How was your party, Susan?"

"Oh, all right." So Mrs Morton had known Olga was coming all the time she was talking to Mrs Merryweather. No wonder she had looked uncomfortable.

"That's good. You can't spend all your time writing to that Donald of yours. If you took my advice, Susan, you'd be finding yourself a nice beau over here and forgetting all about him."

Susan laughed. It was impossible to resent Mary's advice. "I'll think it over, Mary. What kind of pie is it?"

"Lemon meringue for Olga, of course. I'll never have time tomorrow." At least it was easy to distract Mary. "I've seen her eat five helpings when she was a girl. Roger was just the same. How those two did carry on." She closed the oven door.

"Did they?" Susan bent to stroke the old orange cat. "How are you, Ginger?" She tickled him under the chin and he purred ecstatically.

"He's all right," Mary said. "Just restless because of the fish. And if I'm going to get it cooked you'd better be off with you and leave me be."

"Right you are." Susan paused for a minute to look out of the dining room window at the lights of MIT across the river. Mary was quite right about Donald. It would be far better to forget about him. But how could she, when there was nothing else to think about?

She climbed the stairs slowly. A glance into the drawing room showed Mrs Morton quiescent on her sofa. She smiled faintly at Susan: "So tired."

The next floor was heavily quiet. Light from the hall lay across the floor of Mrs Morton's bedroom and caught itself in the great three-fold mirror on the dressing-table. A stronger whiff of Mrs Morton's pervasive perfume came out to Susan as she started up the stairs to her own room. No doubt about it, the elevator had its uses in this high, narrow house with its five floors and two rooms to a floor. Mary, who lived on the top floor of all, was perpetually creaking her way up and down again on some nameless imperative errand. Cheerfully scatterbrained at sixty-five, she rivalled even Mrs Morton in her forgetfulness. The only difference was that she did her own errands. Susan did Mrs Morton's.

The street lamps from Brimmer Street shone in at the high window of Susan's room. Mrs Morton had apologised for giving her a room at the front of the house on that first day when the ground was still active under her feet and she was being swept by recurrent spasms of nausea. The big guest room at the back was kept for the family, she said; this was the room George and Olga had had when they lived there . . . they had always liked it . . .

"I'm sure I shall, too." Susan had managed a momentary heartiness. And as a matter of fact, she did. She liked the view down into the quiet street and the glimpse, through a gap in the houses opposite, of the complicated roofs and chimneys of Beacon Hill. Still more, she liked the room's smallness in a house full of large vacancies, its feeling of privacy. If she could only have shut the door, it would have been perfect. *"Like a high born maiden, in a palace tower . . ."* An ivory tower perhaps, but still . . .

Unfortunately, doors were never shut in that house. Thinking of this, Susan turned on the light and shut hers firmly behind her. She was always a rebel at night, but in the daytime she had largely given in. There had been nothing else to do. If she shut herself in and tried to work, Mrs Morton or Mary would inevitably appear, knock, look in and ask if she was feeling all right. Curious that at the same time one could be so lonely and yet so long to be alone.

And there was no privacy at all. When she gave in and tried

to work with the door open, her morning was punctuated by visits from Mary and plaintive calls from Mrs Morton in her room below. The big central stairwell acted as a kind of whispering gallery in the house, so that Mrs Morton could summon her even from the drawing room two floors below without straining her gentle voice. In fact, if you stood on the top landing, you could hear everything that was going on from floor to floor below. That was why Mrs Morton liked doors left open; she liked to keep in touch. After Susan had counted seven errands in one morning, the plaintive voice from below: "Susan, dear child, would you fetch me my glasses . . .", ". . . my medicine, my head does ache so . . .", "I believe I left my book upstairs . . .", she had given it up and taken to working in the Radcliffe library.

She looked at her watch. Quarter past seven. What an endless afternoon. By now it was hardly worth trying to do any work before supper. She threw her jacket on the bed and sat down at her dressing-table. The too-familiar face looked gloomily back at her from the mirror. Did she look like Father? He had been handsome. "You should have seen him when he was young," Mother had said in one of her rare bursts of communicativeness. "You've got his eyes, Susan, anyway."

Susan looked at them. Too bad that she'd gone and combined them with fair hair. 'The albino', they'd called her at school. If it would only curl it might not be so bad. She shook it angrily back from her face and it fell, soft and limp, on her shoulders. Grace wanted her to have it cut off and have a permanent wave. Of course she couldn't afford it; that would mean no lunch at all. It was all very well for Grace . . .

Donald's picture grinned at her from beside the mirror. Was she running away from him? If she was, how absurd to wait for his letters so impatiently. What had been the matter,

34

anyway? His damp, proprietary kisses? "You're such a dear little thing, Susan." She looked again at the thin face in the mirror. Whatever it might be, surely not the face of a dear little thing?

That had been at the Commem Ball. She shied slightly at the memory. *"Don't forget you don't know how to drink, Susan."* Her mother's voice again. But it was Donald who hadn't. She blushed at an angry memory of fumbling hands. *"Such a dear little thing."* Ridiculous to pretend she was in love with him. What would have happened if she had been? He had insisted on seeing her back to college; the curve of the High quiet in the early dawn. "Are you sure you have to go, Susan? It's very early . . ." She had been sure, and next afternoon had come his red roses (Donald was nothing if not conventional), and they had said no more about the incident. Only, she had been surer than ever that it was a good idea to come to America. Of course it was flight.

She looked at the other photograph. If Father had been alive . . . Gazing vaguely into the mirror she let herself drift into daydream. She and Father were living on Beacon Hill. Donald arrived from England; he could not live without her. She was just trying on her wedding dress (it had a veil like the one in Mrs Morton's portrait), when a plaintive voice hailed her from downstairs, "Susan, it's supper time."

"Coming." She ran a comb through her hair and ran downstairs, brushing impatiently at her shoulders as she went. *"Always put a towel round your shoulders when you do your hair."* Oh, so much advice, and so little else . . .

"Olga's coming up for the weekend." Mrs Morton announced it casually as they sat down.

"Yes, Mary told me." No reason to look more self-conscious than Mrs Morton did. After all, the Morton–Merryweather politics were no affair of hers.

"George arranged it." Mrs Morton felt the need to explain.

"He's taking Betty Jane to the Game, and her cousin Spencer Russell's coming up for the weekend, so they asked Olga. How nice it would be . . ." Her vague eyes surveyed possible developments.

Susan was wondering what Olga would do if she discovered that her visit had been concealed from the Merryweathers. Impossible to tell. She knew nothing about Olga except that she frightened her. It was not only Mrs Morton's endless stories of her social successes; it was the way she took over the house when she came to stay. However little she might be at home, she was unmistakably in command. The gloves in the hall, the breath of a fresher perfume on the stairs, the fur coat over a chair in the drawing room were the signs of her reign. Even when she was out, the old house seemed, somehow, gathered together, waiting for her return, and Susan, going quietly in and out on her academic, uninspiring errands, felt herself less interesting and more of an alien than ever. She neither lived the life nor talked the language.

She was always relieved when Olga left and the house settled back into its everyday shadowy self. The telephone calls, the orchids in the refrigerator, the taxis that stopped at the door were too acute a reminder of everything that she herself was missing. Still, she thought, pushing back her chair, if it came to a battle between Mrs Morton and Olga, it should be worth watching. When Greek meets Greek . . .

Chapter Three

Battle was joined almost at once that Saturday morning. Over coffee and coddled eggs (Mrs Morton thought them indigestible if boiled), Susan watched the first skirmish in silence, oppressed as always by Olga's overwhelming poise.

Only in advertisements, she thought, were people so immaculate after a night on the train. It was unfair. She remembered her own untidy hair and rumpled suit when she landed from the boat. How did Olga do it? There was not a crease in her grey flannel suit, not a crumple in the scarlet blouse that brought out the heavy whiteness of her skin and the lacquered black of her hair. Still to be neat, still to be dressed . . . Only the faint blue circles under her eyes betrayed her tiredness, and, reluctantly, Susan admitted to herself that they were more becoming than not.

Because normally the face was almost formidably calm. More than her general poise and grooming, this was what intimidated Susan. It had a mask-like quality. Worn down by constant admiration, it was smooth and hard and perfect as a stone polished for centuries in the ebb and flow of the sea. Impossible to tell what went on behind the mask. Only, occasionally, there would be a clue, a flicker, as now when Olga, white hands encircling her coffee cup, pursued her elusive grandmother with another question. "Did you tell old Mrs Merryweather I was coming up?"

Mrs Morton was vague. More than usually Dresden this

37

morning in a pale ruffled housecoat, she made an admirable foil to Olga's dark sophistication. The white hair was still neat and faintly blue from its Thursday setting; the hands, playing now a little nervously with her rings, were soft and white as Olga's. "More coffee?" She countered question with question. "I hope you slept all right. Though I can't say I approve of all this running around in sleepers. It's not very ladylike."

Delicately, Olga suppressed a yawn. "Oh . . . ladylike. Come now, Gran, admit that the age of ladies is past. I haven't been offered a seat in a bus for years . . . at least not for the right reason. Anyway, you ought to be grateful I don't sit up. Roger always does. Did you say they knew I was coming?"

Good for her, Susan thought, rescuing charred bread from the toaster. "Have another piece, Susan," Mrs Morton took advantage of it. "Mary, we need some more bread."

As usual, Mary was standing in the doorway, her hand on the doorknob to keep up the pretence that she was in transit. Her habit of listening to the conversation was one that thirty years of Mrs Morton's innuendo had been unable to shake. She returned with the bread. "And how's your mother, Olga?" She played the old family retainer to perfection.

"Oh, very well." Olga smoothed imaginary hair into her pompadour. "She's starting a bridge club like yours, Gran. Tuesday, though. The maids are out on Thursday. I suppose yours is still going strong?"

"Yes, indeed. Martha Merryweather was saying the other day that we ought to celebrate our anniversary next month. It's thirty years since we had our first session."

"Is it really?" Olga pounced. "How is Mrs Merryweather? Did you say they know I'm up?"

"I expect so . . . Coffee, Susan?"

"No, thank you." Susan was wishing she could get away.

Olga might be on holiday, but she had to work. It was half past nine already. She moved restlessly in her chair. But Olga was holding out her cup for more coffee. "You expect so, Gran? You didn't happen to tell Mrs Merryweather, then?"

"Let me think." Mrs Morton pantomimed elaborate thought. "I really can't remember. My poor old mind is getting worse every day; Susan will tell you . . . but George probably told Roger. They have a class together; philosophy, I think, or something."

"Oh, George . . ." Olga breathed sisterly doubt. "Well, I shall call up and make sure. Roger can come to lunch tomorrow, can't he, Gran?" She pushed back her chair and stood up, tall, calm and determined.

Mrs Morton never said 'no' if she could help it. Now she temporised, "Well, I've got the twins and George already. I do think it's a little hard on Mary. Besides, I was thinking it might be nice to ask Spencer Russell. After all, he is taking you to the Game."

"I expect that'll be quite bad enough. He always used to be a frightful drip."

Mrs Morton frowned slightly into the bright morning sunshine which revealed a mass of tiny wrinkles in the delicate skin. "Susan, my dear, would you draw the curtains just the tiniest bit?"

Like its owner, the house was too old for sunshine's revelations. Motes of dust danced in its path, the faded patches of carpet and cushion were suddenly visible; one noticed the cobwebs high up in the corner, the broken tiles in the old fireplace; the marks on the paint.

Pausing, observant at the window, Susan heard Olga's voice at the telephone in the hall. "Oh dear, how maddening . . ."

Mrs Morton rustled the newspaper. "I am so tired of those Czechs. I really don't see why everyone gets into such a state about them. What I say is every one should

mind their own business and there'd be a deal less trouble
in the world."

She said it very often and Susan had learnt to hold her
tongue, if not her temper. To argue politics with Mrs Morton
was like trying to teach a parrot Greek. You broke your
heart, you exhausted your logic, and at the end all you got
was 'Pretty Polly'. If possible, Mary was worse. Taking
her politics readymade from the priest, she saw communists
under every stone. The only time Roger had come to Sunday
lunch she had called him a fellow traveller (her ultimate
in condemnation), because, arguing with George, he had
maintained that there should be a teachers' union. Poor
Roger . . .

Olga was sullen in the doorway. "He's away for the weekend.
I do think you might have told them I was coming up, Gran.
He only decided to go yesterday, his mother says."

Mrs Morton put a thin, smooth hand to her head. "I never
heard of anything so inconsiderate as you children. How do
you expect an old lady like me to remember things . . . Susan,
my dear, don't wait if you've finished."

At Radcliffe, the library was less crowded than usual. Anyone
with any sense was away for the weekend, or at least sleeping
late to prepare for the Game and its attendant festivities.
There was no sign of Grace, who had warned Susan that
she was going out to lunch with a boy from home. Only a
studious few stooped over the tables, round-shouldered and
concentrated, or paused, murmuring, by the desk to enquire
about weekend books. Still, there was the usual muted buzz:
two girls whispering in one corner, the rustle of a heavy page,
the scratching of pencils. Susan settled down to Webster's
plays with a surprised feeling of peace and security. It was
a comfort to be safely out of Olga's orbit.

She lunched alone at the drugstore she usually went to with

Grace. Missing her, she thought with envy of her lunch in
Boston. "Loch Ober's, I expect," she had said, "Tom knows
his way around." A boy from home. Donald. No letter for two
weeks now . . . *A boy from home.* Nice to have such a supply
of stock phrases to cover all the shades of human relationship.
She had noticed it particularly when Grace told her the story
of her life: she had been going with a boy for years; he was
crazy about her . . . It all sounded so easy, put like that. How
different from Susan's own laborious descriptions of Donald:
"A man I know," absurdly pompous, "A friend of mine,"
ambiguous. It would be much easier to be American.

Not that she wanted to be. They were so strange, so rough,
so alien. She paid her bill, failed as usual to count her change,
apologised for being bumped into by a hurrying salesgirl,
and was outside. Normally crowded, today Harvard Square
was pandemonium. Susan stopped to watch a man selling
favours: dolls with purple or green skirts; flags, the crimson
and the green; vast crimson chrysanthemums. Not far off,
the windows of Schrafft's exploded with crimson elephants
and kewpie dolls. How could they be at once so outrageous
and so desirable?

With a pang of envy, she watched a tall young man in a
tweed jacket buying a chrysanthemum for his golden-haired
companion. Laughing, she handed him her fur coat to hold
while she pinned the enormous flower to the lapel of her
jacket. It would smell rich and musky, like autumn gardens.
The young man opened the door of a low-built car, and the
girl stepped in – a flash of long legs in sheer silk stockings,
more laughter; they were off.

The Square's average age was an irresponsible twenty. In
cars, walking, gathered in groups, they seemed oblivious with
lunch and conversation, careless of time's flight. But, no, as
Susan watched, she saw that for all its surface stillness, its
eddies and backwaters, the crowd was drawn on by a steady

41

current. The groups were breaking up, beginning to drift; still talking, laughing, tapping each other on the shoulder, shifting their positions; they moved aimlessly, it seemed, but steadily towards the river.

Susan had to push her way against the cheerful tide to get to the subway station. As she reached it a group of young men debouched suddenly from the exit. They were late. They laughed, they ran, they stumbled, shouting directions at each other. The last of them was waving a Harvard pennant. He tripped on the curb, recovered himself, laughed, shouted to the others to wait, and passed close by Susan, leaving behind an aromatic breath of beer and enjoyment. How barbarous it all looked, and what fun.

Sitting in the empty train (who went to Boston on Saturday afternoon?) Susan thought about Olga's party. They would all be at the field by now, after lunch at the Larrabys'. Betty Jane might have been ill at the last minute . . . They would hurry over and invite her: "Susan, you *must* come . . ." Then the drive to the stadium, a quick pause for their chrysanthemums, George handing her one: "How well it goes with your hair . . ." Afterwards they would go dancing – there were parties in the Houses or something – George would take her home: "D'you know you're very beautiful, Susan?"

But the train had come out into the sunshine. Susan tucked *The Duchess of Malfi* more securely under her arm preparatory to getting off. Ridiculous to let herself dream so. It had been all very well when she was a child and the dreams had been wonderful things full of knights in armour and hairbreadth escapes, but now she was supposed to be grown-up. What would Grace think, or Professor Winter?

She managed to scold herself into working hard all afternoon, with only an occasional restless glance down into the quietness of Brimmer Street; an occasional thought of the cheering crowd at the stadium. It was absurd anyway. She hated games; what on earth made her think she wanted to go to this one?

There was no sign of Olga that evening. "Lucky if she's home by midnight," said Mary, serving rissoles at seven.

"I do hope she and Spencer Russell get on," said Mrs Morton. "Such a delightful family . . ."

The slow evening wore itself out over double dummy and the Russell family history, while Susan dreamed about Olga, about George, about Donald . . . Her bridge suffered and she was sent to bed early, to lie staring at the pattern the street light cast on the ceiling and wishing vague impossible wishes.

She had been long enough in Brimmer Street to know and dread the New England Sunday. At Mrs Morton's it meant a ritual feast attended by formidable grandsons and silent nephews. As the quiet Sunday morning ticked past, Susan would try desperately to think up subjects for dinner table conversation. It was all to no avail. When Mrs Morton's key in the front door announced her return from church with the inevitable quart of ice-cream from Schrafft's, Susan would feel her inspiration slowly and irrevocably draining away; the arrival of the first nephew brought certain paralysis.

And this one was going to be the worst yet. She stood at the drawing room window watching the white-sailed yachts hurrying this way and that on the river. Not *The Duchess of Malfi*, one did not talk about one's work; not yesterday's Game, she did not know enough to ask intelligent questions . . . Oh, it was hopeless, Anyway, George and Olga would do all the talking, they always did, and she and the twins would be properly impressed as audience. At least the twins were harmless.

Mrs Morton's key grated in the lock. Susan moved uncertainly from the window, picked up the *Social Register* and put it down again, then perched herself uncomfortably on the arm of a chair. She could hear Mrs Morton talking to Mary downstairs. "Chocolate and pistachio," she was saying ... The yachts were gathering towards MIT. Their owners would be hurrying back for Sunday lunch. In Dunster House, in Eliot, in Adams, roast beef would be hot and odoriferous on the tables. At Bertram Hall there would be roast chicken. And everywhere, ice-cream; everywhere plates piled high, serious faces, an apology for conversation. Did nothing happen in New England except meals?

"Here I am at last." Mrs Morton looked her best in black. "Such a long sermon. I thought I'd never get home. Where's Olga?"

"I don't believe she's up yet." Susan arranged the rustling quilts and Mrs Morton subsided into them. "Oh dear," she sighed, "my poor old head. Susan, my dear, pour me a glass of sherry." The doorbell rang and her face brightened. "There's my party." A delicate hand smoothed the white hair.

Susan paused helplessly, the unopened bottle in one hand, the corkscrew in the other, and listened to Mary's heavy footsteps in the hall below. The front door creaked. "Hullo, Mary." George's voice. "How's yourself?"

"Not so bad," Mary's voice purred. How did George do it? Everyone seemed to adore him. He made you feel important; that was it.

In a few minutes Mrs Morton was purring as he kissed her. "Prettier than ever, Gran." Then it was Susan's turn. "Still mowing them down at Radcliffe? Here, let me." He took the bottle and bent his handsome head over it. Susan smiled. He really did seem to care about one. Drawing the cork, he threw a bright glance around the room. "What have you done with Olga, Gran?"

"She's not up yet." Mrs Morton rustled on her sofa. "She doesn't care whether she sees anything of her old Gran. Give me some sherry, George, like a dear boy; I declare my head's quite mixed up from that sermon. It was all about charity. Susan, would you run up and see if Olga's awake? I can't have her sleeping through lunch."

Olga was surveying herself with calm approval in the hall mirror. She had changed her scarlet blouse for a dull black one. Susan glanced down at her own navy blue skirt; oh dear . . .

"Hullo there," Olga noticed her. "Is Gran beginning to champ at the bit? I couldn't get up this morning; not with the best will in the world. I didn't get to bed till three." The doorbell rang again. "I suppose that's the twins." Elegant and unhurried as ever, she passed Susan and went to open the door. "Hullo, Ralph. Hi, Randall," Susan heard her say, "how's life with you?"

In the drawing room, George was refilling his grandmother's glass. "Gran's a shocking old toper, you know," he gleamed at Susan. "Have some?"

"Thank you." He handed her a glass. She ought to say something funny about drinking. She ought at least to say something. Instead she stood with one foot in front of the other and stared miserably into the glass. The lengthening silence was broken by the appearance of Olga and the twins. Short, fair and identical, they looked faintly comic beside their tall cousins.

"Good morning, Gran." Olga leaned down to kiss her. Mrs Morton was all smiles, her complaints forgotten.

The twins greeted their grandmother, smiled in shy unison at Susan, and relapsed into placid silence on either side of the sofa. Olga moved over to the fireplace and stood with one arm along the mantelpiece, her smooth dark hair in striking contrast to the blonde curls of the bride in the portrait above her. "Good lord, Gran," she looked down, "don't tell me you've still got those old everlastings? Isn't it time you gave them to the deserving poor or something? They're covered in dust."

Mrs Morton sniffed. "I wish I knew what Mary does with herself all day. The house is a perfect pig-sty. George, I believe I'll have just the tiniest bit more sherry."

George grinned his engaging grin. "What did I tell you?" He turned his full charm on Susan as he filled his grandmother's glass. Dazzled, she said nothing, and he turned to Olga. "I won't be answerable for the consequences if you drink it on an empty stomach."

"Don't worry about me, I can take it. It's a family gift, isn't it, Gran?"

"I don't know why you say so." She bridled, an achievement at seventy-eight.

"Think of Great-Uncle William." Olga caught George's eye and they both laughed.

"He's the family dipsomaniac," George explained for Susan's benefit. "Gran had to haul him out of Freshpond after a party one night. Nobody knows what she said to him; he ran away to sea next morning and was never heard of again."

"Goodness." Susan was tongue-tied. How did one tell stories? There was the mad don who fell into Dames' Delight . . . It was no good. George was listening to Olga anyway. In command at the mantelpiece, she had begun a story about a party in New York. He moved over to stand beside her, taller than she was and still more handsome. Susan moved vaguely over to the window and stared out. The sherry after her morning's work made her head ache slightly.

The two streams of talk flowed on in the room behind her. Olga had reached the climax of her story: "So they took him home in the Black Maria."

Mrs Morton was putting the twins through their weekly cross-examination: "What do you hear from your mother, Randall?"

"She's very well," Randall went a little pink.

"We had a letter on Thursday," Ralph helped him out.

"And dear Rosemary? Does she still like it at school?"

"Oh, yes," said Ralph.

"Very much," amplified Randall.

"Did you ever read a Greek play?" George came over to Susan.

"Yes." Why? she wondered.

"Aren't they exactly like the chorus? You know, strophe and antistrophe, or something."

"I see what you mean." Torn between her longing to impress George and her fear of offending Mrs Morton, she could think of nothing more to say. But Olga had overheard. "Don't tell me you read Greek plays in the long winter evenings, George?"

"Good Lord, no," he was shocked at the suggestion. "I had it in a course."

Susan thanked goodness she hadn't spoken of *The Duchess of Malfi*. She must remember that it was bad form to enjoy one's work. But what did one talk about if one did nothing else?

Mrs Morton had got laboriously to her feet. She always found movement much more difficult when she had an audience, and now she leaned heavily on Ralph and Randall and sighed her way to the elevator. "I'm a lucky old woman to have two nice grandsons to look after me."

"Three, Gran," said George, "and a granddaughter. Don't forget us Horwoods."

"As if I would." She shut herself in the elevator and the others went down the stairs, George whispering something to Olga as they went. She laughed, "Don't be absurd."

Lunch was formal and interminable. George carved the chicken (white meat for the ladies, drumsticks for the twins), while Mary panted her way round with the vegetables and added an occasional word to the conversation. George and Olga were exchanging reminiscences of Vermont: the year

47

they had had the feud with the neighbours' children, the year Olga and Roger had fallen into the millpond, and so on through a succession of sociable memories.

It was odd, Susan thought, when she talked to George, Olga broke through her mask of indifference. Reminding him of the time he had lain in the snow chewing a twig which turned out – much to his cost – to be poison ivy, she was quite a different person. Her laugh was freer and louder, her mouth had lost its slight suggestion of sullenness. Watching her, Susan noticed that Mrs Morton's eye was also upon her. Her catechism of the twins was proceeding relentlessly, but all the time a faintly disapproving glance took in Olga and George. "Not," Susan imagined her saying it, "not exactly ladylike . . ."

She looked happier when George got on to politics. Not for the first time Susan thought what a conversational blessing Bostonians found the New Deal. There must, she supposed, be some who approved of it, but she had yet to meet them. Now George held forth in eloquent imitation of his elders: the country was going to the dogs; they would find next that they were being dragged into a war that was no affair of theirs: "No offence, Susan, but look what happened last time. We won't be catspaws again."

Susan was silent. The twins were suitably impressed (or was that, Susan wondered, a spark of revolt in Ralph's eye?), Mrs Morton purred. She liked an intelligent conversation. Her smile showed her recognition that Susan was properly convinced. Still silent (what was the use?), Susan gave herself up to the familiar feeling of inadequacy. She was hopeless. She had bungled her chance with George before lunch, and now, sitting between him and Randall, she was totally incapable of thinking of anything that would interest either of them. And if she tried to argue politics with George she would only get angry . . . No use at all. The misery prolonged itself from chicken to ice-cream and from ice-cream to coffee. She had hoped that the move back to the drawing room would leave her more strategically placed (she did not ask herself how), but when they got into the hall, George apologised and left.

"Sorry, Gran," he explained, "I promised I'd take Betty Jane out in Aggie and she doesn't like to be kept waiting."

"You're lucky she'll stand being seen in that rattle-trap," Olga's mask was back in place, her drawl superior. "I've got to go, too, Gran. Spencer's driving me back and he said he'd pick me up at two-thirty."

"So soon? Well, I declare." But Mrs Morton's disappointment was obviously modified by her feelings about Spencer Russell. "Have a lovely drive."

Susan had been wondering whether Ralph and Randall would talk more if George and Olga talked less, but the long silences over coffee effectively disabused her. Apparently nothing would make them talk more. After another ten minutes or so of question and monosyllabic answer, even Mrs Morton began to look tired. "Well," she said at last, "it's been lovely to see you boys, but now I think I must take my poor old self off for my rest. Susan will look after you."

Susan was appalled, but so, fortunately, were the twins. They got up.

"Thank you so much for lunch, Grannie," said Ralph.

"It was wonderful," said Randall.

"I really ought to go and do some work," said Ralph.

"Me, too," said Randall.

"Such dear boys," said Mrs Morton when they had left, "but I do sometimes wonder whether dear Ermintrude hasn't let them be together just a little more than was good for them. Of course I wouldn't dream of interfering, but . . ." she paused expressively. "Oh dear, how my poor head does spin. I do think Dr Forsythe ought to realise that forty minutes is too long for a sermon. I really think I must go and lie down."

Thank goodness, Susan thought. She ran downstairs and helped Mary finish the dishes, then put on a jacket and went out. The fine Sunday had brought an unusually large crop of casual strollers out to the river and she threaded her way quickly through them wondering what exactly they came for. To show off their clothes, perhaps. They were all in their Sunday best, the men formal in suits, the women perched and precarious on high heels. Here and there a Harvard student was conspicuous for his more casual clothes and purposeful air; here and there a Beacon Hill lady was walking her spaniels in full panoply of tweeds and fur, but mainly these people were from the nameless heart of Boston. They had escaped for the day from the narrow downtown streets and come here by hordes and families: tired-looking men and women walking side by side in silence while their loud-voiced children chased each other this way and that, threatened to fall into the river, and threw stones at the ducks. Chilly-looking couples were sitting on benches, studiously reading their way through the Sunday papers, with an occasional pause to comment, or to exchange sections. The whole idea seemed to be to avoid having time to think. What other excuse was there for those thirty-page Sunday papers?

But why not? Susan walked faster, brushing through the crowd and aware as she did so of amused glances, an occasional remark: "Look at the outdoor girl." Where did thinking get one, anyway? It only made things more difficult. How much better to be busy, like that red-haired woman, preventing your children from falling into the river. Better to be George, who would be calling for Betty Jane by now, helping her into the car: "Where shall we go this time?" Or Olga, driving down to New York with Spencer Russell. A drip, she had called him. How nice to be able to dismiss people so casually. "Oh,

Donald . . . he's a frightful drip." She imagined saying it to her mother. They did have wonderful words for things . . .

The yachts were out in full strength on the river. They darted here and there, their white sails neat-moving as the seagulls. Susan stopped to watch them, then noticed, nearer to, the iridescence of a pigeon's head as it pecked among the stones. Greedy things, though, and the seagulls had unpleasant expressions. Besides what was the use of noticing things if there was no one to tell about them?

She walked briskly on. There were still children sailing their boats on the ornamental pond, or, more often, standing in admiring and filial silence while their fathers did it for them. Father . . . they would have gone for long walks together; to Brede and Icklesham and Udimore, coming back cheerful and muddy and late for tea. She would have been able to talk to him, tell him things, ask him questions. He would have laughed about Donald: "Well, if he doesn't write to you, don't write to him."

But then what? The winter stretched before her, interminable and dull. But perhaps . . . maybe George . . . He was much better looking than Olga, and, of course, far nicer. He really treated you as if you were someone. He might quarrel with Betty Jane Larraby. He would tell her all about it: "Susan, you're the only one that understands . . ." They were on their way to Trefrey and Partridge to choose their engagement ring, when she had to stop to take a persistent cinder out of her shoe.

She had come a long way: past the landscaped district and under the railway bridge to where the path ran narrowly between the river and the road, and she was perpetually disturbed by passing cars. No place for thinking. Still, she might as well go on now. She could go up to Bertram Hall and call on Grace. It would do her good. All that was the matter with her was loneliness . . .

51

A car pulled up beside her. "You look as if the devil was after you." It was Professor Winter. "Can I give you a lift? I'm going out to Cambridge."

"Thank you very much, but I was just walking, really." *Why did she always say 'no' to things?*

"But you can't be enjoying this bit much. Come on."

"Well, thank you. You do get tired of the cars." She climbed in beside him.

"The best thing's to be in one of them." The car moved forward. "Like taking the house that spoils the view; you never notice it if you live in it. Do you always walk at that speed? I never saw anything like it. Or was the devil really after you?"

"He was a bit." It was surprising that she could admit it so easily. "I'm escaping from a family lunch, actually."

"Oh, lord, one of those Boston lunches. No wonder you looked desperate. I'm escaping from one myself, as a matter of fact. I have an aunt who lives on Beacon Hill and disapproves of me and all my ways, and she always arranges to tell me so over far too much delicious Sunday lunch. I'm afraid we New Englanders have no respect for food at all. It's a terrible confession."

"I have wondered," she agreed. "It all seems to begin and end in pie and ice-cream. Not that they aren't good."

"Excellent in their place, but hardly the be-all and end-all, surely. And besides, it discourages me always to know what I'm going to get. Come to supper on Saturday: Boston baked beans. Come to lunch on Sunday: roast beef, apple pie and ice-cream."

"We have chicken."

He laughed. "I stand corrected. There is always the happy alternative: roast beef or chicken. You might even get turkey round Christmas. It's particularly frightful when you think that nothing ever really happens here but meals."

"That's just what I was thinking today." She turned to him, delighted.

"Look," they were passing Eliot House on their way up to the Square, "do you have urgent business in Cambridge, or can I persuade you to drive out into the country a bit? You oughtn't to work on Sunday you know, they'll burn you for a witch. Besides, I think a little country air would do us both good."

"Oh, it would be wonderful." She was surprised at the enthusiasm in her voice. "I've been longing to see what the country round here is like. It's dreadful to be dumped down in a city and have no idea what's around you."

"Good. I'll see if I can't convince you that there's something to be said for New England, if not for New Englanders. I think we'll go out by Concord. Would you like to see the bridge where they fired the shot heard round the world?"

"Should I?"

"I can't see why, to tell you the truth. It's just a bridge. Besides, some real American is bound to bring you out and want to watch your reactions. It wouldn't be fair to spoil them."

"Aren't you a real American?"

"Not quite, I fear. It's the Rhodes Scholarship I had. Ever since I was at Oxford I've had a fatal doubt about original sin. And of course that puts me right out of court so far as New England is concerned. And as for the rest of America; oh well, I don't think I want the right things."

"When were you at Oxford?" she asked after a pause.

"1929 . . . seems a long time ago, doesn't it?"

It seemed a very long time indeed to Susan, who had been an unhappy child in her first year at boarding school. "Did you like it?" How amazing to be asking him questions.

"I should say so." They were silent, sociably homesick for a magic city.

"Do you like Gerard Manley Hopkins?" he asked, at last.

"Goodness, yes. Except he does baffle me. You mean, *'Towery city and branchy between towers'*?"

"Yes, exactly. I suppose the base and brickish skirt is worse than ever by now. It goes better if you read him aloud, you know."

"But you feel such a fool doing it by yourself. The maid caught me reading Webster to myself the other night and I'm sure she thinks I'm mad."

"You don't live in Bertram Hall then?"

"No, I live in Boston. With a Mrs Morton."

"Mrs Charles Morton? I knew her daughter once. They're quite a formidable family. Does Mrs Morton still call people 'dear boy'? It used to make me furious when I was a serious senior at Harvard."

"She certainly does."

"This, by the way," he gestured lavishly, "is Concord. I'll spare you the bridge, but you have to admit that the town is delightful."

"Yes. I love the low white houses."

"Originally designed by Christopher Wren, as the guide books would say. There's one for your British pride."

"Were they really?"

"We poor barbarians can only build factories, you know." If only she could tell when he was serious and when he was making fun of her. "Now for some real country." The car headed out of town into a gentle mix of woods and fields. "Of course you have to get much farther upstate for anything really exciting, but I'm very fond of this."

"It's lovely." They were off the traffic-jammed main road now and cruising more slowly along lanes.

"I don't want to sound like Ruth Draper showing off her garden," he said, "but of course the colours aren't at all what they ought to be this year, because of the hurricane. You'll have to stay over another year if you want to see a real New England fall."

"This one is good enough for me. I never saw such colours. What's that?" She pointed.

"Sumac. You want to be careful what you pick, by the way. But I expect you've been told plenty of stories about unfortunate English visitors who come back with great armfuls of scarlet leaves and wonder why their hosts start and shriek amain. Do you know what poison ivy looks like?"

"No. People keep telling me about it, but I've never seen any."

"Well, you'd better. With that fair skin of yours you're a natural for it." He stopped the car. "This is a favourite place of mine anyway. That bank is the old streetcar track from Boston to Worcester. And here's your poison ivy. Avoid it like the plague."

"Thank you. It is pretty, isn't it? Did you say streetcar track?" She looked at the wooded bank that intersected the road.

"Yes. In the good old days there was streetcar service from Boston to Worcester, stopping at Framingham."

"It must have been fun."

"Yes, slow but sociable. You can see some of the ties, still. Come and look."

They left the road and walked along the bank. "Don't forget the poison ivy," he said, "but I don't think there's much here. It usually grows along the sides of the road, for some reason; you'd almost think it did it from spite. There are the ties, see?"

They were out of sight of the car by now. On each side of them stretched the woods, shadow-dappled and various in scarlet and gold. A small path ran along the top of the bank and this was fairly clear, although now and then a

55

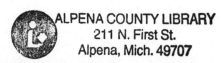

branch would catch in Susan's hair or a briar twist itself around her legs. She stopped to disentangle one of these and looked around. "Isn't it quiet?"

"Well, yes and no. It's odd about woods. Listen."

They were silent. Gradually Susan's unpractised ear began to pick up the small woodland noises. There were crickets by the thousands; birds called to each other or rustled in the leaves; a squirrel went into a tantrum about something.

"I see what you mean," she said, "but somehow these are quiet noises. Except the squirrel, perhaps." Her voice trailed off into the quietness and they walked on silently, listening. *How different*, she thought, *from the agonised silence with George before lunch*. Why was it that this was comfort and peacefulness, while that was misery unrelieved? Because they were outdoors, partly, but it was more than that. She was never uncomfortable with Professor Winter. Even that first dreadful day she had been somehow at home with him.

They came out into a clearing. On one side of the bank stood the ruins of a house, now dilapidated beyond repair. Most of the roof had fallen in, the windows and door were gone, and over everything there grew a riot of traveller's joy.

"When I was younger I used to think it would be fun to buy this place and recondition it," Professor Winter broke the silence, "but I'm afraid it's past praying for now."

"What a shame." She broke off. "Oh, do look at the apples!"

A bent old apple tree grew on the far side of the house. The main trunk was dead, but one low-growing branch was covered with scarlet apples.

"It's done well this year," he said. "They're good apples, too. Have one." He started towards the tree. "You can see I consider this place as practically my private property."

As they went around the house he pointed out a clump of lilac bushes. "You can always tell where a house has been in New England by the lilac. Even when everything else has vanished you'll find it growing. Here you are." He picked an apple and gave it to her.

She bit into it. "They *are* good. They're so much better right off the tree."

They sat down on a ruined wall and munched side by side in the sunshine. The crickets were singing louder than ever. *This is happiness,* she thought. But the silence was suddenly too deep. "It must have been a pretty house, too," she said.

"Yes, very. I'd still like to find a place like this and do it over. Somewhere well and truly out of town. God knows how I'd make a living though." He threw away his core and looked at his watch. "Good Lord, it's five o'clock. I hope you don't have six o'clock supper?"

"No, it's rather vague on Sunday."

"Thank God for one New England habit. Just the same, we'd better be getting back."

"I suppose so. Oh dear, what a lovely place." She stood up. "It is getting a bit cold, though, come to think of it."

"I oughtn't to have let you sit so long in just that jacket. Come on, we'll hurry and warm you up. But first, here's one for the road." He picked two apples and put them in his pocket.

The silence closed in again as they hurried back along the bank. Walking in front, Professor Winter set such a pace that it was all Susan could do to keep up with him. For some reason, she was glad of it. She did not want to talk.

"It's just as well I did notice the time," he said when they got back to the car. "I always forget how quickly it gets dark at this time of year. Here's your apple."

"Thank you. Does it get dark quicker in the autumn?"

"Heaven help me, I don't know. It always seems as if it did. What an English precisian you are, aren't you?"

"Oh dear, I try not to be."

"Don't for my sake. I expect it's good for me." His laugh shaded into bitterness. "I've always suffered from too much fine frenzy. No wonder I don't make a very successful New Englander."

The stories she had heard about him came back to her in a rush. The girl from Schrafft's; the three children; the elopement with the vacuum cleaner man . . . It was incredible; it was ridiculous. He was not old enough . . . People who'd had things like that happen to them would be different; they would not like these things: walking in woods, picking apples . . . There must be a mistake somewhere.

She stole a glance at his face in the gathering darkness. The shadowed profile was set and tense as she had not seen it before. No, there was no mistake; it *had* happened to him. What a dreadful woman she must have been. He was so nice . . . If she had been at Oxford when he was there . . . But that was so long ago: 1929. How odd it all was. He must be thirty. Just a little younger than Father was when he died. Father would have liked him. What a wonderful afternoon . . . If only they could drive on and on . . .

With a gesture whose sudden violence surprised her, Winter opened his window and threw away his apple core. "Traffic's too heavy for eating," he said. "Do you drive?"

"No, we've never had a car. People don't so much in England somehow. The distances are shorter, of course."

"And, saving your presence, the roads are worse."

"I'm afraid they are." She laughed. "Am I such a passionate Englishwoman?"

"You do strike me as being a bit on the defensive so far as England is concerned. I'm sure it would be as much as my life is worth to venture a real criticism."

She thought about it. "I suppose you're right. How tiresome of me."

"I expect you've had plenty of cause. We Americans are

scared to death of strangers, you know, that's why we bully them so. We always think they're going to make fun of us. And when you come to think of it, they often have. Think of the people who came over and wrote us up in the nineteenth century: most of them talked as if we were interesting savages, and you can't wonder we resented it. I suppose it's all bound to make us seem a bit hostile to someone like you."

"Oh, not hostile . . . It's just all the questions: you know, 'How do you like America?' They don't seem to be interested in me at all, really."

"That's just what I mean. We're scared to death you'll think we're ridiculous. Just remember that we're really quite pathetic and insecure and you'll be able to be patient with us."

"Pathetic and insecure aren't exactly the words I'd have used!"

"I don't expect they are. You probably think we're fearfully overbearing, but remember that it's just protective colour for our inferiority complex . . . You might even end up by being quite fond of us." He paused and she looked up and saw that he was threading his expert way through the chaos of Harvard Square.

"Do drop me here," she said. "The subway will get me right home." How was she going to tell him what a wonderful afternoon it had been?

"Don't be absurd. I certainly don't propose to sink your opinion of Americans still lower by leaving you to find your way home by yourself in the dark. Besides, I like the drive along the river."

"It's awfully kind of you." She realised with fury that her voice was formal and even schoolgirlish. *Donald's right, I'm a hopeless prig*, she thought. She looked angrily out of the window for a minute, then exclaimed: "Goodness, it's lovely." She had not driven along Memorial Drive at night before. The dark band of the river was decorated on either side by

reflected lights which shimmered and twinkled on the water.
"*Would I were heaven . . .*"

"You'll like Boston when you let yourself."

"I hope so."

They were silent again. How could she thank him? What
could she say? Too late to wonder; he had stopped at the
turning for Brimmer Street. "I think," he said, "if you won't
think me too churlish, I'll drop you here."

She was relieved. Now she would not have to explain
her return by car to Mrs Morton and Mary, who noticed
everything. How considerate he was. But now she really had
to say thank you. "That'll be wonderful," she said, "and thank
you so much for a lovely afternoon." A voice echoed in her
ears: "*Now, Susan, say thank you for your lovely party.*" She
sounded like a reluctant child. Why was she such a fool? She
got out of the car.

"On the contrary, thank you for coming," he was almost
invisible. "It's done me a world of good. I hope it has
you."

"It's been wonderful."

"Good." He was businesslike. "I'll see you on Friday.
Don't forget to read Bradley."

"No, indeed." The car slid forward and was gone. Susan
walked slowly towards the house. How was she going to
explain her long absence? She did not want to tell Mrs
Morton about the drive. It would spoil it, somehow. Besides,
it was ridiculous. There was no reason why she should tell
her everything she did. She was suddenly angry. It was all
so childish; this talking and talking that destroyed things.
She would just say she'd been over to see Grace. That
would do it.

Fortunately, Mrs Morton was too pleased with the outcome
of Olga's weekend to take much notice of Susan. She talked
about the Russells all evening. Spencer was a delightful boy.

His mother was charming: "I must find out if she plays bridge. Eliza would know . . ." It was so lucky that Spencer Russell lived in New York . . . What did he do? (Susan had been rather proud of thinking of the question). "My dear, the Russells don't need to *do* anything. Of course if he wanted to . . ." The world and its kingdoms lay at his feet. "A most intellectual young man . . ." Susan was left with the impression that, as a matter of fact, Spencer Russell did nothing.

But Mrs Morton was talking again. "I really must have a party. I can't think why I haven't thought of it sooner. Let me see: Olga and dear Spencer, George and Betty Jane, and we must find a nice boy for you, Susan. I'm sure George would know someone. I must write to Olga about dates."

Susan did her best to listen to the plans: a theatre, perhaps. "The Russells are such a cultivated family . . ." A little dinner beforehand. "It'll be such a chance for you, Susan. I hope you've got a pretty evening dress. It's your bid, my dear."

It was hard to pay attention to the cards; it was hard to make herself care whether they had chicken or roast beef for the party. She did her best, but all the time her truant thoughts kept wandering to the woods, where the brambles caught at her ankles and leaves gleamed scarlet in the sunshine. Finally she revoked, and was sent to bed as incorrigible.

Chapter Four

'*Dear Donald, this is a very difficult letter to write ...*' Susan paused, stared out of the window at the grey Monday morning, and bit at the end of her pencil. It certainly was difficult. But it was no use putting it off, even if it did mean she missed her twelve o'clock class. It had to be written. She had decided that the night before.

The street was quiet. She wrote again: '*We had such a good time at Oxford, and I have so loved getting your letters.*' His letters were quite dull, it occurred to her; Father would have laughed at them. She must get on; Mary would be up to do the hall any minute now. '*I do want to say thank you for everything. It was so nice.*' She thought of long, golden days on the river. But was it the river or Donald that she regretted? Anyway, the main thing was not to sound as if she thought any of it more important than it was. '*But now I'm such a long way away,*' she went on in a rush, '*don't you think it's a little silly to go on writing? Letters always make things seem so much more important than they are.*' Donald's recent ones certainly had not, but still . . . '*So it seems to me maybe it would be a good idea if we stopped writing to each other. Of course, I'll always love to hear what's happening to you. After all, we've been such good friends. But I do think it would be better if we left it at that.*'

She blew her nose and re-read the letter. It did not make very good sense, but it would have to do. She copied it carefully onto a sheet of Mrs Morton's letterhead paper and decided that it did not look too bad. She was also overwhelmed by a tidal wave of loneliness.

The only thing to do was get it over with. She addressed the envelope, licked it up and hurried downstairs and out to drop it with a sense of finality in the mailbox across the street. Then she went back to her room, put Donald's picture in her stocking drawer, and read Bradley's *Shakespearian Tragedy* with frowning concentration till lunchtime.

Passing the spinach to Mrs Morton, she wondered if she would see Professor Winter on her way to class. He had a four o'clock lecture at Radcliffe on Mondays and she had sometimes met him outside Longfellow Hall. He might stop and talk to her; ask if she had got home all right, or something. It would be a chance to thank him properly for the walk. What an idiot he must have thought her. Still, he had said it did him a world of good . . . He really had seemed to be enjoying it. Perhaps he would ask her again? After her next tutorial, maybe. "Won't you come for another walk on Sunday? I did so enjoy our last one." He had talked about Cape Cod . . . perhaps they would go there . . .

On the train to Cambridge she sat staring out the window at dark vacancy and wondering if she would meet him. They would take lunch next time, or maybe have it on the way. He would tell her about his plans for his book: "You're such a good listener." Perhaps he would ask her to help him with the research for it. He did think she was good. "My model student," he had called her.

But there was no sign of him on the Longfellow steps. Instead, Grace appeared, hurrying, almost at a run, from the library.

"Hullo," she panted slightly, "waiting for me? We're going to be late, something tells me."

They were. Fortunately, it was their composition class and Susan could dream her way through it in peace. Someone was reading aloud a short story full of split infinitives. It was called *Dust*. Perhaps she would see him afterwards.

"Come on," Grace urged her as she lingered on the steps, "no use waiting around here. I want you to come down to St Clair's for a drink. It's my party," she anticipated Susan's protest, "it's my birthday."

"For goodness sake, why didn't you tell me?" There was no sign of him. "Many happy returns. But isn't it a bit early for a drink?"

"Some people would say it was never too early. Have a heart, I've got to celebrate somehow. Tom's taking me to the theatre, but he had to get the tickets for tomorrow; I'll go nuts if I have to go back to Bertram all by myself."

Susan rather liked being bullied by Grace. And after all, she had been longing to see her yesterday. What a long time ago . . . But Grace was telling her about her presents. "It sounds lovely," Susan managed, "red will suit you . . ."

At St Clair's the afternoon had paused to catch its breath. Tea was over, the cocktail hour hardly begun. In a corner booth, a man and a girl sat preoccupied over empty cups. A waitress lingered nearby, anxious that their belated crumbs should not mar the sophistication of six o'clock.

The leather seats in their booth were cold to the touch. "What's it to be?" Grace asked, as the waitress hovered towards them. Then, quick to notice Susan's bafflement, "How about an orange blossom? Cheap and cheerful. It's high time you learned something about drinks, you know, Susan."

"I suppose it is, really. I feel an awful fool when there's no menu and I don't know what to ask for." It was a long time since she had found herself in that position. She had always had sherry with Donald, anyway. Donald . . . Had her letter been all right? Too late to worry about it now.

Grace was explaining her theory of drinking. "Just ask for a dry martini and you can't lose. If you want to be extra fancy, make a fuss of insisting that it's got to be *really* dry. There's nothing to it."

Susan laughed. "I'll remember. You'll have me quite a social character by the time you're through."

"I don't see why not. This business of being shy is so silly. All you have to do is forget about it, and that's that."

"It's quite true." Susan considered. "D'you know, Professor Winter picked me up in his car when I was out walking yesterday and took me out to Concord and it seems to me I talked a blue streak the whole time." She was blushing slightly, but on the whole rather pleased with herself for having worked the announcement in so neatly.

"Think of that." Grace was impressed. "And how was his sardonic lordship?"

"He was awfully nice; I can't think why you don't like him, Grace."

"Probably because he doesn't like me. Besides, I get tired of that melancholy pose. And he must have been an awful fool to go and marry that girl."

"I don't see why," Susan's blush deepened, "he must have been frightfully young, and everyone says she was perfectly lovely."

"He didn't have to marry her, though." Grace was worldly wise about it. "And I bet he gave her a hell of a time afterwards. I'm not at all sure I blame her for running out on him. You can see he's selfish as the devil, just looking at him. It's all very well for you. He likes you," Susan had tried to interrupt, "but you try working with him if he doesn't. Tom says he never listens to a word he says; you might just as well have tutorials with a fish."

"I think you're very unfair," Susan's voice rose slightly. "I expect Tom doesn't work properly for his tutorials. You can't expect someone like Professor Winter to bother about people who don't."

"Some would say it was his job," Grace smiled. "I'm sorry, Susan, I didn't mean to insult your fair-haired boy. I expect I'm just prejudiced and he's an angel of light, really. What's the news of Donald, talking about fair-haired boys?"

"Oh, I meant to tell you. I wrote to him this morning and suggested we stop writing to each other."

"For the love of Pete: *Why?*"

"It all seemed so silly somehow. I'm not a bit in love with him any more; I'm not sure I ever was," Susan explained, full of a warm lucidity.

"But, my good woman, if you insist on being in love with people before you'll even associate with them, you're going to have an awfully lonely time. You really are the oddest creature I ever met. How's he going to feel about it d'you think?"

"He'll be frightfully relieved. I haven't heard from him for two weeks, you know." Her voice sounded loud in her ears.

"Oh, well, maybe you're right. It's always nice to turn them down first, if it's going to happen anyway. How about another drink to celebrate?" But the waitress had disappeared.

"I couldn't, thank you, really." Finishing her drink, she felt the lucidity gradually lose itself in the warmth.

"What a hopeless abstainer you are. Still, I suppose it's time I went and rescued poor Beowulf; he's been swimming around underwater for days. I wish he'd go drown himself." Grace paid the bill and they got up to go. "Well, goodbye, and don't do anything rash."

"I'll try not to." They parted at the door. Susan found she had to make a separate effort of concentration for each step of the stair down to the subway, and then had a little difficulty persuading her dime to fit into the slot. *How very funny*, she thought, *I'm drunk.*

It was a relief to sit down in the train. Funny of Grace not to like Professor Winter. But she was obviously prejudiced by Tom. Ridiculous to say he was selfish. Monday today. Tuesday, Wednesday, Thursday, Friday. Only three whole days. At school they used to make calendars of the days to the end of term and colour them off as they passed. A red letter day. She might even meet him before then . . . "What luck meeting you . . . Come on, I've got the car. I've been hoping I might run into you . . ."

The week passed in a succession of dreams. He had invited her to go for a really long walk with him on Sunday; they were climbing Monadnoc; at the top, he told her how unhappy he had been till he met her . . . They were dancing together; "It's so easy to be with you . . ." His wife had died suddenly; the news came when she was at her tutorial . . .

There was always a hitch in the dreams, and Susan would be glad to be distracted by Mary or Mrs Morton. Anything not to have to listen to the cold and penetrating voice of reason. He had taken her walking because he was sorry for her. He was kind to her for the same reason. He would be kind to anyone who was unhappy (absurd of Grace to say he was selfish), but that was all there was to it. Of course it was. But still, he might ask her again, he might be sorry for her again . . . Why not? And so, slowly, imperceptibly, back into the world of dreams . . .

It was hard to decide what to wear on Friday. Not her blue suit; she had worn that to the tea where she'd met him; not a skirt and jersey; they made her look all angles. Her black dress? Grace had approved of it. But was it all right for a tutorial? She finally put it on and then wished all the way to Cambridge that she had worn a jersey and skirt. She felt self-conscious and ridiculous. The dress had a vast bow at the neck, it was far too dressy; he would think she was a complete idiot. He probably did already.

She was as nervous as before her first tutorial. It was absurd. She stopped for a minute halfway up the cold stone steps to his office and brushed a long hair off her shoulder. Her hand shook a little. What a fool.

The Dunster House clock was striking four as she knocked at his door. At least she was on time. But he was on the telephone. He motioned to her to come in and sit down and she shut the door quietly behind her, took off her coat (the bow was enormous), and perched uncomfortably in one of the big leather chairs.

"That'll be fine." He sounded as if he was talking to someone he liked. "No, of course it'll be no trouble at all. Tell Julia I'll pick her up at about five-thirty, that'll give us lots of time; it only takes an hour . . ." He listened for a minute, smiling to himself. "Yes, I'll be on time, just tell her to be sure that she is, or we really *will* be late." The voice at the other end crackled and he laughed. "Don't be silly, I'll be there at five-thirty and no nonsense about it. Goodbye till then." He rang off. "Sorry to keep you," he said to Susan. "And now we'd better get right down to it. I'm afraid I'm going to have to run like a hare at the end of the hour. I hope you were none the worse for your walk last week, by the way? I was stiff next day, I'm ashamed to say."

"Oh, no," Susan managed, "it was lovely."

"That's good. And how did you find Mr Bradley?"

So that was that. Susan was somewhat incoherent on the subject of Bradley. Her thoughts were out of hand. When she should be paying particular attention to what he was saying, her mind gnawed restlessly at the telephone conversation she had heard. Julia could not be his wife, her name was Josephine. It was none of her business. They were going away for the weekend, of course . . .

"Yes, it really is a romantic approach," she realised that she had said exactly the same thing five minutes before. Fortunately, he did not seem to notice. At five to five he paused. "You know what," he said, "I believe I've been pushing you too much. How about our taking a week off so we can both catch up on our reading?"

Susan's heart sank. She was about to protest, but he went on. "I'm sure that's a good idea. You go off and relax a bit; you've really been working like a Trojan you know; and then take a look at Beaumont and Fletcher and come along two weeks from today and tell me all about them. Good lord, I really must get going. I hope you'll excuse me."

"Of course." Susan fumbled for the sleeve of her coat.

"Here." He helped her into it. "There you are." He picked up her books from the table and handed them to her. "Lord, what a load; you need a truck to cart them round in. Now, have a good holiday and I'll see you in two weeks."

The light on the stairs shone mercilessly bright in her eyes. A *truck*, indeed. There was no need for him to make fun of her. She settled the books more securely under her arm as she came out into the gathering darkness. It would be the last straw to drop them. Not that he would know, of course. She looked up at his lighted window. He would be busy picking up his pipe, his overcoat, getting ready for his weekend. As she watched, the clock struck five with a hollow note and the light was switched off. He must have been longing to be rid of her. Julia was waiting for him.

She walked up Plympton Street blind with humiliation. Once she apologised after running into a tall young man with a green bag of books over his shoulder, once a car swerved to avoid her, hooting angrily. Of course, it was a one way street. He had been interested in her for a while. "*Do you drive?*" She had wondered if he would offer to teach her. And then all the talk about England. The memory of it tasted bitter.

Sitting in the subway, she caught a glimpse of her own reflection in the window opposite. The outline of the face was angular, the long hair straggled on sloping shoulders. Julia would be a Boston girl with a professional hair-do and a fur coat; older than Olga, of course, but with the same air of practised perfection. After all his hurrying, she would keep him waiting.

Serve him right. She was surprised at her own bitterness. For the first time she realised that she had actually been counting on another walk this Sunday. What a fool. Talk about castles in Spain . . . "It's all right if he likes you," Grace had said. He *had* liked her for a while; surely she had been right about that? What had she done to spoil it? Something on Sunday? It had all seemed so right at the time. Or had it? What had he been thinking about all that time when he was so quiet and grim-looking on the way back? Maybe he had been bored to death.

That must have been it. And she had thought they were getting on so well. He would probably tell Julia all about her: "Sorry I had to ring off, I have a wretched little English girl for tutorials."

Her room looked empty as an abandoned grave. She drew the curtains against the black sky, but there was still something achingly wrong. Of course, Donald's picture was missing. Smiling derisively at herself, she got it out of the drawer and put it back on the bureau. What a blessing Mary hadn't noticed. It might be supercilious, but it was company.

*   *   *

71

It was all the company she had that long, blank weekend, and for once Monday morning was almost welcome. Over breakfast, she decided that she would go to the library early. Grace might be there. Would she see him outside Longfellow? *Oh, stop it*, she told herself, *aren't you enough of a fool?*

Mrs Morton had a letter from Olga. "She thinks the party's a lovely idea. The first Thursday in November – she *would* pick my bridge day. Goodness, that's just a week from Thursday." She went on reading and her face fell. "She wants to ask Roger. Isn't it *too* provoking? I told her I wanted to have Spencer Russell. We really owe it to the Larrabys. They've been so sweet to George. She is the most inconsiderate girl."

Susan was only half listening. She had a letter of her own from Donald.

"So you've got a letter from the boyfriend at last," Mary missed nothing. "Heaven help us all; if I just had ten cents for every time you blushed, Susan, what a rich woman I'd be."

Still blushing, Susan escaped to her room. Donald had not had her last letter when he had written. As she re-read his, she was glad she had written it. As usual there were protestations of how much he missed her, but instead of reappearing in almost every paragraph as they had at first, they were decorously disposed of in the opening sentences. The letter went on to describe his life as an apprentice in the family business. '*You would be scandalised,*' it said, '*to see me devoting myself so exclusively to pounds, shillings and pence. But there are compensations, and life in London is not the least of them.*' How self-conscious it sounded. Susan read on and realised why. There had been dances; he had taken a girl, who was mentioned very casually as '*a friend of the family's called Sally – you wouldn't think much of her; she's not at all the intellectual type.*'

So much, thought Susan, for the intellect. She decided not to answer the letter and put it carefully in the desk with Donald's others. Then, for the last time, she got up and removed the photograph.

When she got home from Radcliffe that night she found Mrs Morton again gleeful with plans for the party. "Isn't it lucky," she said, "I met Eliza Larraby at Stearns and she says Spencer's going to be up that Thursday. So, of course, as I was asking dear Betty and Priscilla, I just had to ask him. I'm sure Olga will understand; she always was a dear reasonable child. Oh, and I called George and we're going to have the twins for you and Priscilla Larraby. Wasn't it clever of him to think of them? They'll be such nice company for you."

"It sounds lovely." Susan was depressed.

"It'll be a bit of a change for you. I think you work far too hard, Susan. A little more social life would do you all the good in the world. Now, how about taking it easy this evening and having a little double dummy?"

So, over hearts and spades, the long, dull evenings drifted by. Mrs Morton remarked that Susan's game had improved. "You're really paying attention these days, my dear."

"Two hearts," said Susan. Of course she was paying attention. Anything to distract herself from the monotony of her own thoughts.

The evenings stretched out. Mrs Morton indulged in too many catnaps in the daytime to be a sound sleeper at night, and now Susan, too, was finding it hard to get to sleep. She was used to drifting down from daydream to daydream until the last control gave way and she was lost in sleep. But now, turning this way and that on an unsympathetic pillow, she could find nothing to dream about. Her usual cast of characters resisted her: Donald was a ghost, lifeless, useless; there would be no more imaginary drives through the autumn woods with Professor Winter. She tried Merton Dennison (but he had never invited her round for that drink), she tried a

gallant stranger who saved her from drowning; it was all no
use, they remained obstinately inert. In desperation, around
two o'clock one night she tried an imaginary walk across the
marsh at home, but that only made her miserably homesick.
Finally, she was reduced to reciting poetry and fell asleep at
last at: "*No, no, go not to Lethe.*"

Still, there was Mrs Morton's party. Next night she got
out her evening dress and tried it on. The deep blue and the
long, full skirt suited her. Donald had said she ought to wear
evening dress all the time: "You look positively stately." She
recoiled from memories of the rest of that evening. There
would be eight of them. Mrs. Morton had ordered two
bottles of wine; Mary was cleaning the house from cellar
to garret. The old everlastings had been thrown away and
the halls had an unfamiliar smell of furniture polish, while
the conversation over meals ran more and more on charlotte
russe and chestnut stuffing, with Mary taking an animated
part from the kitchen door.

After all, she thought, hanging the dress at the back of the
closet, all she needed was something to look forward to. At
school she had always had to have some future point – a half
term holiday or breaking-up date – towards which to look.
It was just the same here, and the trouble with her now was
that she had come to look on her tutorial as a sort of focal
point around which the week revolved. It was absurd to let
a little thing like skipping one of them upset her so.

The party was going to be great fun. She covered an
incipient spot with cream and got into bed. Of course it
was. This was going to be *the* success. The twins would
be dazzled; Spencer Russell would take no notice of Olga;
George would be at her side all evening: "You should always
wear evening dress . . ." At the theatre: Professor Winter
and Julia. He would come over to them: "May we join
you afterwards?" Amazement among the Mortons. Julia

would sulk. Almost convinced, smiling to herself, Susan fell asleep.

The trouble about daydreams, she thought bitterly as she sat between Ralph and George at the theatre, was that the reality was such a catastrophe.

In cold misery she reviewed the events of the evening. Dinner had been a glorified Sunday lunch, with wine instead of sweet cider, and George and Olga rivalled for once. Spencer Russell might not be much to look at (spectacles and sandy hair and a profile like a horse), but he was magnificently sure of himself. Older than the others, an established bachelor with an apartment in New York, he patronised them charmingly. He was the kind of young man who called his interlocutor 'my dear' at frequent intervals, largely regardless of sex. Visibly aware of his aristocratic background, he made a point of his liberal and intellectual connections in New York. He had taken pains over dinner to tell them at some length about the night he had spent sitting up talking about life with a young poetess (her name, carefully concealed, slipped out absent-mindedly in a parenthesis). Bolt upright at her end of the table, Mrs Morton pretended not to hear, but, Susan was sure, kept repeating the magic formula: "Such an intelligent family," to herself.

Incurably sceptical herself (she would still have liked to know what Spencer Russell actually *did*), Susan was surprised to see that Olga, too, seemed impressed. She had never seen her defer to anyone before, but she seemed fascinated by this blend of admiration and patronage. And, of course, Susan told herself, it must be satisfactory to be so singled out for attention. Spencer Russell had soon made it clear that Olga was the only person in the room that he considered worthy of the slightest attention.

Altogether, once she had resigned herself to total submersion, dinner had been entertaining enough. It was afterwards that the real blow had fallen. She had run upstairs to get her coat while the others lingered over coffee. Coming down again, she paused to find a refractory sleeve, and as she did so, heard Olga and George talking below.

"I bet you can't," Olga said.

"I bet I could have her eating out of my hand if I wanted to, but what a chore." George's voice was cheerful. "I've never heard her say more than three words together yet."

"That's because she's so learned," Olga again. "She's reserving judgement."

"I'll have a stab at it," George concluded, as Susan started, scarlet-faced, back up the stairs. "Betty's in a tantrum about Aggie and it'll serve her right."

Betty Jane had refused to freeze herself, as she said, driving in George's old car. As a result, when Susan finally came down, more silent than ever, in the elevator, she found that she was to drive in with George.

"And very handsome you look tonight, Susan," he handed her in. "What a comfort you don't have notions about draughts."

If only she could have thought of a really scathing answer that would have put him in his place, without showing that she had overheard his conversation with Olga. Instead she had merely blushed, and she was blushing again with mixed fury and discomfort when the curtain fell on a play she had hardly seen.

They were to go out to the Stage Coach Inn for drinks afterwards and she found that again she was to go with George, while Olga and Spencer Russell dazzled each other and the twins took the Larraby sisters in their closed car. Silent on the way out, George became very much the gallant when they arrived. It was: "Have another drink, Sue?" ...

"How did you like the play?" . . . all with his head close to hers, the full battery of his charm playing on her; and one eye watchful for how Betty Jane was taking it. Susan sat tense with embarrassment and fury. If only she could think of the right, the final thing to say. He was using her; he used everyone; devouring them with his charm and then spewing them out when he was tired of them.

But she could think of nothing. She could only watch the Larrabys and the twins in cheerful conversation; Olga and Spencer deep in tête à tête, out of which from time to time Olga would emerge to throw a quick, amused, surreptitious glance at George. Absorbed in his own effort to impress, Spencer noticed nothing, but each time Susan writhed.

"Time we were going home," she shrank from George's casual, possessive hand on her shoulder. "How about it, Betty, d'you want to risk your life this time?"

"No, thank you." Betty was definite. "I'm going with the twins. You can have Susan."

On the way back, George stopped the car at a dark turning, put a practised arm round Susan and kissed her. It was the last straw in a bitter evening. She wrenched away from him into the corner of the car. "Don't waste your time. Betty Jane's not here to see." She was appalled at the fury in her voice.

"*Tiens*, as we say in France." Even George was temporarily taken aback. He recovered quickly. "I beg your pardon," there was insult in the over-elaborate gesture of apology, "I must have got my signals crossed. What *do* you want then?"

Already, he had her hopelessly in the wrong. "I want to go home," she said, a vision of black Atlantic before her eyes.

"And so you shall." Humming faintly under his breath ("*Au près de ma blonde . . .*"), he put the car into gear.

Susan finished the drive in furious silence, hunched up in her corner of the car. "*I got my signals crossed . . . what do you want, then?*" Was that the kind of impression she gave?

"*You're so transparent, Susan.*" It was Mother's voice; of
course, it would be. But what *had* she wanted? She moved
restlessly. She didn't know . . . but not this, anyway. If she
could only think of something devastating to say . . . Grace
would know how . . . Anyone but a fool would . . .

She still had not spoken when they got to Brimmer Street.
George was in command of the situation as usual. "No hard
feelings, Sue, I hope?" It was no use. Anything she said would
only make her look more of a fool than ever.

"Oh, no." Her voice was dull.

"Good. Then I think I'll be shoving along. Goodnight."

There was a note for her in the hall. '*Professor Winter
called,*' it read. '*Will you go to his house, 40 McCarthy Road,
for your tutorial tomorrow. His office is being painted.*' She
crumpled the paper in her cold hand and went upstairs to
bed, but not to sleep.

Chapter Five

Morning brought no consolation. Just when her sleep seemed sound at last, cold light in her face, cold sounds from Brimmer Street warned her that it was time to get up and face Mrs Morton and Mary, and, worst of all, Olga. She had been in the drawing room with Spencer Russell the night before and had glanced up to say goodnight as Susan passed. Had they noticed anything?

Why should they have? Susan swung reluctant feet out of bed. There had been nothing to notice. George's frustrated kiss would hardly show like a brand on her cheek. Why all the fuss about it anyway? What a joke he must have thought her.

Across the hall, the guest room door was still mercifully shut. Relieved, she immured herself in the bathroom and turned on both taps. Her head ached and her eyes were gritty from lack of sleep. It had been after two when she had finally turned out her light. Heavy with rum and misery, she had fallen asleep at once, to wake again as the hall clock struck three. With the fierce clarity of the small hours she had reviewed the events of the evening, twisting and turning this way and that for comfort, and finding none. When the clock struck four, calmly, ruthlessly, she had realised that this, already, was Friday. Today was to be the tutorial she had hardly dared look forward to through an endless fortnight.

Without sleep, she would be useless. Ice-calmed by the

79

thought, she had lain rigid, compelling sleep. She had counted: in fives, in tens; sheep, elephants, hippopotami; at last the houses round the square at home. Unable to remember what stood between the New Inn and Miss Mincheon's cottage, she was broad awake again at the half hour. This was disaster. And in the lowest deep . . . She began reciting from *Paradise Lost*: "*Thrones, dominations, princedoms, virtues, powers . . .*"

Sleep was full of nightmares. A tutorial with George: "*Quite hopeless; why don't you go back to England?*" His face, diabolic, turning slowly to Donald's, then to Professor Winter's. Somewhere, far away, Father, disapproving, had given her up: "*You're so transparent . . .*"

No wonder her head ached. But the bath, fiery hot, would revive her. She lay, almost in agony, watching her legs and arms turn scarlet. Better if she could have slept late, but the hall clock, striking eight at the climax of another dream, had been final. "*Macbeth does murder sleep . . .*" Besides, she might get out of the house before Olga waked to tell Mrs Morton about the evening: "Poor Susan, she *did* make a fool of herself."

Her eyes closed. But she must get out of the house. She stood up, dizzy for a moment from the heat, and reached for her towel. The mirror over the basin was clouded with steam. It was a comfort not to have to look at the weary face that she knew lurked there. But under a sudden compulsion she rubbed the mirror with her towel and watched the dull, familiar features reveal themselves. Yes, under the temporary flush were pallor, dark circles, all the insignia of despair.

Oh God, what an idiot. Why shouldn't he kiss you? She stepped into her bedroom slippers. No reason in the world. *The trouble was that she had wanted him to.* There it was. The flush was darker. She turned away. Better no kisses than second-hand ones. She had proved that, for what it was worth.

Olga's door was still closed. Thanking God, she dressed quickly and hurried downstairs. The smell of haddock in the hall turned her suddenly sick. Friday, of course. Mary always gave them fish, saving them whether they liked it or not.

Mrs Morton was reading her mail, but looked up, eager for details of the party. Mary leaned against the kitchen door to listen. Listless, Susan did her best. What had the play been about? Yes, the Stage Coach Inn . . . About two . . . A wonderful evening. Her orange juice tasted bitter. "No haddock, thank you Mary, I really couldn't."

At last she was safely away. And still no sign of life behind the guest room door. She made her bed, looked out for a weary minute at the raw, grey day, and turned to leave. When she stood still for a minute, the tiredness enveloped her, her eyelids flickered, longing to close. Better not stand still.

A few cold drops of rain fell as she came out of the subway by the entrance to Harvard Yard. As always, the paths were full of hurrying young men, busy as the last autumn leaves that blew this way and that across the grass. Susan threaded her way through them. It would be much less lonely at the North Pole. There, at least you would not be lonely in the middle of a crowd. I could fall down dead, and they would tidy me away, she told herself; I could go mad, and they would put me in an asylum; I could burst into tears, and they would politely take no notice. *Nobody would care.*

No, Grace would. The thought was comforting. But when she got to the library, Grace was not there. She had been clinging to the idea of telling her all about it, soothed by the thought that under her cheerful eye, the tragedy would become drawing room comedy at the worst. She went over to Longfellow Hall and looked in the smoking room. No Grace. She wandered forlornly back to the library and looked through it again. No Grace. She investigated the ladies' room,

81

again without success. At last, reluctantly, as the clock struck twelve, she gave in and went to her class.

After an abstracted hour, in the course of which she gathered that Hardy's novels were full of tragic purpose, but his way with his characters sometimes high-handed, she returned to her search for Grace. It was no use. There was still no sign of her in the smoking room, and none in the library. She was not in the cafeteria nor yet in any of the ladies' rooms. Giving up in despair, Susan realised that she was actually hungry. After all, she had had no breakfast. She went to their usual drugstore, hoping that she might find Grace there. Disappointed again, she ordered split-pea soup and a cheese and bacon sandwich and ate without tasting them.

Outside again, she paused on the sidewalk. Brattle Square was full of Cambridge ladies on their way to the Post Office and the Personal Book Shop. It was a curious no-man's-land, she thought. Harvard Square belonged entirely to the students who strode into the Co-op or the Harvard Garden Grill. In Brattle Square it was different: respectable Cambridge raised its head and student and old lady were all one in the eyes of the Post Office.

But the Square's activity only intensified her own loneliness. She turned and walked back towards Radcliffe. She ought to go to the library. She was more and more aware that, for once, she was badly prepared for a tutorial. She had been too restless in the last two weeks to work well. Perhaps if she were to spend the next two hours reading some essays on the Elizabethan drama – Eliot, perhaps, or Lamb – she could sharpen her dull thoughts. But a kind of desperation drove her to go on looking for Grace. She walked up to Bertram Hall, which was deep in an afternoon quietness. Grace's room was empty and silent like the rest of the building. There were signs of a rapid change. A black skirt had been thrown on the bed; a drawer was half open, revealing a tumbled pile of sweaters; a pair of shoes lay by a chair where Grace had stepped out of them.

The air of the room was cold and dead. Automatically, Susan closed the gaping drawer, shut the door behind her and walked slowly back to the library. It was three already. Her long hair fell in her eyes as she turned the uncomprehended pages of Eliot's *Essays*. At half past three she gave it up and went to the ladies' room. It was cold and empty as her own future. One of the wash-basins was blocked with pieces of damp paper towel; a tap dripped sullenly into it. Presently, there would be a flood. The shelf above was littered with mouse-coloured hair, hair-grips, smudges of spilled powder.

Why was all hair mouse-coloured off the head? Susan dug in her bag and brought out the lipstick Grace had made her buy: "No need to go round looking like a charity child." But today, the scarlet mouth merely made her face look paler than ever. Everything she did was in languid slow motion. "All you need, my girl," she told her pallid reflection, "is a good night's sleep."

When she got to the bottom of Plympton Street her watch was still obstinately at ten to four. This time she would not be early. She went straight on to the river and sat on a bench staring unseeingly across at the Business School. The cold wind blew through her coat. She was a hopeless, ridiculous failure. She was so busy dreaming about fantastic social successes that she didn't even do her work properly. No wonder everyone made fun of her. No wonder George thought she would be grateful even for Betty Jane Larraby's cast-off kisses. After all, they went well enough with her second-hand clothes.

How tired she was. Her head ached worse than ever. If she had ever known anything about Elizabethan drama she had forgotten it. Professor Winter would think it was a waste of time even to be sorry for her. If only it was five o'clock and the tutorial was safely over. If only she was back in England. *Would God 'twere night . . .*

It was five to four. She got up and walked slowly past Dunster House. The sunlight was fading; soon it would be dark. Two young men in shorts and heavy sweaters passed her at a trot; "Serve you right if we miss tea," one of them was saying. She ached suddenly with homesickness for an English tea by the fire, with buttered toast and the curtains drawn against the outside world. "Not *another* slice," Mother would say, "You'll be fat as a pig, Susan." Even Mother's constant criticism would be better than this blank loneliness.

That must be the house. It was small and white and sat sideways to the road as if it did not care to associate with it. She climbed the neat white steps to the porch and rang the bell. In the silence that followed she took a drowning look up and down the street. Beaumont and Fletcher, dramatists; Beaumont and Fletcher . . .

Professor Winter opened the door himself. "Hullo," he said, "how've you been all this time? Come on in. Sorry to make you come here, but my office is full of painters." He took her coat and led her into a square blue living room full of books. "Sit down. I recommend the sofa." He closed the hall door and moved over the the large armchair opposite. "Cigarette? Oh, sorry, I forgot." He got out his pipe.

The sofa was dangerously comfortable. Susan looked around. No photographs; one big oil painting – strange blues and greens with a touch of gold – over the mantlepiece; no flowers; only, everywhere, books. They filled the bookshelves that lined two of the walls; they overflowed into piles on the floor and broke in a wave over the desk. Feeling an unexpected angle in the corner of the sofa, Susan brought out *The Love Song Of J. Alfred Prufrock*.

"Sorry." He got up to take it from her. "Fine way I treat my first editions, I must say." He balanced it on top of a pile of books on the desk. "Do you like Eliot?"

"Oh, yes." She sounded schoolgirlish again. If only she could think. "Specially *Ash Wednesday* . . . all the sunlight bits."

He smiled. " '*Weave, weave the sunlight in your hair* . . .' It's not *Ash Wednesday*, though, you know. I used to mix those two up myself. Well," he knocked dry ash out of his pipe against the hearth, "I suppose we'd better get down to it. How did you get on with Beaumont and Fletcher?"

Her mind froze. "I can't say I liked them as well as Webster."

"I'd be scandalised if you did. But why not?"

"It's all so artificial," she floundered, "and I don't seem to be able to get interested in the people."

He laughed. "You ought to have been a historian. You always come back to people. There's more to it than that, you know. How about craftsmanship? Can't you give the poor things any credit for that?"

"I suppose so. It's neater than Webster; but that's just it, it's all so clever and – I don't know – full of imitations of Shakespeare and things, and I just can't get worked up about it."

"And you insist on getting worked up? You're as bad as the magazine crowd; all you ask is a good emotional orgy and you're happy. Is that it?"

"Oh, dear, perhaps it is." Sinking further into the corner of the sofa, she was too tired to do anything but agree with him.

"Don't apologise," he relit his pipe. "At least it's an honest approach, with no false pretences and talking about art; but it's not exactly the most comprehensive one, you must admit. I hate to think what's going to happen to you when we get to Restoration Comedy. If you go in for identification and wish fulfilment and all that, you're going to end up fairly confused,

I'm afraid. I don't quite see you as Millamant. That's the trouble with women scholars: they will take everything personally. It's the trouble with women, come to that. And for God's sake don't say 'I don't' or I'll throttle you."

"I wasn't going to," said Susan meekly.

"I'm glad to hear it. Are you planning to teach?"

"I had thought of it." Susan was surprised at the sudden question.

"For God's sake don't. You'll end up as bad as the rest of them. Oh, of course there are a few who get away with it. I've known two or three who managed to be educated without being blue-stockings. They were the ones who had the sense to stick in fields they knew something about it: women novelists, you know, and maybe the romantics. But, oh my God, the others! They get to be as passionate and stupid about their subject as adoring mothers about their children, and quite as tiresome. I know an expert on Pope who becomes positively violent if you dare suggest that his philosophy might have left something to be desired. And then, of course, they dry up. They're so busy being Pope, or Chaucer, or even Shakespeare that they've no time to be themselves." He got up, long and angular in the gathering dusk, and turned on a reading lamp on the table behind Susan's sofa. "Sorry about the oration; I don't know why I have to scold you about female scholars." He drew the dark blue curtains with a rattle of curtain rings. "You're in no danger yet."

He doesn't even think I'm good enough to be one, Susan thought, I'm just a little fool who takes things personally.

"But to come back to the matter in hand," he went on, "what are we going to do to convince you that there's something to be said for the craftsmen? Don't think I'm going to let you get away with this fine romantic attitude of all for passion and the world well lost. I think perhaps it's time we rubbed your nose in a little technique. For a beginning, what can you tell me about Beaumont and Fletcher's use of prose as compared to Shakespeare's?"

She had not been listening. She was a fool who pretended to be a scholar because she was no good at anything else. Even as a scholar she was a failure. He had stopped talking. He must have asked her a question. "I'm awfully sorry," she said, "what did you say?"

He looked at her. "I do believe you've been sleeping through my lecture on the female of the species. Well, it serves me right."

"Oh, no, really. I—" Susan stopped. It was the last straw; she was beginning to cry. Tears hung heavy in her eyes and she fumbled in her bag for a handkerchief. At any rate she had her back to the light.

"What I said," he repeated himself patiently, "was that it was time we paid some attention to technique. What can you tell me about Beaumont and Fletcher's use of prose?"

She blew her nose. "Well, they use it for comedy, don't they, and of course Shakespeare did too." She stopped.

"Look," an idea struck him, "did you *read* the plays I suggested, or has your social life been interfering, by any chance?"

"Oh, no, it's not that. I did read them." It was easier if she talked in short sentences, "I'm sorry. I'm afraid I'm not much good today." A tear escaped and fell with what seemed to her a resounding splash on her bag.

Still he hadn't noticed. "That's too bad. Then I suggest we call it a day and you can brood about prose for next week. You might even do me a learned treatise on it. In the meantime, how about a glass of sherry? I think I owe it you for lecturing you when you're not feeling well." He got up as he spoke. As he collected a bottle and two glasses out of a cupboard in the corner of the room, Susan mopped at her eyes surreptitiously. When he

87

came back she was sitting up very straight in the corner of the sofa.

"There," he said, "that'll fix you up."

"Thank you so much." It tasted faintly of tears.

"I hope it isn't America that's got you down so." He sat down again. "Remember I've got a bet with you that one of these days you'll tell me you want to stay."

"I doubt it." Difficult to control her voice.

"Is it anything you want to talk about? After all, if this was Oxford, I suppose I'd be your moral tutor. I wish you'd consider me as such, if it'd be any help."

"I don't know." She sipped her sherry. "It's everything, really."

"Everything's rather hard to cope with. Is it your work that's bothering you? Because there's no reason why it should; it's going very well."

"No, it's not that . . . Oh, it's so silly."

"It must be more than that if it's upset you like this."

"It's nothing, really. I'm awfully sorry to be such a nuisance. I'd really better be going." Her head was spinning from tiredness and sherry. She did not want to go. She felt safe here. Outside were darkness and memories of last night. *What do you want*? But she must go. She would start to cry again if she stayed.

"That's a fine way to treat your moral tutor." He filled her glass and knelt down by the fire. "I'm going to light a fire and you're going to drink another glass of sherry and tell me all about it, if I have to shake it out of you. For another guess, I bet it's the Mortons. Does Mrs Morton beat you or something?"

"Heavens, no." She started to laugh and was appalled when the laugh turned into a sob.

"Why, Susan." He was beside her on the sofa; his arms around her. "What on earth's the matter?"

88

It was no use. She sobbed helplessly into his shoulder. "I am so sorry," she managed through her tears.

"Don't be sorry. It's all right." He was stroking her hair. "Just cry it out, Susan. It'll do you good."

She sniffed and looked up at him. "I'm dreadfully sorry," she said again.

"You're perfectly ridiculous," he said, and kissed her. The bleak world of the morning vanished; she was warm and safe and part of her was singing. All she knew was that she did not want him to stop. At last he drew away and looked down at her. "Oh, Susan; oh, my dear." He kissed her again. The fire was crackling; when she opened her eyes she saw its light dancing up the walls and on the ceiling. She curled closer to him and her bag fell on the floor.

"Leave it," he said, "darling."

"But I need a handkerchief."

"I should say you do." With his free hand he dug in his pocket and gave her his. "Here."

"Thank you." She blew her nose.

"Thank goodness," he said, "now you can breathe." He kissed her again.

How strange it was suddenly to feel so secure. "How I have wanted to do that," he said at last. "I hope you give me credit for my strength of character. Not that this is exactly the moment to boast of it. I thought I'd got you safely out of mind, with this two week holiday and all, and then you go and burst into tears. It's all your fault."

She looked up at him in surprise. "Was that why you told me not to come last week?"

"What a silly little thing you are. Of course it was. I've been fighting you off ever since you came stalking into my office hating the whole pack of us. It's nice to have given in, though. Happy?"

"Incredibly."

He pushed her hair back from her face. "And I suppose when I took you walking you just thought it was kind professor feeling sorry for lonely student."

"Of course."

"I'm afraid I'm not that philanthropic. I've been wanting to ask you again ever since. And then you walked in today looking like a ghost, and I went and scolded you."

"You certainly did."

"How nice to see you laugh." His finger traced the dark circles under her eyes. "What have they been doing to you, Susan? You do look dreadfully tired." He moved over and swung her legs up on to the sofa. "There, that's better." He settled her head more comfortably on his shoulder. "Now tell me the tragic story of your life."

She smiled up at him. "It isn't tragic any more."

"Oh, Susan." She drowned in his kiss. All she wanted was to be nearer and nearer to him. She clung to him and felt his hands travel about her as she pressed closer. Her only defence from this sudden violence of feeling lay in her closeness to him. Her lips pleaded with him for some slackening in the tension and were overruled. Somewhere in the back of her mind, she heard a chorus of familiar, disapproving voices, but her only safety from them, as from everything else, lay in his arms. He moved slightly and she held him desperately to her. She felt his lips form the word "Susan," as his hands moved more strongly about her. And then, rearing up to look down at her: "Are you safe?"

"Of course I am." She had never felt safer.

"I'm glad. It's better—" He was kissing her again, pulling away her clothes, and she was in a frenzy of helping him. Even the pain, when it came, was pleasure.

The fire burned low and quiet shadows crept in from the corners of the room. Then a log fell with a cluster of sparks; a car started up in the street and there was a sudden burst of voices outside. A telephone rang in the house next door and a dog barked persistently, forlornly in the night. Susan lay and listened, peaceful, now, and quiet; at home as she had never been before.

"Susan," his arms were gentle now. "Aren't you angry with me?"

"No," she said. "Should I be? I love you."

"My darling." He kissed her, gently now, and for ever. "But you ought to be. You ought to rush to the Dean and have me thrown out of Harvard. I ought to be ashamed of myself."

"But you're not." She was almost triumphant.

"No, I'm not. I love you so, Susan. But I should be ashamed."

"Don't be. I'm so happy, and I was so miserable."

"Were you? I must say you looked it."

"I looked frightful."

"You did, rather."

She laughed. "I suppose I ought to care, but I don't, not a bit. I don't seem to care about anything any more."

He sat up suddenly. "You'd better, though. Are they expecting you home to supper?"

"Heavens, yes. What time is it?"

"Late. Can't you phone and say you'll be out? Please."

"I suppose I could. I don't want to move, ever. But what'll I say?"

"Oh, say you're up at Bertram." The telephone had a long extension and he picked it up and brought it over to her. "There you are. You make your call while I go and look in the ice-box."

She sat up and pulled on her skirt. How strange. How incredible. A vague, drugged hand pushed her hair back from her forehead. As from a great distance, she imagined the house on Brimmer Street . . . Mrs Morton . . . Mary . . . She sat up straighter, picked up the receiver, and dialled.

91

"Hullo, Mary. This is Susan. Would you be an angel and tell Mrs Morton I won't be home to dinner?"

"Such goings on." Mary's voice was hurt. "And me with the chicken frying on the stove."

"Oh, Mary, I am so sorry. Save some for me cold, won't you?"

"Oh, no doubt you'll see it again. All right, I'll tell Mrs Morton." Mary rang off.

David reappeared. He was David and not Professor Winter at all. How strange it all was. She smiled at him dreamily.

"All right?" he asked.

"Yes, perfectly. Except the maid's cross because it's fried chicken."

He laughed. "Too bad. And all you're going to get here is bread and cheese."

"It sounds wonderful. I do believe I'm hungry."

"You'd better be. I don't like to see you so pale." He made her a sandwich and poured her another glass of sherry. "Here's to you," he raised his glass.

She ate what he gave her obediently, without noticing it. The fire was burning up again now and shadows danced and faded on the ceiling. From time to time the sound of voices outside intensified her feeling that here she was safe. Outside were the heat, the fury and the fret; here there was nothing but the fire, and quietness, and David. She finished her sandwich and settled back more comfortably. She never wanted to move. Nothing should disturb this peace. She closed her eyes.

"Don't go to sleep, my darling," David looked up from the fire.

"Why not?"

"It's hardly polite, for one thing. And besides, you've got to have some more to eat."

"Oh, I couldn't."

"Yes, you could." He picked an apple out of the bowl of

fruit on the floor beside him and gave it to her. "Not as good as the ones on my tree, but not bad. Would you like it cut up so you can eat it like a lady or would you rather have it as is?"

"As is, thank you."

"I had a feeling you were no lady. What a comfort." He gave it to her.

She laughed. "That's what George says." The memory of last night was comic now.

"That you're no lady?"

"No, that I'm a comfort."

"Does he, indeed? And who, pray, is George?"

"He's Mrs Morton's grandson."

"Should I be jealous?"

"I don't believe I'd bother." She laughed. "As a matter of fact he thinks I'm a prig and a bookworm and dying to be kissed."

"He does, does he?" He kissed her. "Have another apple," he established himself on the sofa beside her, "and tell me more about George. He sounds like a deplorable character to me. Has he anything to do with what was the matter with you today?"

"Well, a bit." It was amazing how easy it was to talk to him now she had her head safely buried in his shoulder. "Him and a lot of other things."

"Like what?"

"Oh, I don't know. Homesickness, I suppose, and not knowing what it was all about, and being such a fool."

"What kind of a fool, if I may ask?"

"Well, not being able to talk to people, and getting stuck at parties, and things like that."

"In fact, what it all comes down to is that there was a party last night, and you didn't enjoy it, and George kissed you, and you didn't enjoy that either, which shows your good taste."

She laughed. "You make it all sound so silly."

"So it is. As far as I can see you're thoroughly upset just because you're not a Boston beauty. Is that right?"

She rubbed her nose against his shoulder. "I'm afraid so."

"You ought to be spanked. If all those dark circles were just because your name's not Cabot, I'm afraid I've been wasting my sympathy."

"That wasn't quite all," she was shy again.

"Good Lord, more confessions. Well, what now?"

"Well, I . . ." she paused. How hard it was, after all, to say it. She went on in a rush. "I'd sort of got used to counting on our tutorials to get me through the week, and then we skipped one, and it was such a long time, and you were going weekending with people." She was blushing fiercely.

"That," he said, "is much better. I call it a really respectable reason for looking tired." He kissed her. "I suppose you mean Julia, and it's high time I confessed that she's my oldest and dearest friend." He was laughing at her; she was suddenly rigid in his arms. He shook her slightly. "I do love you, Susan. Julia, my darling, is my older sister. She saved me from drowning when I was three and gave me my first watch when I was fourteen. She's about the nicest person in the world and I'm sure she'd be flattered to death to hear you were even a little jealous of her. We must go up and see her."

Susan took a long, cold plunge. "Won't she mind?"

"Not Julia. But don't let's think about that tonight. It's too good just having you here. And you really aren't angry with me, darling? You ought to be, you know."

"I suppose so. But it's no use, I'm not. I'm too happy. It's all very confusing."

"And you're very tired," he looked down at her, "you really are going to go to sleep on me any minute. I'm afraid I'd better take you home, Susan."

"I don't want to."

"Nor do I, but I'm going to." He pulled her to her feet. The ground was unsteady.

"Goodness," she leaned against him. "I do feel strange."

"You'll be all right out in the air." He fetched her coat and helped her into it. Then he kissed her for the last time. "Please don't look so dazed, darling."

"I can't help it. It's just . . . it all feels so unreal."

"Oh, my dear." He took her arm. "Look, we must go."

They went out into a cold, clear night. In the fresh air Susan realised how tired she was. The world was dizzy round her. She leaned back in the car and closed her eyes. Almost immediately, it seemed, he was stopping the car. "I'm afraid I'd better make you walk home from here. I hate to. But you'll be all right, won't you? And don't hate me tomorrow. Remember I love you, Susan."

"Yes," she said.

"And, darling, will you come walking with me on Sunday? I'll pick you up at the corner of Cambridge and Charles Street at two-thirty. All right?"

"Yes." Again she answered almost mechanically.

"Goodnight, my dear."

"Goodnight." She stood for a while looking with vague eyes at the lighted river and the stream of traffic. Then she turned and walked slowly along Brimmer Street.

The street was quiet and the house itself dark and silent. She stopped under a street lamp and looked at her watch. After eleven. Mrs Morton would be in bed, Olga would be out still.

The hall was dark with only one small lamp burning. It looked a long way upstairs and she rang for the elevator. Waiting for it, she leant, half asleep against the cool wall, and when it came she was glad to sit on Mrs Morton's stool in the corner. She had never been so tired. She undressed slowly,

95

watching herself with puzzled eyes in the mirror. It should all
be different, somehow, and yet it was all the same. She took a
last look at the white, tranced face in the mirror and turned out
the light. She had not washed her face, or brushed her teeth.
She had not even bothered to put on pyjamas. In the silent
dark she opened the window and climbed with slow, drugged
movements into bed. She ought to feel wicked. Perhaps she
would in the morning. She was asleep.

Chapter Six

She had never slept so well. She was oceans down in sleep, protected even from dreams by the waters above her. Faintly and luxuriously, was it at the last moment before she fell asleep, or all night, or just as she awoke, she was aware of this? Blissfully conscious that never had she slept such a sleep. When she first waked, sunlight was streaming in at the window. She had forgotten to pull down the shades. She smiled vaguely, decided she did not care, and fell asleep again. Now, through her lighter sleep, she almost consciously enjoyed the knowledge that outside the world was waking up. There were noises in the street, not the early morning noises of the milk, which would mean that a sleepless night was almost over, but late, reassuring ones: men whistling, a dog barking, a bicycle bell. She was almost awake. She turned over and buried her head in the bedclothes.

When she woke next it was high noon. This time she was wide awake at once. Her thoughts picked up where they had left off the night before. Now she would feel wicked. She turned over luxuriously. She had never been so happy. David had a nine o'clock on Saturday. He must have been up for hours. Poor David. She looked at her watch. Twelve-thirty. How nice it would be to lie in bed all day. But lunch was at one. She threw back the bedclothes and stood up. The air was cold and she shivered, pyjamaless, and went to the closet for her dressing-gown.

It was impossible to hurry. She lay long in the bath moving her legs rhythmically so that the water ran over her in waves. Then she dressed leisurely, broodingly, with frequent pauses to gaze, thinking beatifically of nothing at all, out the window.

When she finally got downstairs she found Mrs Morton already in the dining room. "What a sleep you had," she said. "I hope it did you good. Mary saved your orange juice."

"Lovely." It had been put back in the refrigerator and was cold and refreshing. "I'm famished," it occurred to her.

"I don't expect you had enough for supper." Faint reproach in her voice. "You were at Bertram, I suppose?"

"Oh, yes." Susan was vague.

Mary brought in the lunch. "So you woke up at last. Olga's been out for hours."

Susan forgot to answer. Would David be having lunch at home? It was a long time till tomorrow afternoon.

"I do believe you're still asleep, Susan." Mrs Morton was in the minor key today.

"I'm so sorry." Susan pulled herself together. "What did you say?"

"George phoned this morning to ask if he could bring Betty to lunch tomorrow. And Olga's insisted on asking Roger, so we're going to be a party again. It's very inconsiderate of her. She knows what a hard week Mary's had. I hope you'll be in, Susan; Mary'll be needing some help with the dishes."

"Oh," Susan said. "Actually I'm supposed to be going for a walk at half past two. But if I skip coffee I can do the glasses and silver."

"Don't think of it for a minute," Mary was at the kitchen door as usual. "I've got all afternoon to get the dishes done, without a lot of amateur help cluttering up my kitchen."

"You know I'm no amateur, Mary."

"Yes, I must say," Mary admitted it grudgingly, "they do

98

bring a girl up in the old country. I've never found smears in the teaspoons you dry."

Susan sang as she walked to the subway. Happiness was a funny thing. Today the whole world shone. She thought of the bleak afternoon she had spent yesterday. Years ago, it seemed. It was hard to believe that she was the person who had stood, lonely and miserable, in Brattle Square and watched the old ladies chatter over their library books. It was hard to believe that they had all had the sad, dull faces she remembered. Today they would not look sad, but then today everything was different. The river shone in the sun, even the people in the subway looked pleasant. She smiled to herself and caught the eye of a woman opposite who smiled back. The whole world seemed happy.

As she came out into the Square she thought she saw him. Her heart turned over. It was an occurrence she had read about and refused to believe in. Now she threw science and scepticism to the winds. Today, anything could happen. But it was not David. She would have to wait a whole day. Sobered, she turned up towards Radcliffe.

There was no sign of Grace in the library, but she met another girl from Bertram Hall in the stacks. "Have you seen Grace?" she asked her.

"She's away for the weekend. Her father turned up; he's East for a convention and she's gone to New York with him. She's going to get dreadfully behind with her work. You haven't seen an Anglo-Saxon Grammar lying around have you? I left mine here last night and I can't find it anywhere. And I've got all the irregular verbs to learn over Sunday."

"You poor thing. But maybe it's a blessing in disguise. Haven't you noticed it's Saturday and a fine day?"

"What's that got to do with it?"

Susan laughed and went on her way. She collected two

volumes of Restoration plays as well as the Elizabethans she needed. Why had David said he could hardly see her as Millamant?

She started *The Way of the World* on the subway back to Boston and decided regretfully that he must think she was too serious-minded. She hardly felt so today. She was singing again as she let herself into the house.

"There's my girl," Mrs Morton called to her from the drawing room. "You're just in time for a cup of tea."

"How lovely. May I come in as I am? Hullo, Mrs Merryweather, how are you?"

Roger's grandmother was even more impressive than usual today, monumental in black satin. "I hear you had quite a party the other night." She was eating bread and butter with her usual concentration.

So she had heard about it. "Yes, indeed," said Susan. "It was great fun." Well, entertaining at least, she thought.

Mrs Merryweather and Mrs Morton looked surprised. They had been talking about her, Susan realised. Olga must have said something about Thursday night. They had been feeling sorry for her and enjoying every minute of it. How funny. She offered Mrs Merryweather more bread and butter and helped herself.

Mrs Morton sipped abstemiously at her tea and visibly counted Mrs Merryweather's slices of bread. "I was telling Mrs Merryweather how sorry I was we couldn't have Roger the other night. A party doesn't seem the same without him." (*Old hypocrite*, Susan thought.) "I must say, though, Spencer and Olga made a charming couple. He couldn't keep his eyes off her. I know you'll sympathise with me, Martha; I'm an old woman, with not much to look forward to, and I would like to see my Olga well settled."

"I know just how you feel." Mrs Merryweather helped

100

herself to chocolate cake. "Roger's coming to lunch with you tomorrow, he tells me."

"Yes, indeed." Mrs Morton smiled her most saccharine smile. "I told Olga we really ought to have him ... after all, she mustn't quite forget her old friends."

The shot went home. Mrs Merryweather paused, silenced, between bites. *I ought to say something*, Susan was suddenly angry. It was Olga who had insisted on inviting Roger. But what could she say? One did not go round calling old ladies liars to their faces.

In the suddenly tense silence, she heard the grandfather clock's slow, unsympathetic tick from the hall. Like the dentist's waiting room. Mrs Morton rustled in her quilts. "Are you feeling all right today, Susan? Olga thought the cold air in George's car was really a bit too much for you the other night."

She's trying to distract me, Susan smiled inwardly. My cue is a crimson blush. But she had no blushes to spare. "Yes, I was tired, and of course it was depressing having poor George in such a state about Betty Jane. I hope they've made it up." The old ladies looked more surprised than ever. *They really think I'm in love with George*, she thought. *If they only knew*. The tension in the room had slackened. "If you'll excuse me," she got up, "I think I'd better go and do some work." Pausing on the upstairs landing, she listened to the muted buzz of the old voices below. They must admire her self-control. She smiled again to herself.

She woke up on Sunday morning with a problem. If she had to help Mary with the dishes she would probably not be able to get out to meet David by two-thirty. She ought to call him up and tell him so. But the telephones at Brimmer Street were strategically placed in Mrs Morton's room, the drawing room and the front hall. If she tried to call from any of these points, Mrs Morton, or Mary, or even Olga would be bound

101

to come drifting into the room. Impossible to talk to David in front of any of them. Your motto, she told herself, turning over another unread page of *The Maid's Tragedy*, is, "*Oh, what a tangled web we weave.*" She decided that there was nothing to be done except hope that they would get through lunch promptly.

But even after deciding this she could not settle to her book. Her mind was restless on a deeper level, too. The golden glow that had kept her insulated from the world the day before had faded. She was tired, and dull, and doubtful. She remembered what David had said, so long ago, about suffering from too much fine frenzy. Perhaps one could. Perhaps a golden glow was not enough. She shivered a little as she wondered what Mrs Morton would say if she knew. Yesterday it had seemed supremely comic to hug her secret as Mrs Morton and Mrs Merryweather probed at her feelings about George; now, it seemed merely furtive. The thoughts came and went as she turned the pages of *The Maid's Tragedy*. Suddenly its theme of adultery and betrayal was overwhelmingly unpleasant and she closed it with a bang.

She ought to write to her mother. The habit of a Sunday letter home had stuck from her schooldays and she knew that her mother counted on it. She got out pen and paper. '*Dear Mother*,' she must tell her about the party, of course. The pen moved slowly: '*It was great fun. I wore my blue dress and Mrs Morton lent me her fur jacket. She really is fearfully kind. And the theatre was wonderful. Afterwards we drove out into the country for drinks . . .*' The stilted sentences crawled across the page like snails. Mother would be bound to know something was wrong.

Wrong. The golden glow had vanished indeed. She got up from the desk and wandered to the window. Staring down into Brimmer Street she wondered if she wanted to see David. Perhaps she should just stay at home. He would understand.

He understood everything. But that was just why she *must* see him. She could not face the midnight blackness that swept over her at the idea of staying at home. If she did, Brimmer Street would smother her.

And she wanted to see him. It was all very well to argue it this way and that, but all the time something inside her was already out there waiting for him at the corner of Cambridge and Charles Street. Ever since they parted, she had been suspended, waiting . . . Would they get through lunch in time? Perhaps she should have telephoned. Of course she should have done it from Mrs Morton's room immediately after breakfast, when Mary was clearing away and Mrs Morton was safely involved in the Sunday paper. She had been afraid that Olga would appear, but she had slept late; she always did. Now the chance was gone.

She sat down and re-read her letter to her mother. Perhaps it was not so bad. No word about David, of course, or, for that matter, about Donald. But then ever since she had gone to school – or was it since Father died? – she had found it increasingly difficult to tell her mother things. Her letters had become mere chronicles of events, her holidays at home silent times when she buried herself happily enough in her books. It was much easier to talk to David.

It did not matter where they started, her thoughts always came back to him. But she would not meet him. That was so clear it was incredible she had ever considered it. It was no use wondering how it had ever happened. No use thinking about it at all. It had happened, but it must not happen again. She ought never to see him again. Time enough, though, to worry about her next tutorial when Friday came. In the meantime, she would not go. She looked at the letter again. '*And of course,*' Mother had said before she left, '*I don't need to tell you to be careful with boys, Susan.*' She remembered the scene: Mother bending over her trunk in crimson slacks ("I can't think how you manage to have a grown-up daughter," people said); the one bit of advice thrown almost casually over her shoulder; the smell of mothballs in the room.

Too late now to be careful. She ought to feel wicked. Why did she even want to see him again? (Not that she would, of course.) What would Father have said? But he was so long ago; for once it was impossible even to imagine. She had never been so lonely. If she could only talk to David about it; he would help. But she must not see him. Her thoughts circled round again relentlessly. All the time they had avoided the focal point: *he was married*. She dived suddenly and faced it. *He had three children*. Two tears fell onto the letter. No use thinking about it. Suddenly and illogically she was furious with her mother. *"Be careful with boys."* The bald advice mocked her dilemma.

But it was no dilemma. There was no choice. She would not see him again. That was all. She sat down and finished her letter: more details of the party; a little about George and Betty Jane (that would amuse Mother); a good deal about her paper (that would not); no mention of David. It would do. She signed it, '*Your loving daughter, Susan.*' She was not the loving daughter who had signed that way last week. She was someone quite different. Better not think about that. As she sealed the letter, the gong rang for lunch.

Her hair was tidy. There were two bright pink patches in her cheeks. *I look as if I've used rouge*. Olga came out of her room yawning. "Hullo, Susan. Isn't it a depressing day? I hate grey Sundays."

Perhaps it would rain and he would not come. No, he would come. How long would he wait for her? "Yes, isn't it dismal." What would he do when he realised she was not coming?

"The gong's gone," said Olga, "we'd better be getting a move on."

Downstairs, George and Betty were taking off their coats while Roger talked to Mrs Morton. Less good-looking than George, he had the kind of face which encouraged people to stop in the street and ask the way. He would tell them, too, Susan thought, without all the humming and haaing and confusion of right and left that most people went in for. He would make a good teacher; clear and patient and humorous.

"Hi, Olga," George noticed them. "I hope you didn't catch cold the other night, Susan." He grinned at her, part superior, part conspiratorial.

"Oh, no. We English are tough." Tough enough not to go? *You're not going to*, she told herself, *you can't*.

"That's good." Missing the reaction he expected, George turned back to Betty.

Olga brushed past Susan. "Hullo, Roger, I haven't seen you for ages. How are you?" *I believe she's really fond of him*. It had never occurred to Susan.

"I'm thriving. I can see you are." Always quiet, he was almost brusque today. *Mrs Merryweather must have told him Olga didn't want him invited*, Susan thought. But what could she do about it? As she wondered, her chance to say something vanished; Mrs Morton was shepherding them into the dining room.

Susan sat opposite the big clock on the mantelpiece. At one-fifteen George was carving the beef and Mary was passing vegetables. She was even slower than usual today. With an eye on Roger, Olga had embarked on a story Spencer Russell had told her and did not notice the roast potatoes and creamed spinach at her elbow. Susan chafed.

"Have some vegetables, Olga," Mrs Morton's voice saved her from exploding.

Just before two, Mary served the ice-cream. The clock was racing. *But you're not going*, Susan reminded herself. At five

105

past, the telephone rang. Susan's heart turned over. *He can't come. He doesn't want to.* But Mary was smiling from the door: "For you, Olga. Another of your boyfriends."

Olga looked across the table at Roger, who had hardly spoken throughout lunch, shrugged her shoulders and went to the telephone. Betty and Roger broke simultaneously into self-conscious speech. "How's the bridge, Mrs Morton?" from Roger.

"What time do we start, George?" from Betty.

They kept it up valiantly till Olga returned. She smiled, faintly triumphant, at Mrs Morton. "Spencer's going to drive me down, Gran, he's picking me up at two-thirty. I hope you don't mind?" Sitting down opposite him, she managed not to see Roger.

At last they were moving upstairs for coffee. It was a quarter past. Susan hung back.

"Don't you bother with the dishes," Mary said, "you're excused."

"You're an angel, Mary," Susan said, "but I don't think I'm going out after all. I'll do the glasses and silver anyway." *You are not going. There is no hurry at all.* The words ticked over and over again in her mind, remorseless as the old grandfather clock. Far, far worse than the dentist's . . .

Roger opened the kitchen door. "What's the matter, Susan, are you running out on us?"

"I'm just going to help Mary with the dishes."

"Good. I don't like coffee and I'm an expert at dishes. You wash and I'll dry and Mary can serve the coffee in peace."

How courteous he was. It would never have occurred to George to help; not in a million years.

Mary beamed. "That's the boy. Susan's got a date at half past and I want to get her out of here."

Oh, hell, Susan thought, but Roger was rolling up his sleeves and took no notice. She finished stacking the dishes and started rinsing glasses under the hot tap. This was her chance to tell Roger that Olga *had* wanted him asked to the party and had insisted on his being invited to lunch today. But how could she? It must be casual. It must spare Mrs Morton. You cannot call your hostess a liar. Should you interfere with people anyway? *Mind your own business*, Mother would say. What would David do?

Drying a glass, Roger smiled approvingly. "That's the way to do it. No soap, no grease, no trouble at all. But aren't you scalding yourself?"

"Goodness, no. Women's hands are always tougher than men's. It's terribly nice of you to help." *Better mind your own business.*

"Not a bit. You'd better hurry, though, if you're going to make that date."

"Oh, that's all right." *You're not going. You are not going.*

Mary reappeared with the empty coffee tray. "Well, aren't you the speedy pair. The clock's just struck half past, Susan, you'd best be on your way." The doorbell rang. "That'll be Spencer Russell." Her voice breathed scorn. "Oh, well." Deliberately, she dried her hands on her apron, took it off and started for the front door as Susan passed her to take the stairs two at a time.

She changed her shoes, combed her hair and put on a jacket. Then she walked to the window and stood there staring out. *She must not go.* She would have to see him on Friday, but today she must not go. Friday would be time enough to try and explain to him. *What would he do now?* No use thinking about that.

Very slowly she walked to the door and closed it. Slowly and deliberately she took off the red jacket and hung it in her closet, took off her shoes and stood them under the chair. Long sobs were beginning to work their way up through her.

107

With a violent gesture she pulled the quilt off the bed and lay down flat on her face. As the sobs rose more and more violently she buried her head under the pillow to smother the noise.

A long time later – but it was only fifteen minutes when she looked at her watch – she heard the telephone ring. A sudden, irrepressible hope surged through her. Mrs Morton called from downstairs, "Susan, it's for you."

As she passed, she caught sight of her face in the mirror; it was ugly and shapeless with tears and she was glad to find Mrs Morton's room empty. She picked up the receiver. "Hullo?"

"Susan." It was his voice. "What happened to you?"

"I can't come." Her voice was lifeless.

"Susan, you *must*. I was afraid of this. I know you can't talk from there, darling, and I've got to talk to you. I've been desperate, worrying about you. Please, Susan."

She could not face her lonely room. "All right," she said, "I'll come. But only this time." She heard Mrs Morton at the foot of the stairs. "Goodbye." She put down the receiver and ran upstairs on stockinged feet as Mrs Morton rang for the elevator below.

She washed her face in cold water and put on the jacket and shoes again. "Have a good time, Susan," Mrs Morton called as she passed her room. "I'll expect you when I see you."

At the corner by the subway she had a moment of panic. Where was he? Then she saw his car parked a little way along Cambridge Street.

"Thank God." He opened the car door. "I was getting worried that you'd changed your mind again."

"I nearly did." She was still surprised at herself.

"I'm glad you didn't." He took her hand for a minute as she got into the car. "It's just as well, too, because if you

108

hadn't come I'd have come to Brimmer Street and dragged you out by the hair on your head."

"Would you really?"

"I should say so. I don't think you realise what a desperate character you're dealing with." His voice changed. "Susan, I've missed you terribly. Did you really mean not to come?"

"I thought I did."

"I was worried to death you wouldn't. I've thought about you all the time. You mustn't be unhappy, Susan." He picked up her hand and kissed it, then let it fall. "If I don't pay attention to my driving I'll get us both killed, and that'll be no help at all. We're going to Cape Ann, in case you're interested."

"Where's that?"

"North of Gloucester, if you know where that is. D'you mean to tell me you don't know your T S Eliot? What an ignoramus, I don't see how I stand associating with you."

"Nor do I." The world was golden again. *It was all right.* It was much more than that. She had been staring straight ahead at the traffic. Now she turned towards him. "Goodness," she said, "it's nice to see you."

"I'm glad." He was silent for a few minutes. Presently he said, "That's Faneuil Hall. They have the market there in the week; like Covent Garden, more or less. We must come down and see it when it's open; it's a wonderful place. And I want to show you North Boston some time. That's the old Custom House. Striking, isn't it?"

"Enchanting. I wish they made public buildings like that these days." She turned to stare.

"But they have to be so much larger now. You can hardly imagine the Custom House twenty times its size, can you?"

"No, I can't quite." *But we sound like an afternoon-tea party. What's the matter?*

109

"You ought to go to New York. I'd love to show you Radio City. There's a building for you."

But how can he? Her thoughts were grey again. They went on talking carefully on the surface of things as he drove through the Sumner Tunnel and out on to the Shore Road: British architecture compared with American; outdoor advertising; even the Elizabethans ... And every time he spoke of things he wanted to show her and places they must go, there was a cold hand on her heart. The only excuse for having come was that she had to explain why she could never come again. They fell into an uneasy silence.

At last, "This is Gloucester," he said, "but I don't feel much like sightseeing, do you?"

"No," she said, "not really."

"Then let's go right on. I'm taking you to a favourite place of mine, Pigeon's Cove. My Aunt Beatrice used to have a house up here when I was a boy, and I spent a lot of my holidays with her. I've always loved the place. I was as bad as you are, you know, Susan, and it used to be wonderful to get away from the New Bedford parties and safely off up here."

He parked the car and they walked out on to the cliffs. The sky was still grey, but it was a light, cloudless grey with no threat of rain. The sea below was quiet, working restlessly to and fro and beating patiently against the rocks, as if it knew it had all time to destroy them.

"How I love the sea." Susan stood with her head back staring out at it.

"I thought you would. It's wonderfully soothing, too. One of these days I'm going to make a collection of poems to go to sleep on. They'll all be either about sleep itself or about the sea."

"What a lovely idea." A small, erratic wind blew through her hair. "I suppose England's over there."

"Yes. A bit north, of course. Are you still homesick?"

"Not exactly homesick, but I wish I was there."

"You mean you wish you weren't here?"

"I don't know." Her voice was desperate.

He took her hand. "Come on. I know a sheltered place where we can sit."

It was a cleft in the rocks, just below tide level, where they could see nothing but the sea turning and returning below them, and hear nothing but its voices. They sat on his coat with their backs to the cold rock and he put his arm around her. She shivered slightly.

"May I, Susan?"

"I don't know," she said again. She sat and stared greyly out at the grey sea. "I don't know."

"Susan," his arm was still there. "Why don't you let yourself be happy? We could, you know."

"But we *shouldn't*!" She turned towards him vehemently, her long hair wild for a moment as she moved.

"Why not?"

"Because—" she stopped.

His arm was reassuring. "I know. For one thing, you've been brought up to think the whole thing is scandalous and immoral, and to make it worse, there's my wife."

"Yes." It was all she could say.

"How much do you know about that, Susan? I've taken it for granted you'd have heard the gossip. Everybody does."

"Yes," she said again.

"You know I married her when I was twenty – younger than you, Susan. God knows why I did it. I was mad, I think. I'd just got back from England and nothing seemed to matter very much. My friends were all businessmen by then, and started in life, and I was lonely as the devil, and homesick for Oxford – I was, too, you know, Susan – and Josephine was kind, and company. Sometimes I even think

111

she was in love with me a little when I asked her to marry me; I don't know, she might have been for a while. But there had been too many men before; there were bound to be more after." He stared at the sea for a moment. "I hate to tell you all this, Susan, but you've got to understand. I married her because I was lonely and miserable and needed someone. And she made me far more lonely and far more miserable, so that when she left me it was nothing but an unbelievable relief. Only I needed someone worse than ever. You know what it's like to be lonely, Susan."

It was hardly a question, but she nodded, the tears heavy in her eyes. "And then you walked into my office," he went on, "with your pale hair in the sunshine, and your own loneliness, and how could I help falling in love with you?"

She had not known that one could be so unhappy. It was a slow misery that ebbed and flowed in her like the sea below, washing resistlessly over every part of her. His voice came from far off; she was alone, lonely in a world of loneliness. "I don't know." It was all she could say.

"Susan, hasn't it made you happy at all?" The pleading voice was nearer.

"Oh, yes," she said. "But . . ." She stopped. If only there were words.

"Why the 'but', then?" he asked. "Who do we hurt, Susan, tell me?"

A voice rang in the back of her mind, "*Alas, alas, who's ruined by my love?*" "I don't know," she said, "but is that the point?"

"If it isn't, for God's sake what *is*? Look, Susan," his free hand waved towards the sea, "there's the world – a fairly unhappy place. And here we are, lonely and discouraged, finding we can comfort each other. Is that wrong? And please, darling, don't say 'I don't know' again."

She laughed unsteadily. "I'm afraid I was going to."

112

"I could see you were." His voice rose. "Susan, what's the use of my knowing what you're going to say before you say it? What's the use of your making the whole world a better place, if you won't let me love you? Why should we throw it away? It's too good."

"I know." The tears were streaming down her face.

"Then *why*?"

"Because I'm a fool, I think. Oh, David, it's so difficult. I do love you so," she talked fast, once she had started. "But, I don't know; I must be the last of the Victorians, I think."

"I know." His voice was gentle. "It's hard to fly in the face of all the things you were brought up with. But weren't you brought up to be a reasonable human being? And shouldn't you be able to decide things for yourself, rather than running blindly off to a set of rules?"

"I suppose so." The taste of tears was salt in her mouth.

"Maybe I'm just immoral," he went on, "though I don't think so. But it seems to me it would be much worse if we went on seeing each other and loving each other and making each other unhappy. And we can't stop seeing each other, even if we wanted to. Anyway, I can't imagine making myself want to. I love you. It all comes back to that, and isn't it more important than anything?"

His arm was urgent around her as she stared at the sea. "Yes," she said at last, "it really is." Giving up, she felt happiness surge back. *It was going to be all right*. The outside world was nothing, negligible. He was right: they were all that mattered.

Presently it began to get cold. She moved a little in his arms. "We're going to have to move pretty soon, or I'll freeze to death."

"You poor darling, why didn't you complain?" He got up and pulled her to her feet.

"I was far too comfortable."

113

As they neared the road she turned for a last look at the sea. "What a heavenly place." Sea gulls dived and swooped around them. "But why Pigeon's Cove?"

He laughed. "You have a wonderfully literal mind. Maybe there was a pigeon here once. Now, into the car with you and you'll find a rug in back."

On the way back they stopped at a small cafe and had hot chocolate and toasted English muffins. "I was starved," Susan said. "I was so busy wondering whether I'd be late at lunch that I feel as if I haven't eaten anything at all."

"I thought you didn't mean to come."

"I didn't, but all the time I was worrying about being late. Very confusing."

He laughed. "It must have been. I'm very glad you were confused, though. Have another muffin."

"I don't believe I could." She was regretful. "I never tasted anything so good, but I'll be getting as bad as Mrs Merryweather."

"Good Lord, I know her. Where does she fit in? Pretty soon you're going to have to settle down and tell me all about yourself so I'm not confused all the time."

"All right. Mrs Merryweather is Roger's grandmother. He's a friend of Olga's. Oh dear, and she's Mrs Morton's granddaughter, George's sister."

"How complicated. You mean the deplorable George who kissed you in the car?"

"*Tried* to kiss me."

"I beg your pardon." He paid the check. "I think we'd better get back to the car ourselves or I shall kiss you right here, which would be shocking."

She laughed. "It certainly would. Oh, darling, it's incredible to be so happy."

"I told you you shouldn't fight it."

It was dark now and the street lights were on. They drove

back quietly through the night, Susan a chrysalis of warmth and content in her rug. Once, David pointed to a turning. "That's the way to Julia's," he said. "When are we going up there?"

"I don't know. How can we?"

"I'll talk to her about it," he said. "She'll think of something. You'll love each other." He had heard the misery in her voice. "It'll all work out, Susan. I'm sure it will. It must."

"Yes," she said, "it must."

Chapter Seven

The last leaves had fallen from the trees and the roller-skating season was in full swing on the Esplanade. Mrs Morton complained dulcetly about the children as she wrapped Christmas parcels in the evening, and Susan found it necessary to interrupt her dreams and dodge them as she walked out to Cambridge. Mary, who never took any exercise beyond her rather desultory efforts with a mop, defended the children. "After all," she said, "it's flying in the face of Providence to bring children up in the city anyway, and if the poor little creatures can get some fun, it's not for us to stand in their way."

Susan agreed with her, but Mrs Morton, whose heart occasionally permitted a decorous stroll on the Esplanade, still objected. It always surprised Susan that a heart so easily upset by a random child, should survive the rigours of Christmas shopping. Mrs Morton and Mrs Merryweather spent two or three afternoons a week in raids on the Boston shops, from which Mrs Morton would return triumphantly to show her trophies to Susan in the evening.

Susan enjoyed the quiet evenings in the drawing room, when the card table was given over to a pile of coloured paper, ribbon and gift-tags. She much preferred the nightly consultations over whether Cousin Jessamine should have pink paper with gold ribbon, or green with red, to the bridge they superseded.

Wrapping the parcels with long, neat fingers, Mrs Morton talked to Susan about the relatives they were to go to. Cousin Jessamine was a silent old maid who lived in a huge house in New Bedford. "It's the strangest house. I think the green paper, Susan." Mrs Morton wrapped the soft wool shawl neatly in green paper and went on, "Jessamine's lived alone there ever since her mother died – twenty-five years it must be now – getting queerer every year. She was the prettiest thing you ever saw when she was young. I remember going down there to a Christmas party when I was eighteen. Jessamine was two years older than me and all the boys were wild about her. We were supposed to be very much alike, as a matter of fact." Mrs Morton glanced quickly up at the portrait over the mantelpiece. "Of course, being first cousins it wasn't surprising, but I was hardly out then and she was quite the belle of the ball.

"What a cold Christmas that was. I used to wake in the morning and find the water frozen in the glass by my bed. That always was a cold house; Jessamine will be glad of the shawl. There, now the red ribbon. I never did understand why she didn't get married. It wasn't that she didn't have plenty of offers, I'm sure – Roger's grandfather, for one; everyone was amazed when he married Martha. But then nobody'd ever heard of the Merryweathers, and Jessamine's mother had her mind made up right from the start that nothing but the best was good enough for Jessamine. I always did wonder what went wrong, though. I think one of the Santa Claus tags, Susan. She always liked things gay. That Christmas she had a scarlet dress my mother thought was quite shocking. I wish I could get down and see her some time, but I'm afraid my poor heart would never stand the drive. Would you pass me the scissors, please?" She cut the scarlet ribbon at a neat angle.

"I do wish I could make parcels look as pretty as you do," Susan said, "how do you do it?"

"Just practice, my dear. I'm an old woman and I've been wrapping Christmas parcels for a great many years. I ought to be good at it by now. How about your Christmas shopping, by the way? It's Thanksgiving next week, remember, and after that Christmas will be here before you know it."

"I suppose so, but really, I haven't got much to do this year." She would have to get Mrs Morton and Mary presents; and then there was David. What in the world could she afford to buy that he would like? She could hardly consult Mrs Morton about that, though! For the hundredth time she thought with astonishment how easy she found her double life. She was so used to the tangled web now that she wove it almost automatically. Mrs Morton had been slightly querulous when she first announced that she was going to stay and have supper with Grace at Bertram every Friday after her tutorial, but she had soon got used to it. It had meant telling Grace, of course. There was no use risking discovery by a telephone call. When Susan had haltingly told her a somewhat abridged version of the story, Grace had been first astonished, then horrified, and finally, somewhat to Susan's own astonishment, amused. But she had agreed to help. "Mind you," she'd said, "I'm against it, Susan. I hope you won't be sorry." "I won't," Susan had said, and meant it.

One evening a week seemed pathetically little, though. "The trouble is," David said, "I want you with me all the time." Failing that, they managed to escape together into the country for occasional afternoons, and had picked the last apples from David's tree before the frost came. It was not enough, Susan thought, handing Mrs Morton the scissors (what a blessing that she talked so much). Would David really have managed to arrange something with Julia? She was just back from New York and he had spent the weekend with her. "I'll need more time than that to tell her all about you, Sue." If only he could have

119

telephoned her today, but they had agreed that that was impossible.

The evening dragged on. Olga was to have an evening bag. "Of course she has dozens," Mrs Morton said, "but this is such a pretty one. Martha Merryweather's giving her a compact for it. I wish she wouldn't. I told her there was no need to. She will go on acting as if Roger and Olga were engaged. As if Olga hadn't more sense."

It was an increasingly sore point with Susan. Helpless, she had watched the breach between Roger and Olga slowly widen under expert, delicate pressures from Mrs Morton. After that first Sunday, there had never been a point at which actual intervention had seemed possible to her. It was all so trivial, so gossamer. The pool merely rippled, concentric circles starting outwards from Mrs Morton's gnat touches. Speech from Susan would be violent, the splash of a rock. How could she? When she'd told David about it, he had laughed, "I'd let them work it out for themselves if I were you. People are never grateful if you interfere."

So she had left it, but it worried her to see Olga more and more taken up with Spencer Russell ("that drip", she had called him, and nothing had happened to make the words less true). As for Roger, he hardly ever came to Brimmer Street now. It was only the blind obstinacy of hope that made Mrs Merryweather persist in her plans and presents.

"I met Eliza Larraby in Stearns' today," Mrs Morton's remark was no *non sequitur*. "Spencer's coming to them for Christmas. I do hope Gertrude decides they can all come up here. I really don't believe I'm going to be up to going to New York. Besides, what would happen to you if I went off and left you? I must write Gertrude again; it would be so nice for George to be near Betty Jane." Mrs Morton always preferred to mention her secondary motive. She put her hand to her head. "I've got a little bit of a headache tonight; all

the Christmas shopping. I believe I'll take my old self off
to bed."

They put the finished parcels in the drawer Mrs Morton
devoted to Christmas and Susan said goodnight and went
slowly upstairs. If only David had arranged something. It
was strange that the more you saw of someone, the more
you missed them.

They met in Scollar Square next day. It was a Tuesday, which
meant that Susan was through for the day, while David had a
late class. "Hullo, darling." He was there first. "It certainly
is nice to associate with a punctual woman. I thought it was
a contradiction in terms till I met you."

"Am I really on time?" Susan was breathless. "I was afraid
I was going to be frightfully late. We didn't get out of class
till a quarter past."

"I'm surprised at Chavendar. What does he mean by keeping
you so late? I've a good mind to speak to him about it."

"It might be a bit difficult to explain why you cared."

He took her arm. "It might at that. I suppose you've
been bolting your food as a result. What did you have for
lunch?"

"Mushroom soup and a sandwich. It was very good."

"You're incorrigible. I do wish you'd let me start a sinking
fund to buy you decent lunches."

Susan shook her head. It was a vexed point between them.

"Well, if you insist on being unreasonable, I suppose you'll
have to explore North Boston on an empty stomach. But I
know one thing we can do about it." He led her through the
narrow streets to a little, dark-windowed candy store. "Now,
what'll you have?"

The window was full of plates piled high with slabs of
nougat, its ivory whiteness studded richly with brilliant greens
and reds.

"It all looks perfectly wonderful." Susan loved to have him make up her mind for her.

He bought her a bar of nougat. "There, chew on that. I doubt if you'll ever be hungry again."

She bit into it. "It's delicious. Don't you want some?"

"No, thanks. I ate a respectable lunch."

"Don't be superior. Are you sure you don't mind walking about with someone who's chewing candy? It's not exactly ladylike, you know."

"Darling," he took her arm, "if you have been deluding yourself with the idea that I love you because you're ladylike, it's high time you were disabused. Besides, this suits me down to the ground. I get a chance to do some of the talking."

Susan chewed for a minute before she could answer. "Isn't it amazing when you think how silent I used to be?"

"It certainly is. Sometimes it scares me. I like it, though."

"Do look," Susan's eye lit on a shop window, "what extraordinary things."

It was a tiny gift shop, its window full of strange and wonderful objects made of shells. "Why are they so enchanting," Susan asked, "when you see such ghastly boxes and things made of shells in the big shops?"

"Maybe it's because these are made by hand. Which do you like best?"

"The Madonna's rather wonderful." She stood on a scallop shell, with another rising behind her.

"Just so long as you don't mix her up with the birth of Venus. Come on, let's go in."

The Madonna was two dollars-fifty. "I'll have her, please," David said.

"Oh, you shouldn't," Susan protested.

"I certainly should. You need a guardian angel, and she ought to do nicely for you."

The old woman behind the counter beamed. "She will bring the signora much happiness."

"I told you it was an Italian district," David said as they left. "Did you see the gorgeous thing on the counter?"

Susan had noticed it too: a conch shell holding a glass ball half full of water, in which grew a red and green spiral. "Yes, it ought to have been dreadful, yet it was lovely, and I don't understand it at all."

"We're just over-complicated," he said. "But come along, we'd better hurry if I'm to show you my fish shop." He persuaded her past windows full of religious pictures and statues, and other equally fascinating ones that held marine hardware or, best of all, gorgeous and elaborate pastries, with, usually, an ornate wedding-cake in the middle. Once, she stopped.

"Do look; think of hiring your wedding dress." A sign in an upstairs window advertised wedding or confirmation dresses for hire, at reasonable prices. It was illustrated by a limp grey-white dress and a pair of old white shoes.

"I suppose the theory is better hired white than no white at all." He saw her face change. "Darling, you mustn't worry. Josephine's bound to agree to a divorce in the end. She isn't really a good Catholic at all; it's just her family that makes her stick to it. Oh, and I told Julia all about it," he was trying to distract her, "and she's longing to meet you. I knew she'd help. We talked about you all weekend; you've no idea how wonderful it was to be able to."

Susan's face had cleared. "Yes, I know. I'm afraid I bore poor Grace dreadfully. But what did you decide?"

"Julia thinks the thing to do is play it perfectly straight – or at least as straight as possible. She's coming down for the weekend, so she's just going to go and call on Mrs Morton on Saturday."

"For goodness' sake!"

123

"Simple, isn't it? She's known her for ages, of course; that's the beauty of Boston. And don't be surprised if she takes a sudden fancy to *you*."

Susan giggled. "I know it oughtn't to be so funny, but it is, isn't it?"

He smiled down at her. "I love it when you laugh. There's my fish store. Come on in. I just want to show the lady the eels," he explained to the proprietor. "I'm afraid I can't buy anything today; I'm eating out, worse luck."

"That's all right," the man smiled at them. "You come in any time, Mr Winter."

The eels were coiling and turning irridescently in a glass tank. As they watched, a man came in and selected one. "Oh, dear, let's go, they're so pretty," Susan said. "I don't want to see the poor thing killed."

"Do you like oysters?" David asked.

"I'm afraid so. It's not very logical, is it?"

"Not very. How are you on snails?" He pointed to a barrel full of them which stood at the shop door.

"Heavens, aren't they huge?" She looked up. "Do look, there's one in the gutter."

"Yes, they're very enterprising, they're always escaping. I'd hate to live in the house next door and have them coming in at the windows all the time. How about some tea?"

She finished her last piece of nougat. "I don't know that I could. Besides, isn't it getting rather late?"

"I suppose it is. Are you coming out to Cambridge?"

"I oughtn't to really."

"Oh, come on."

Susan always gave in. They caught a Park Street car and as they got out there, another streetcar was starting up across the platform. Susan caught David's arm. "There's Mrs Merryweather; Roger's grandmother." She felt numb, suddenly.

"Did she see you?"

"I don't know. I think she must have, but someone moved in between."

"Well, at least we weren't holding hands. See the advantages of doing what Emily Post tells you. I'm afraid, darling, that means you'd better go right home. Where do they think you are this afternoon?"

"At Radcliffe."

"I hate to ask you to, Susan, but I think you'd better tell Mrs Morton you and Grace went exploring in North Boston. Then you can say she went home by Lechmere and you met me on the tram. But for God's sake work me in casually."

"Must I? I don't see how I could be casual about you."

"You really must, Sue. If Mrs Merryweather really did see you with me, she's bound to tell Mrs Morton, isn't she?" He was getting to know the family.

"I'm afraid so. All right, David, I will. But I wish I could come with you."

"So do I. But I'll see you Friday and mind you're punctual."

They parted, and loneliness closed round Susan like a fog. *But it's all right as long as you're lonely for somebody*, she told herself. Just the same, she dreaded telling her story to Mrs Morton.

She found Mary and Mrs Morton in consultation about Thanksgiving Dinner. "I think wine," Mrs Morton was saying, "the children do enjoy it so. Why, Susan, you're nice and early today. Don't you think wine's a good idea for Thanksgiving Dinner?"

"Lovely. Grace and I took the afternoon off and went exploring in North Boston." Might as well get it over with.

"What fun," Mrs Morton was not interested. "Then that's settled. I'll get a bottle of red wine, Mary, and don't forget we must have chestnut stuffing as well as the ordinary kind. George loves it. I *do* wish Olga could come."

"Isn't she?"

"No, I'm very disappointed. We'll only have George and the twins. I wanted to have Betty, but she has to stay home. I think it's miserable. I'm so glad I have you, Susan." There was something wrong in the tone of her voice. *She's not glad*, Susan thought, *why not*? But she had not finished her story. "Look what I got." She showed Mrs Morton the Madonna.

"What a funny thing. Where on earth did you get it?"

"At a little Italian shop. Isn't it lovely? And guess who I met on the way back?"

But Mrs Morton had remembered something. "Mary," she interrupted, "for goodness' sake don't forget the nuts and raisins this year. The children were dreadfully disappointed last time."

"I'll do my best," Mary sounded hurt, "but Thanksgiving Dinner in this house is no joke. You'd best make me a list."

It was no use. Susan could see no way of bringing in David's name. She gave up and left Mrs Morton and Mary at the cranberry sauce. In her heart of hearts she was relieved. The sudden need to lie point-blank had come as a shock. Again, as on that first Sunday, she found her happiness suddenly faded. Between themselves it was so perfect. Why could the outside world break in and tarnish it? She put the question resolutely to the back of her mind and went to work.

On Friday night David reminded her to stay at home next day so that Julia could take a fancy to her. "After all, she can hardly do it by remote control."

"But what do I do if Mrs Morton decides to go out?"

"Make her stay at home, of course."

She laughed. "I can see you don't really know Mrs Morton." She settled more comfortably in his arms.

Chapter Eight

Waking next day to the sound of rain against her window, Susan knew that at least one problem was solved. Mrs Morton never went out in the rain.

Just the same, she thought over breakfast in the grey dining room, she should have asked David what time Julia would be coming; now she would have to spend the whole long afternoon in the drawing room for fear of missing her. As David said, she could hardly take to her by remote control. How could he be funny about it? For a moment, she was disgusted with the whole complicated business. She climbed gloomily to her room. It was unfair that things should be so difficult. But the moment passed, as such moments always did, and she settled down for a peaceful morning of *Far From the Madding Crowd*, soothed by the pervasive sound of the rain.

"Mary tells me you're staying at home today?" Mrs Morton looked in around eleven. It was hopeless trying to work at home.

"Yes," Susan put a finger in her place, "my lecture's been cancelled."

"How nice. Will you be in for tea?"

"Why yes, I think so. It's not much of a day for going out." *Would Julia venture?* She had not thought of that.

"That's lovely." Mrs Morton's voice was unconvincing. "George and Betty are coming in." *Good Lord*, Susan thought,

127

she really does think I'm in love with George. How fantastic.
"Well, I mustn't disturb you at your studies," Mrs Morton
lingered by the door, "I was just wondering if Mary had got
it right. Oh, you haven't seen my spectacles anywhere, have
you? I've looked all over for them."

Susan got up dutifully. "I'll see if I can find them." Half
an hour later she found them in Mrs Morton's purse ("but
I know I looked there first of all"), and returned to her
interrupted chapter. But what would Julia Winter be like?
"You'll love each other," David had said. If only they did.
Her sister-in-law . . . How strange. She sat and brooded as
the north-easter beat itself out against the window.

George and Betty had just arrived and they were all still
dealing socially with the weather when Mary appeared to
announce Miss Winter.

"I call that delightful," Mrs Morton said, "I haven't seen
Julia Winter for *ages*."

Susan was suddenly struck with acute stage fright. What
would Julia *do*? Suppose she disapproved of her? She might
refuse to help. And David adored her; what would he do if
she told him she thought he was making a mistake?

But here she was. Tall and calm, she had grey hair and
eyes that were astonishingly David's in the strange face.

"Julia, my dear, this is a nice surprise," Mrs Morton greeted
her. "I didn't know you were in town."

"I do hope you'll forgive my bursting in like this," she
had David's smile, too, "but I thought you'd probably be
at home on such a wet day." She looked quickly round the
room, caught Susan's eye and smiled at her. No need to be
afraid of her, after all.

"It's the nicest thing you could have done." Mrs Morton
introduced George and Betty and finally, Susan. Julia Winter's
hand shake was firm; she smiled David's smile again; *it was
going to be all right*. Mary appeared with the tea and there

128

was a brief flurry to decide the important questions of cream
or lemon, cinnamon toast or bread and butter. At last they
were settled; Mrs Morton on her sofa with Susan beside her
to pass the cups, and Julia Winter in the easy chair opposite.
George and Betty had withdrawn slightly and turned on the
radio to listen to the Yale Game. "Thank goodness it isn't
raining there."

"You're looking very well, Mrs Morton." Julia threw the
first ball. "It's ages since I saw you."

"Yes, you're quite a stranger since my children have all
left me. I'm sure it's very good of you to remember a poor
old woman."

"I'm ashamed it's been so long," Julia could make anything
sound natural, "but really, I'm in town very little these days.
I've settled down in the house at South Kingston, you
know."

"I heard you had." Mrs Morton heard everything. "Don't
you find it forlorn out there in the country all by yourself?
It seems a dreadful way to live." It would hardly suit Mrs
Morton, Susan smiled to herself.

"I'm ashamed to confess I love it. But of course, I have a
good deal of company over the weekends. David comes up
all the time. You remember my brother, David?"

"Indeed I do. Susan, pass Miss Winter the toast. Susan's a
student of his, by the way. He must be a regular slave driver;
I never saw anyone work the way she does."

Miss Winter smiled reassuringly at Susan, who had gone
scarlet. "David's often spoken of Miss Monkton. She's quite
his favourite student."

"Well, all I can say is she deserves to be, the way she
studies."

To Susan's relief the doorbell rang again. "This is certainly
my lucky day." But Mrs Morton's face fell slightly as Mrs
Merryweather's voice resounded in the hall. She recovered

herself quickly. "It's worth having it rain if it makes all my friends remember me."

Mrs Merryweather's face was flushed and her hair untidy. "I'm so glad to find you home, Emmeline. I've been all over town in this dreadful rain, and I thought maybe you'd give me a cup to cheer . . . I can see I picked the right day, too. How are you, Julia? I haven't seen you for years. I saw that nice brother of yours the other day, though." She looked at Susan. She *had* seen them; that was why she had come. Susan was cold all over.

"Oh, yes," Julia took it up. "David said he'd seen you. It just shows what a small world it is, doesn't it?" She gave platitude for platitude. "And goodness knows, Boston's smaller still. Could I have another piece of that delicious toast, Miss Monkton?" Susan got up gratefully to pass it to her. "I hope you got home all right," she went on, smiling at Susan. "David met this child way over by North Station the other day," she turned to Mrs Morton. "He said he felt quite badly at not being able to escort her all the way home. Do you think she should be wandering round North Boston by herself?"

Mrs Morton looked reproachfully at Susan. "You never told me. I certainly don't want my girl running around in that kind of district."

Mrs Merryweather was looking at her, too. She had to speak. "Don't you remember, Mrs Morton? I told you. It was the day I got the Madonna." She paused, boggling. *Must she repeat the lie about Grace?* Somehow it was worse in front of Julia.

"Oh, that's right." Mercifully, Mrs Morton lost interest. "What brought you in town on a day like this, Martha?"

Mrs Merryweather helped herself to toast. "It never rains but it pours," she said. "My miserable car's out of order and I had to bring it in to the garage." As she plunged with gusto into a description of the errands she had then had to do on foot, Julia beckoned to Susan. "Come along over here and tell me all about yourself."

Susan settled on a stool beside her with the same feeling of safety that she had with David. It was almost as easy to talk to her as to him. They talked about Oxford; Julia had been there when David was a Rhodes Scholar. But at the mention of him, Susan was suddenly self-conscious again. Julia noticed it. "Good heavens," she looked at her watch, "it's nearly six. I must run, Mrs Morton, I'm going to the Symphony. It's been lovely to see you again." She stood up. "And now I've got a great favour to ask you. I wonder if you'd lend me Miss Monkton for Thanksgiving? I expect you'll have all your family here, and it's at times like that that I do find the country just a little lonely. It would be wonderful to have a child about the place. Excuse me!" She smiled at Susan. "And Miss Monkton has confessed she hasn't seen much of our New England country yet."

Mrs Morton was surprised and delighted. "What a nice idea. I'm sure Susan would love it. I often think it must get dull for her, being cooped up here with an old lady like me all the time."

Susan felt she should protest, but Miss Winter had turned to her. "That's lovely. You will come, won't you?"

"I'd love to."

"Good. I'll be driving up Thursday afternoon. Why don't I pick you up at three? And now I really must be going. Please don't get up."

Mrs Morton poured herself a cold cup of tea. "Well, Susan, she certainly took a fancy to you. I must say I hardly recognised her. Do you remember what a charming girl she used to be?" She was talking to Mrs Merryweather now. "I do wonder why she never married. But I expect there were reasons . . ." They exchanged a wise old glance.

131

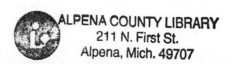

Susan raged internally. What a disgusting place Boston was: nothing but food and scandal . . . But George and Betty had got up to go.

"I'm glad to see those children together again," Mrs Merryweather settled down for a little adult conversation after they had left. "It's really quite touching. Jack shall have Jill . . ." She glanced quickly (was it sympathetically?) at Susan.

"Yes, George is really devoted to Betty. Susan, my dear, would you tell Mary she can clear away the tea things? And don't let us two old things keep you from your studies."

She was dismissed. When she came upstairs after giving Mary the message, she saw the two old ladies deep in talk. She smiled to herself. They would be discussing how she was breaking her heart over George. How amused David would be. She would have to wait till Thursday (what a tremendous time) to tell him about it, but then they would have the whole weekend together. She lost herself happily in dreams of Thanksgiving.

Julia arrived alone on Thursday afternoon and Susan's heart sank. She had taken it for granted that David would be there.

"Don't worry," Julia said, as they got into the car, "he's coming all right, but he had a conference, of all things, so he's driving up later."

Susan laughed. It was obviously no use trying to conceal anything from Julia, and it was a wonderful relief not to have to. Just the same, she could think of nothing to say.

"I'm glad, in my selfish way," Julia went on. "It gives me a chance to have you to myself a little, which is more than I'll get when David arrives. I hope you brought walking clothes, by the way? If I know my David he'll have us all over the countryside before the weekend's over. I do hope the weather keeps fine for you." As she manoeuvred the car skilfully through the traffic and out on to the open road she told Susan about the old family house at South Kingston. "It's David's and mine, really," she said, "but of course he has to live in Cambridge, and Josephine loathed the country." Her hand rested lightly on Susan's shoulder for a minute and then returned to its place on the wheel. "I'm so glad I've met you at last, Susan," she said. "I can see how David feels now. I've never known him so happy, you know; but I do hope it isn't too hard on you? I've been worried to death about you since he told me."

Susan was astonished to find herself crying. Julia, however, did not seem surprised at all. "That's right," she said. "It'll do you all the good in the world. There's Kleenex in the glove pocket."

"Thank you." Susan blew her nose. "I can't think why I'm so silly."

"You're not silly at all. I've been very angry with David; not that it's any use, of course. You cry it out and don't worry about anything. It'll all work out, I'm sure." *That was what David said*, Susan thought, leaning gratefully back in the car and letting the tears flow as they would.

Julia's house was half a mile outside South Kingston. It sat well back from the road behind a screen of bushes and a lawn deep in dead leaves that whispered under their feet. The rich smell of turkey met them in the doorway.

"Easy to tell it's Thanksgiving," Julia said. "Hullo, Bertha," she called. "We got here."

"And high time, too," replied a voice from the back of the house. "Will you be wanting tea?"

"Yes, I think so. It's getting cold out. But don't bother with anything but cookies, we've got to save up for dinner. I'll show you your room." She led Susan upstairs.

It was a tiny room at the back of the house, with a sloping

ceiling and dormer window that looked out over more lawn to fields and a dark band of wood.

"I hope you'll be comfortable," Julia said. "This isn't the proper guest room, but David said you must have it because of the view. My room's just across the hall, if you want anything."

Susan got downstairs first and found a fire burning brightly in the living room. It was a long, low room at the front of the house, full of firelight and quietness. A big bowl of leaves on a table by the fire threw Disney shadows on the ceiling. She had just settled on the hearthrug with her copy of *Illyrian Spring* when Julia appeared with the tea tray.

"Bertha's a little excited about dinner," she explained, "so I thought I'd better cope with tea. Cream or lemon?"

"Cream, please. What a lovely room."

"I'm glad you like it. David always says it's the most peaceful room he knows. Don't get up; you look so comfortable on the floor."

"Thank you." Susan put her tea cup on the floor beside her. "I do think it's nice to have Beatrix Potter in your spare room."

"Which have you got?"

"*The Tailor of Gloucester*. The cat's one of my favourite characters."

"It is a nice one, but I'm old-fashioned; I like *Peter Rabbit* best. David gave me a complete set years ago, so you'll find them all over the house. He's a great one for complete sets. He gave me Jane Austen last Christmas – an awful waste, really, I had so many single copies – and he's been threatening me with Trollope for years."

They had just got to Henry James when the front door banged and David appeared, rubbing his hands. "Good lord, it's getting cold. How are you Julia? Well, Susan, how do you like it?"

"It's wonderful."

"You look comfortable, I must say. I warn you, you're going to have to move over when I've got my coat off. I'm frozen. Where am I sleeping, Julia?"

"In your own room, of course. David sleeps downstairs to take care of the burglars," she explained.

"What happens if they come when he's not here?"

"It would be very inconsiderate of them," David said. "I'll be right back."

"I suppose we really ought to clear away the tea things," Julia got up.

The kitchen was full of Thanksgiving smells, and Bertha, vast and cheerful at the stove.

"This is Miss Monkton, Bertha," Julia said, as they deposited the tea things on the one available corner of the kitchen table.

"I hope you've got a good appetite?" Bertha acknowledged the introduction.

"I can't help it when everything smells so good."

Bertha beamed. "Well, if you ever want to eat, you'd better get out of my kitchen. Leave the tea things, Miss Julia, they won't make any difference in the washing up I'll be doing presently."

Looking at the piles of plates, saucepans and bowls that occupied every bit of space on the table and draining board, Susan was inclined to agree with her. She and Julia returned to the living room, where they found David pouring out sherry.

"I hope you two have managed to entertain each other?" he said, handing a glass to Julia. "Susan, you get served last as youngest member of the party."

Julia laughed. "Poor Susan, I can see you're bullied already."

135

"She loves it. Don't you Susan?"

"Yes, I do really. Isn't it funny?"

"I told you women were kittle cattle," David said. "Your health, ladies."

Julia raised her glass. "Here's to you both, and, David, if you think you're going to be let deliver your lecture on women tonight, you're grossly mistaken. Besides, I expect Susan's heard it long ago, haven't you, Susan?"

"I certainly have," Susan said. "He read me a frightful sermon about women teachers once." What a long time ago.

"Don't believe a word he says. He's just a sour old New Englander. Aren't you, David?"

"I'm afraid so." He sounded unrepentant. "And I'll be sourer still if you two are going to bully me all weekend; I might have known it was asking for trouble to let you meet. And what were you talking about so comfortably when I came in? You looked as if you were having the time of your lives."

"You'd be surprised," Julia said, "Henry James."

"Good Lord, have some sherry and spare my feelings. Remember, it's Thanksgiving! Sherry, Susan? You're very quiet."

"I'm very happy," Susan said.

"Ah," he said, "that's what I wanted to hear. D'you remember my betting you you'd like this place in the end? How about it now? Admit it's grown on you a bit?"

"That's not fair, David," Julia protested. "If she says, no, she's insulting her hostess."

"Oh, I think her hostess can take it. What about it, Sue?"

She smiled at him over her wine glass. "I must say it is rather nice."

He laughed and drank to her. "British to the last. I hope you'll confess that's something of an understatement."

136

In bed that night, somnolent with wine and turkey, Susan admitted to herself that he was right. She had never been so happy. She lay in the dark, listening to the silence outside and thinking vaguely of David and Julia, of the firelit room full of after-dinner peace and of the long, miraculous weekend before her; finally, thinking again how happy she was, she fell asleep.

She woke to a great sense of stillness. The light on the ceiling was so bright that it must be late, and yet there was not a sound outside. It was not just the silence of the country, but a deeper, softer silence. She got out of bed and went to the window, the floor cold under her feet. Outside was a magic world. The view she had seen the night before had vanished, submerged and transfigured by the winter's first snowfall. The ground was deep in snow and every black twig had its soft white inch of it. It was a fairy world, far too exciting to allow of any more sleep. Dressing quickly, Susan was grateful to Julia for sending her to bed early the night before, though at the time it had been a bitter disappointment not to be left alone with David.

Julia was already down. "Hullo. Did the snow wake you, too?"

"Yes, isn't it lovely? Why should it wake one, though?"

"I suppose quietness is just as disturbing as noise, when you aren't used to it. Besides, it's always so light when the sun shines on the snow. That's your orange juice."

Susan was drinking her second cup of coffee when David appeared. "See what we arranged for you, Susan?" He sat down beside her. "This'll teach you to be ungracious about America. I hope you've got some ski things you can lend her, Julia? This is no weather for skirts."

"I'm sure I have." After breakfast, Julia took her upstairs and fitted her out in a ski-suit and overshoes. "There," she

137

said, when Susan had put them on. "Now I think you're ready for anything David takes you through. And I warn you, he'll take you through plenty."

"Aren't you coming?"

"No, I think I'll stay home and write some letters and keep the fire burning for you."

David laughed when he saw Susan. "Americanised at last. What a triumph. When's lunch, Julia?"

"When you get here. Cold turkey can wait, and don't imagine you're going to get anything else this weekend. I don't want to be eating it till Christmas."

They went out into the cold, white world. The snow crunched underfoot as David led the way out of the front gate and along the road to the woods. "Happy?" he asked.

"Oh, David, you've no idea . . ."

He took her mittened hand. "We'll make you like America yet."

Chapter Nine

For once, their favourite table in the corner of the drugstore was free.

"Well," Grace deposited her books under a chair and pulled off her gloves, "how's the great romance? I must say you look as if you were thriving on it." She laughed and picked up the menu. "You are a most surprising person, Susan."

"Why particularly? Cheese and bacon on white, and some coffee, please," Susan told the pausing waitress.

"And I'll have chicken salad on wholewheat and coffee." She turned back to Susan. "Just look at you. There you were making a great to-do about being shy and not able to cope with people, and a poor little helpless English girl, and next time I turn round you're having a wild romance with the campus glamour-boy. D'you wonder I'm surprised?"

"I do wish you wouldn't call him that."

"I'm sorry; I keep forgetting. But he is, you know. You should hear them talk about him at Bertram. They'd have your eyes out if they knew."

"I think it's horrid." Susan took a limp bite of sandwich. "I wish I'd had this toasted; I always forget. He's just a person, after all; I don't see why they have to talk about him so."

" 'Just a person' is good. You will forget the romantic background. What's the news of Josephine anyway?"

139

Jane Aiken Hodge

"Nothing." Susan looked worried. "David wrote at Thanksgiving and said she really had to give him a divorce, and he hasn't heard a word. I do wish he would."

"Does he think she'll agree?"

"Oh yes. He's sure she will in the end. It's just her family that's so difficult, you know."

"Just the same," Grace had said it many times before, "I do wish you weren't seeing so awfully much of him. Do you really think it's a good idea?"

"Of course it is. You sound like a worried aunt."

"Goodness knows I feel like one. It's this hole-and-corner business I don't like. What's going to happen if someone sees you with him and tells Mrs Morton? There's going to be the most frightful row, you know, and people are going to jump to all kinds of conclusions."

Susan played with the handle of her coffee cup. Their conversations always seemed to come round to this point in the end and she always felt guilty about everything Grace had not been told. It was odd that it was only in reference to Grace that she ever did feel guilty these days.

"Oh, well," she said now, "let them jump. I wish you wouldn't worry so, Grace. It'll be all right, really it will."

Grace finished her coffee. "I hope so. But if I was really your worried aunt, I'd say I wished you'd picked something a bit simpler. You're such a baby, Susan."

"D'you think so?" Susan tried not to look superior.

But Grace was looking past her to the front of the store. "Oh my God," she said, "what was the name of that incredible man from Texas who came to the Student Union tea?"

"You mean 'call me Bud'?"

"That's it. Well, hold your horses, here he comes."

"Just look who's here," Merton Dennison's voice came from over Susan's head. "Miss Lawrence and Miss Monkton

140

as I live and breathe. And how's the world been treating you young ladies since I saw you last?"

"Nicely, thank you." Grace stood up. "Only we're going to be late for class. Coming, Susan?"

"No, I'm going shopping. It's a scandal, but it's the last chance I'll get before Christmas."

"Then I suppose I won't see you again before I go?" Grace said as they stood for a minute in the newly-piled snow of Brattle Square.

"No, we're driving up tomorrow. But have a good journey and a merry Christmas. I hope you find your family thriving."

"Thank you, and same to you. And don't do anything rash." Susan laughed. Grace always said that. *If she only knew . . .*

Merton Dennison had been standing in the cold snow looking from one to the other. Like an audience at a tennis match, Susan thought. Now, as Grace turned away towards Radcliffe, his mouth dropped a little further open so that the gold tooth gleamed. "So you're both going away for Christmas?" he said to Susan.

"Yes, Grace has never been away from home and her family said she'd got to come." Susan's feet were getting cold.

"Lucky Grace." He giggled. "But you can hardly be going home."

"No, hardly." She looked at her watch. "I must be getting started. Merry Christmas."

But he was not to be shaken off so easily. "Christmas shopping. What fun. You've no idea what a poor rolling stone I am. I haven't gone Christmas shopping for years. And where are you going for yours?"

"To Boston."

"Delightful," said Merton Dennison. "Then I can come, too. Let me take your case."

Susan surrendered her briefcase because she could think of nothing else to do, and they turned through Brattle Square towards the subway station. There would be plenty of time before they got to Park Street to explain that her shopping trip was not to the centre of Boston, as he clearly thought, but to North Boston. What a nuisance he was, though, and how he talked.

"So you're doing a long paper for Professor Winter, you lucky girl," he was saying. (*How did he know?*) "I bet all the girls are crazy with jealousy. He must be quite an inspiration, with his literary background?"

"Literary background?"

"Don't tell me you don't know?" He loved to give information. "Professor Winter's a descendant of Emerson."

"Oh, really?" It would be difficult, Susan thought, to be less interested.

"Yes, indeed . . . Allow me." With a chivalrous gesture he pressed a dime into the slot and stood aside to let her pass. Then he discovered that it was his last one and hurried over to the change window. A train was about to leave and Susan longed to get on it and leave him safely behind. But he had her briefcase. He rejoined her, panting and apologising, as the doors closed in their faces.

"Yes," he stuck to a subject like a dog to a bone. "A grandson, I believe, though it may not be as close as that. I just heard the other day myself. It's funny, he seems to keep rather quiet about it."

It would puzzle you, Susan thought. "How interesting," she said.

"Yes, ma'am," he repeated, "a grandson or something. As a matter of fact that's why I'm so tickled at running into you today. I've been meaning to call up and ask you round for that drink, but you know how it is . . . We newspapermen just can't call our time our own. But I've been wondering if

I could persuade you to ask Professor Winter if he had any of Emerson's letters he would consider parting with. I've tried to catch him a couple of times, but he's a brute to get hold of – such a popular lecturer of course," he hastened to explain it. "So I thought that maybe if you were to put in a word . . .?" he let the sentence trail hopefully.

"Oh," Susan paused as a train slid out of the tunnel towards them. She remembered David's comments on people who tried to catch him and ask him silly questions after lectures. How comic, too, to think that there had been a time when her feelings would have been lacerated by the discovery that it was not from pure love of her company that Merton Dennison had attached himself to her.

He misinterpreted her hesitation. "Of course, if you don't feel like asking him," he stood aside to let her get into the train. "I'll quite understand. But I hear that you're such a favourite of his . . ." He smiled knowingly.

"Do you?" She was amazed at her own coolness.

"Yes, sirree. And how do I know that, you ask?" He was delighted with himself. "We newspapermen have our sources of information, you know. There's not much you can keep from the press. Not if the press wants to find it out."

Susan was cold with sudden rage. "And what did the press find out?"

"Why, that Winter changed your tutorial to the afternoon so he wouldn't have Joe Robertson crashing in before he was finished with you. Yes, ma'am, I told you we had our sources, and it just so happens that old Joe's a friend of mine."

Susan almost laughed with relief. "Yes, he did change my tutorial. How clever of you to have heard."

"Of course I heard. There isn't much that gets by Bud Dennison. But where are you off to?" She had got up as the train slowed down for Park Street.

"I'm getting off here."

"Then so am I. But let me take your case. At least in Texas the age of chivalry is not dead."

"I can see it isn't." Susan kept hold of the briefcase. "But as a matter of fact I'll have to leave you here. I'm going over to North Station."

"Shopping at North Station?" He raised pale eyebrows.

"I'm going to a shop in North Boston," she let herself be irritated into telling him.

"How very interesting. In that case I shall most certainly come too – with your permission, of course," it was taken blandly for granted. "It would never do to have a little English girl wandering round North Boston by herself."

He took the briefcase and he came too. She tried politeness, she tried persuasion; finally, in despair, she tried to be rude, but, blandly aware that he was doing her a favour, he was impervious to it all. When they got to North Station it occurred to her that he might be waiting for her to say something about the Emerson letter. She made a final effort. "Do give me the briefcase," she held out her hand for it. "I'll be quite all right, really. And of course I'll ask Professor Winter about the letter. I'll let you know what he says."

"There," he said, "I knew the British never went back on their friends." (*Friends*, indeed). "But of course I won't desert you. The age of chivalry – must I tell you again – is not dead."

If you do tell me again, Susan thought, *I shall throw something at you.* She turned silently and led the way out of the station. There was no help for it. She would have to buy David's Christmas present with Merton Dennison for company. In a state of controlled rage she led him past David's fish shop and along the narrow streets to the shop where he had bought her the Madonna. As he wove around her in his efforts to keep on the outside of the sidewalk, Merton

Dennison was loud in exclamation about the quaintness of the place and in admiration of Susan for having discovered it. "A real antique hunter," he said, as they paused outside the shop. "A girl in a million."

But Susan was already inside. The shell with the spirals that David had liked was still there and she bought it, while Merton Dennison exclaimed, admired and patronised all in a breath. "Quite the professional, I see," he said as they left the shop, "but let me carry the parcel for you. The—"

"No, thank you," Susan interrupted him in time. "I'll carry it. And now I must get home."

But he had hailed a taxi that was wandering forlornly down the street, far from its usual haunts. "Not," he said, "before we celebrate this happy meeting. The Statler," he told the driver, before Susan could even protest.

So she drank sherry and Merton Dennison told her about the articles he had been sending to the Texas *Evening Journal*. "A very intelligent paper – I really think I'll go and work for them when I'm through here. After all, there's no place like home, is there, Susan? And what do you reckon to do, I wonder?"

What fun to say, "Marry Emerson's grandson." Instead, "Really," she said, "I haven't any idea."

He blinked at her. "But surely . . ." Then he giggled. "I suppose you're planning to go home and marry a lord?"

"That's it exactly," she finished her sherry. "A duke, I think. And now I must be going."

Outside, he hailed another taxi, was surprised to find she did not live in Bertram Hall and impressed by the Brimmer Street address: "What a lucky girl." She was getting used to his habit of blinking pale eyelids for emphasis. "And when are you coming round to see my autographs?"

Susan suppressed a giggle. It should have been etchings. She was ashamed to think that such an invitation

145

had once figured in her daydreams. "One of these days, I hope."

"Not one of these days at all. Why not tomorrow?"

"Thank you very much," the taxi was stopping, "but I'm afraid I'm going away tomorrow."

"Just like my luck." He opened the taxi door. "Well, I'll call you after Christmas, Susan, and don't forget, it's a date." Standing there in the cold snow, he looked as if he was going to make a speech about the age of chivalry. In the early dark, the light of a street lamp gleamed on his spectacles and illuminated the one gold tooth.

Susan looked at her watch. "Goodness, it's frightfully late. Thank you so much, and merry Christmas." She passed him and hurried up the steps. Looking back from the front door, she saw him still standing there with his mouth slightly open; the frog footman, of course.

Mary was in the hall. "So it's you, is it? Gallivanting around in taxicabs. I thought it'd be Mrs Morton."

"Is she still out?" Susan took off cold overshoes.

"Yes, she and Mrs Merryweather went downtown to finish their shopping." Mary snorted. "How they manage to take so long over it certainly beats me. I don't hold with all this business about Christmas. Presents for the family are one thing, but not all this fuss and feathers."

Susan rang for the elevator. "Roger's here," Mary went on, "waiting for his grandmother. I've got him shelling nuts in the kitchen. You'd best come and help; the furnace is out and it's warmer down there."

Susan hesitated. There really was hardly time to do any work before supper. Anyway, she was far too excited to work. This time tomorrow they would all be in South Kingston. Exulting in the thought, she followed Mary into the kitchen.

Roger was sitting in his shirtsleeves cracking walnuts. "Hullo, Susan," he smiled at her. "Have you been pressed

into service, too? I never saw such a slave-driver as Mary.
But they're very good; have one." He held out a walnut in
two perfect golden-brown sections.

"Thank you." Susan ate it, enjoying the bittersweet flavour,
then pulled up a chair and went to work.

Mary was making pastry at the other side of the room.
"What happened to the furnace?" Susan asked her.

"Oh, it'll be in one of its moods," Mary said cheerfully.
"It's all right so long as the weather keeps warm, but when
it gets cold, out it goes. Every spring Mrs Morton says she's
going to have it fixed, and every summer she forgets. Why
this house hasn't fallen to pieces round us years ago is more
than I ever could understand. But I expect it'll last our time
now. Put the almonds in the glass dish, Susan, like a good
girl. I don't want them mixed up with the walnuts."

"D'you know if there's any news of Olga, Susan?" Roger
asked.

She was surprised. "Haven't you heard? They're all coming
up tomorrow. Mrs Morton decided she wasn't well enough
to go down there after all."

"Yes," Mary chimed in, "such a confusion and changing
of plans I never did see. First it was to be turkey for everyone
here, then we're going to New York, and then when I'd told
them *not* to send the turkey or anything, here we'll be after
all. They'll be lucky if they get anything at all to eat, and
me hardly started on my mince pies."

"They only settled it this weekend." Susan did not want
Roger to feel he had been kept in the dark about it. Though
he probably had, she thought.

"Oh, I see. That's probably why Olga hasn't answered my
letter. She never writes if she can help it."

"Not Olga," Mary said, "she's too busy with her social life,
if you ask me. It's time she was safely engaged to someone,
Roger, I'm thinking."

The door upstairs banged. "That'll be them," Mary said. "You children had better scoot, and thank you kindly for the help."

They ate a nut each and scooted. Mrs Morton and Mrs Merryweather were sorting out their packages in the hall. "And the big blue one's mine," Mrs Morton was saying. "Oh, how are you, Roger?"

"Very well thank you. Susan tells me Olga's going to be up for Christmas." Roger helped her out of her coat.

"Yes, I'm delighted. I was just saying to your grandmother how sorry I was we shan't have room for you at Christmas dinner, but with all the Horwoods, I can't think how we're to manage as it is. Susan, be a good girl and take these up for me."

Taking the armful of packages, Susan looked at Roger's set face. She should have said something long ago. But what could she do now? Besides, if Olga really had stopped writing to him . . . She paused on the stairs, hoping for an opportunity (*but for what?*).

"Well, merry Christmas." Roger collected Mrs Merryweather's share of the packages, opened the door for her, smiled up at Susan and followed her out. The door banged definitely behind them.

"Such an exhausting afternoon," Mrs Morton took off her hat. "But thank goodness it's all done now. Sometimes I wish there was no such thing as Christmas; it's just work, work, work, and little enough thanks at the end of it. And now you're going off to Julia Winter's and I'm sure I don't know how Mary's to manage with the great crowd that's coming."

"Don't you worry about me." Mary was at the dining room door. "I can manage. Goodness knows I've been doing it for long enough. And where's George to sleep if Susan doesn't go away?"

Susan was grateful for the intervention. She was perpetually in terror that Mrs Morton would decide she could not spare her.

"That's true," Mrs Morton was temporarily satisfied, "and it will be nice for dear George to be so close to the Larrabys. Eliza says he's at their house from morning to night these days. I really believe I'll ask Betty Jane to Christmas dinner – you could manage one more, couldn't you, Mary? – I wouldn't be a bit surprised if we didn't have an engagement in the family one day soon. So suitable, too; I'm delighted with dear George." She fixed the usual suspicious eye on Susan. "I used to think he was just the least little bit wild, but this is most satisfactory. I must say I never thought he would be getting engaged before Olga. But of course you never can tell . . . Oh dear, I suppose it would be rude to ask Betty Jane without asking Spencer, since he's their house guest. And one more would never make any difference, would it?"

Susan agreed absent-mindedly. She was still thinking about Roger. But what could she do now? As Mrs Morton went to work once again on the Larraby and Russell family trees, her mind wandered back to the horrid moment Merton Dennison had given her that afternoon. If only she and David could drift placidly and publicly towards an engagement the way George and Betty Jane were. But it was no use thinking about that. It was impossible, and that was all there was to it. And she would be seeing him tomorrow. They were to have a whole week. Before that thought, Merton Dennison, Mrs Morton and all the world they stood for vanished like bad dreams at dawn. She would be seeing him tomorrow.

Chapter Ten

"Just the same, David," Julia said, "I wish you'd hear from Josephine."

Susan stirred unhappily on the sofa, but David sounded unconcerned: "Oh, I'm not worrying," he said. "She was always hopeless about writing letters. She'll answer when she gets around to it. I'm not sure it isn't a good sign she's taking so long. It probably means they're off somewhere with their vacuum cleaners and the further she's away from her family the better. She'd have agreed to a divorce ages ago if it hadn't been for them."

Julia looked at Susan's worried face. "I expect you're right, and of course no one's very businesslike around Christmas time. David, now we've waked the child, you'd better take her for a walk. It's too nice to stay indoors, and besides I have to write 'thank you' letters and I'll never get it done with the two of you here distracting me."

"So much for us," David laughed. "Come on, Sue, up you get. And never tell me women aren't worse bullies than men. What were you dreaming about there, anyway?"

"Just about how nice it all is. Think of having a whole week."

Susan was wearing the ski suit Julia had given her for Christmas and they went straight out into the snow.

"You mean you weren't daydreaming at all?" David asked. "Not even a ghost of a fairy prince?"

151

Susan picked up a handful of snow. "I'm going to be sorry I ever told you about that. I said I was a reformed character these days."

"And a good thing, too. It's very humiliating to be jealous of a daydream, I'll have you know." He put a firm hand on the collar of her jacket. "If you are entertaining any idea of throwing that snowball at me, I'd get it out of my head at once. I'm a dangerous man when roused."

Susan looked up at him. "I bet you are. What a disconcerting thought. Will you beat me when we're married?"

"Of course." He took the snowball from her, aimed it carefully at a tree, and missed. "Every night at eight, regular as clockwork. I can hardly wait. Have you told your mother yet, by the way?"

She frowned into the bright sunlight. "No, I haven't actually. I'm awfully superstitious, David, and I'm scared to. I know it's silly."

"It certainly is. Do you mean to say she doesn't know anything about me at all?"

Susan blushed. "Isn't it awful?"

"It's going to be when you do tell her, and serve you right. I can just see you sitting down one fine Sunday for your weekly letter. Let's see, how would it go: 'My dear Mother: you know my tutor that I told you was such a slave-driver? Well, I've been sleeping with him all winter and I'm going to marry him just as soon as he gets his divorce.' That'll start a fine family scene. It's lucky I've got you safe over here."

She was blushing harder than ever. "You make it sound so awful."

"Oh, no I don't. It's the beating around the bush that makes it sound awful, and you know it. I won't have you getting yourself mixed up about it again. God knows I've had enough trouble with you already. I'll never forget that first Sunday. I really thought I was going to have

152

to come and drag you out from under Mrs Morton's
astonished nose."

Susan was holding his hand inside the pocket of his coat. "I
won't forget it either. What a long time ago it seems, though.
I have grown up a bit, haven't I, David?"

"You certainly have. Sometimes I'm quite proud of you."

"Julia's right," Susan smiled up at him. "I can see you're
going to bully me like anything and patronise me between-
times. I wonder why I stand for it?"

"Maybe you're fond of me."

"Come to think of it, maybe I am. Do let's take the hill
road, David. Surely we'll have time today?"

They got home half an hour late for tea and found Julia
waiting for them with a worried face. "Children, it's awful,"
she gave them no time to apologise, "but I've got to break
the party up. I've had a wire from Aunt Beatrice, David.
She's got pneumonia down in Florida with no one to look
after her."

"Good Lord, poor old Beatrice. You'll have to go, I
suppose?"

"I'm afraid so. I've called up South Station and they can
get me on tonight's train. I'm most dreadfully sorry, Susan,
but I'm afraid it means you'll have to go back to Mrs
Morton's. I really can't leave the two of you here, can I,
David?"

David took Susan's hand. "No, I'm afraid you can't, Julia.
But we can't turn poor Sue out into the cold tonight. I don't
think even Mrs Grundy would demand that, do you?"

Julia hesitated. "Well, I suppose you could get Bertha to
stay the night."

"Don't be ridiculous, Julia. That would be just asking for
scandal. And remember that grandson – what's his name
– George – is in Sue's room at Brimmer Street. We can't
dump her back there with no notice at all, even if we wanted

153

to. Look, when you get to Boston you can telephone Mrs Morton and tell her all about it and say I'll deliver Susan safe and sound tomorrow evening. After all, I am her tutor. Tell the old thing it's a blessing I'm here and she'll never give it a second thought."

Julia thought for a minute. "Well, I hope you're right, David. I must say it does seem to make sense. What do you think, Sue?"

Susan managed a steady voice. "I do think it'd be an awful crisis if I suddenly arrived back tonight."

"There, you see." David was triumphant. "It'll be bad enough to throw her to the wolves tomorrow. I suppose you've *got* to go, Julia?"

"I'm afraid I must, David. I am most awfully sorry."

She went upstairs to pack and David put his arm around Susan. "Never mind, Sue," he said, "there'll be lots of other times."

"I suppose so."

Lots of other times, she repeated to herself later that night as they stood on the desolate platform at South Kingston. Nothing so sad as a station at night. They said little, but walked to and fro, stamping numbed feet. The cold finger of the parting was on them already, making ordinary conversation impossible. The simplest remark took on the quality of valediction. "Mind you write me, Sue," from Julia. "Of course I will." They might have been parting for ever.

It was a relief when they heard the melancholy hoot of the train and saw its light approach bleakly over the snow.

"Give my love to Aunt Beatrice," David handed up Julia's bag, "and for goodness sake get her well and come back as fast as you can. We're going to miss you horribly, aren't we, Sue?"

"We certainly are."

Julia smiled down at them from the step. "Take care of

yourselves, children." The train started to move. "Don't let David do anything silly, Susan."

They were alone on the cold platform. "I do hate having her go." Susan blinked back her tears.

David took her arm. "Never mind, Sue. After all, you still have me, for what it's worth to you."

It was hard to laugh. "Why, so I do. How careless of me to forget."

They sat up late over the fire. Susan was finishing a handkerchief she was hemstitching for Julia. The monotonous movement of her fingers soothed her and helped dull the sharp thoughts of tomorrow that kept rising in her mind. David was restless. He fidgeted with the radio in a vain attempt to get some music, then gave that up and offered to read aloud, but found it impossible to choose a book. At last he got up once again and fetched two glasses of rum and milk.

"Bertha's gone, thank goodness," he said, "I was really afraid Julia was going to insist she spend the night, bless her heart."

Susan broke off her thread. "Bless whose heart?"

"Both of them, of course. Have you nearly finished that infernal handkerchief? I never saw anything so domestic. To look at you we might be a thousand-year-old married couple."

"I wish we were."

"Oh, come now, Sue." He moved over and settled on the floor at her feet. "Admit we have a pretty good time as it is. And don't you really find it rather funny to think how scandalised poor old Mrs Morton would be if she knew? Such a prim little thing she thinks you are . . ."

"No." Susan could never see it that way. "It's no good. I suppose it's all right for you, it's just a game you're playing, but I can't, somehow. I feel frightful sometimes: that time

Mrs Merryweather saw us in the subway . . . It's so horrible to feel guilty about you."

He turned quickly to look up at her. "I'm sorry. I know it doesn't suit you, and I promise it'll all be over soon. It's the children, you know. If I make Josephine angry she'll insist on keeping them, just out of spite, and I can't let that happen."

They had been through it all so often. "I know," her voice was dull. "It can't be helped, but I do wish she'd write."

"Don't you worry. She will." He was determined to be cheerful. "Aren't you ever going to finish that handkerchief? I really am quite sufficiently impressed."

"It's my one domestic talent. D'you blame me for showing it off? There," she dropped it over his shoulder, "it's finished."

"Thank God for that." He looked it over critically. "I must say it's a fine professional bit of work. I can see you'll do me credit. Now finish your milk like a good girl. It's high time all good people were in bed." He pulled her down onto the floor beside him. "Why waste good firelight?"

She sat slightly withdrawn in his arm, sipping her milk and staring into the fire. It was curiously difficult to find herself alone in Julia's house with David. There had always been a tacit agreement between the three of them by which she and David remained scrupulously apart when they were staying with Julia, although she was sure that Julia knew all about her Friday visits to McCarthy Road.

David was looking at her. "What are you thinking about so seriously?"

"I was thinking what a hardened character I'm getting to be."

"You won't be that if you live to be a hundred, so don't get your hopes up. Hardened indeed . . . And here you are behaving as if I was the parson on a duty call. What's the matter?"

"Nothing." She went on staring resolutely into the fire.

"Oh yes there is. There always is when you say 'nothing' in that tone of voice. I bet if I kissed you you'd slap my face like an outraged Victorian. Come on, Sue, own up. You're thinking about Julia."

"Thought-reader!" She laughed with relief. "Why do you bother to ask when you know everything I think about, anyway?"

"I just like to have my dark suspicions confirmed. And now will you please stop thinking about Julia, because I told her that if she left us alone in the house she must expect the worst."

"Oh, *David* . . ."

"And don't 'Oh, David' me. Julia's a reasonable woman, even if you aren't. Besides, she knew if she wasn't reasonable I'd carry you off to Atlantic City or somewhere for the rest of the holiday. In a way I wish she hadn't been, come to think of it."

"In a way so do I." She settled closer to him. "It's dreadful to have to go back tomorrow."

"I know. But I'll be back next week, and it'll soon be all over; it really will. Please don't cry, Susan, not tonight."

He kissed her and then pulled her to her feet and looked at her. "That's better." His finger touched her eyelids. "Not a sign of a tear. And now, young woman, you are coming to bed without any more objections, which is what you get for looking like the Mona Lisa all evening. And don't you dare say 'Oh, David' again either."

"Do you always know what I'm going to say?"

"Of course I do." He put up the firescreen and turned out the light. "Didn't I ever tell you that I love you, Susan?"

Chapter Eleven

"And don't think I'm going to let you go till the last minute, either," David said over kippers next morning.

Susan protested, but without much conviction, and at last it was settled that he should put her on the five o'clock train.

"That'll get you there for dinner and hours of double dummy," he pointed out.

"I expect at least I'll be spared that with all the Horwoods there," she said. "I'll be bored to death, I expect. Oh, David, I do wish you were coming, too."

"So do I, darling, but you know I can't. I've got to hold the fort here for Julia. Goodness knows she's done enough for us. And if you're bored you can always do some work. It would be embarrassing if you were to go and fail your mid-years."

"Wouldn't it just. Specially when the Mortons think I'm such a scholar. Goodness, how I used to work for my tutorials. Weren't you impressed?"

"You've no idea," he said. "And you've got to keep it up, too. One nit-wit's enough for anyone's career. You've got to do me credit, darling, and see if you can't save my reputation for me. By the way, I don't think I'll write to you this week, though I know I'll want to. It'd just complicate things for you, wouldn't it?"

She hesitated. "I suppose it would really. But a week's a dreadfully long time."

"I know it is. If I have my way it's the longest we'll ever be separated. But after all, what's a week? Just seven days. They'll be over before you've started to count."

As the train carried her away from him that night, Susan repeated to herself that it was only for seven days. Six really. She would see him on Friday. Six days will quickly steep themselves in night . . . But still, the monotonous rhythm of loneliness beat itself out with the sounds of the train. *Six days; going away; away; six days . . .*

It was almost a relief to get out into the busy brightness of North Station. She climbed to the elevated platform and stood under the cold stars thinking of the first time she had been there with David and how they had seen Mrs Merryweather. One of these days there would be an end to all this concealment. They would announce their engagement. That was no daydream, but sober fact. She thought of the astonished faces: Mrs Morton, Mrs Merryweather, George, Olga . . . What fun it would be.

She put down her suitcase and felt for the chain around her neck. David had been scandalised when he discovered that she was wearing his mother's ring on a piece of string around her neck and had bought her a thin gold chain for it. "After all, if you're going to behave like a romantic heroine there's no use stopping at half measures." There was something reassuring about the feel of the ring, her one solid token of this daydream that had become reality, and she twisted it with chilly fingers as she waited for her train.

The house in Brimmer Street was full of lights. A great wreath hung on the door, its aromatic scent heavy in the cold night, and when she opened the door warm air and a tumult of voices rushed out at her. She stood still for a moment, dazed at the change from the cold silence outside, then put down her suitcase and rang for the elevator. As she did so Roger came out of the drawing room above and leaned over the head of the stairs.

"Why, it's the prodigal returned," he said. "We thought it might be. Come on up, we're celebrating."

She paused with her hand on the elevator door. "What's going on?"

"George and Betty are engaged. Come and drink their health."

"Goodness." She dropped her coat on a chair and looked quickly in the mirror. For once her hair was tidy. "When did it happen?" She climbed the stairs slowly, postponing the plunge.

"Just this minute, for all I know. Friday's engagement's full of grace." There were dark circles under his brown eyes. "And now there's nothing but alarms and excursions and the fatted calf. More power to them." He stood aside to let her into the drawing room.

It was full of people and the smell of cigarettes. She paused on the threshold, dazzled anew after the darkness.

"Come on," Roger was still at her elbow. "Might as well get it over with."

"I suppose so." She turned to him, grateful for his support, "But where's Mrs Morton?"

"Over there. She's sitting down because of her poor heart." His voice made it a sober statement of fact, but his eyes betrayed him. They exchanged a glance of sudden complicity as he steered her across the room to a thicker knot of people by the fireplace. In their midst, Mrs Morton was enthroned on her sofa, resplendent under her grandmother's Indian shawl. It must indeed be a festive occasion, Susan thought.

George and Betty were standing by the mantlepiece. Hand in hand, smiling, absorbed, they looked, Susan thought, faintly ridiculous. She could feel Roger thinking so, too.

161

Following his eyes, she noticed Betty's left hand stretched casually along the mantelpiece, the large diamond gleaming on her finger. David's ring was an opal, "Diamonds are so vulgar," he had said.

But Mrs Morton had noticed her. "Why, there's my wandering girl. You're just in time for the party. George and Betty are engaged, isn't it lovely?"

"Roger was telling me," Susan said. "I'm so glad." What did one say when people got engaged? There was something about who you congratulated. She gave it up and looked around for another topic. "But where's Olga?"

"I don't know." Mrs Morton was her vaguest. "She's been out all afternoon with dear Spencer. So inconsiderate, when I had all George's things to move out of your room. Poor Mary's been working like a horse."

"I'm awfully sorry," Susan began.

"That's quite all right, my dear. I'm glad you had somewhere to come back to. I never did think much good would come of that sudden fancy Julia Winter took to you. Easy come, easy go, you know. I didn't like to say so at the time, but I always thought it wouldn't last."

Susan was astonished. "But, Mrs Morton, her aunt's sick," she began to explain, but Mrs Morton interrupted her:

"Oh, yes, of course. She called up and told me all about it. Very convenient to have a sick aunt in Florida at this time of year. I'm sure I only wish I had one myself. But I was really shocked at her leaving you alone with that brother of hers. From what I've been hearing, he's no better than he should be. I'm not at all sure you ought even to be studying with him, and then she goes off and leaves you alone with him. But of course it's just like Julia Winter. I do wish you wouldn't work so hard." She turned to her daughter who had come up with a tray of canapés.

"What on earth's the matter?" Roger had reappeared and

looked at Susan in surprise. "Here, have a drink. I brought you sherry, I hope that's right."

"Lovely, thank you so much." She took it gratefully. Something – was it the noise, or the cigarette smoke, or Mrs Morton's outburst – had made her suddenly giddy. Perhaps it was the heat of the room. She was glad when Roger steered her over to two stiff chairs behind the piano.

"I never did like cocktail parties." He glowered out at the crowd.

"Me, neither." Sipping at her sherry, Susan fought down the conviction that this was pure nightmare. Any minute she might wake and find herself in her room at Julia's with the silent snow outside.

She pulled herself together. "It doesn't seem real at all," she tried to explain it to Roger.

"Too real by half, if you ask me." He finished his drink. "Are you as hungry as I am? You must be after the train. How about our going down and seeing if Mary's got anything to eat? Anyone can see this crowd's not going to break up for hours."

Susan looked around. He was obviously right. The conversation was still rising in a steady crescendo, punctuated now and then by a shriller laugh or a louder exclamation; hands stretched out for drinks or semi-surreptitious handfuls of peanuts; cigarette ash fell wide of ashtrays; over everything hung a soft pall of cigarette smoke. Her head was aching with a dull repetition of the rhythm of the train: *Six days*, it throbbed, *going away*.

"Do you think it would be all right?"

"I'm sure it would." He stood up. "I'm not sure it isn't a question of life-saving. You look all in."

"I do feel rather peculiar." She steadied herself against the piano. "I didn't have much lunch, come to think of it." They had picnicked in David's favourite wood; hours and hours ago.

163

The sherry had given a new intensity to her dizziness. She had to concentrate desperately on every step of the stairs, and the effort made her head ache more than ever.

Mary was knitting creakily in her wicker armchair. "Well, only look who's here. How's the wanderer?"

"I think she needs something to eat," Roger said. "I've brought her down for first aid."

"You do look tired, you poor lamb." Mary got ponderously up. "Come along and sit down."

Susan had been leaning uncertainly against the kitchen door; now she moved forward and sat down by the big table. Its metal top was cold to her touch; she was unspeakably tired. *Tired to death, tired as the weary dead, so tired . . .*

"And I suppose you're hungry, too?" Mary turned to Roger. "Where's Olga, by the way?" She opened the refrigerator and took out half a cold chicken.

"I'm starved." Roger answered only half her question as he took the chicken and put it on the table by Susan.

"Let's see," Mary reached into the refrigerator again. "A glass of milk, I suppose, and here's the potato salad. Never you worry about Olga," she gave the potato salad to Roger, "she'll settle down in her own good time; we can't all be born wise, like this one."

Susan took a dry mouthful of chicken. "Heavens, Mary, what makes you think I'm wise?" The light hurt her eyes and a great hammer was pounding inside her head.

"Oh, you're one that knows your own world," Mary said. "Now, Olga, she's always looking . . . Come on, children, eat up."

Roger needed no encouragement, but Susan found it hard to swallow. She played with the chicken and drank her milk slowly, moving as little as possible so as not to exacerbate the pain in her head. Roger and Mary were talking about the engagement. She heard them as from a

164

great distance, grateful that there was no need for her to join in.

The kitchen door opened and Mrs Morton stood for a minute surveying the scene. "Well," her voice was sour as old buttermilk, "there you are. Roger, your grandmother's been looking all over for you."

"I hope you don't mind my making myself at home like this," Roger got up. "I thought Susan really needed something after her journey."

Mrs Morton smiled her surface smile. "I'm so glad you do feel at home here, Roger. But your grandmother's waiting for you." She stood aside to let him pass. "Olga just telephoned, by the way. She won't be home till late."

"Oh. Well, thank you very much, Mary. Goodnight, Susan, I hope you'll feel better in the morning. And thank you for a grand party, Mrs Morton."

Her smile faded as he closed the door. "I thought we were to have the chicken for lunch tomorrow?"

"Why, so we were." Mary was cheerful about it. "But the children were hungry. I can make an omelette tomorrow."

Mrs Morton turned to Susan. "Didn't they even feed you before they turned you out?"

"They didn't turn me out, Mrs Morton." Susan tried hard to say it politely.

"I don't know what else you'd call it."

"But . . ." Susan got no further. Surely it was a nightmare. *Going away*, said the voice in her head, *away . . . away . . . away . . .*

"I do believe the child's sick," Mary's voice broke the silence. "Are you all right, Susan?"

"I don't know." Susan stood up, and then leant quickly against the table. "I do feel rather queer." The whiteness of the kitchen dazzled her eyes, and Mrs Morton's set face in the doorway was now near, now infinitely far away. From

165

a great distance Susan heard her say, "I suppose she picked up something in New Hampshire. I've a good mind to write Julia Winter . . . Get her up to bed, Mary, would you? I must get back to the party. I never heard of anything so inconvenient."

Mary's firm arm was under Susan's. "Come along, then, and don't you worry about anything. It'll all come right in the morning."

That was what David had said: *"It'll be all right."* All right. "Will it be all right?"

"Of course it will," Mary said reassuringly. She must have spoken aloud. Panic seized her. She must not talk about David. *Going away*, said the voice in her head, *away, away*.

She looked quickly at Mary. Surprisingly, they were in the elevator. Mary was pressing the button and seemed not to have heard anything.

"I'm awfully cold," Susan complained.

"You'll be all right when you're in bed." All right . . . all right.

The sheets were cold. The ceiling was miles away, a sheet of snow in the sky. No, it was close overhead, threatening to stifle her. "Mary," her voice sounded odd. "I do wish the ceiling would keep still."

"Now don't you worry," Mary's voice was soft and far away. "Take these, and have a good sleep and you'll be better in the morning."

Susan took the aspirins obediently and settled back on the pillow. "Just the same," she said, "I do wish it would keep still."

Mary was miles away at the door. A sudden burst of laughter came up from below. "Just listen to them," she said, "how they do go on. I'll shut your door so they won't disturb you. Now, are you sure you'll be all right?"

"All right? Of course I will." With a great effort she

166

smiled at Mary as she closed the door. It made her head ache more than ever. *All right*, it throbbed, *goodnight . . . all right . . . goodnight.* Suddenly Susan sat up in bed. But that's Ophelia, not the Duchess! Only the darkness answered, and she shivered and lay down again.

First there were dreams and then there were nightmares. Her father was looking for David to kill him; she must warn him, but she could not get her feet to the ground to run. And it was Donald, not David. David had disappeared, and when she called him, her mother came out of the drawing room and said crossly, "*I told you you couldn't get away with it.*" Only it was not her mother, it was Grace, who said, "*I'm against it, Susan, I tell you.*" And then the telephone rang and Olga answered it, and David said, "*You'd better come or I'll come and drag you out by the hair of your head.*" "But I went," Susan said, and found that she was sitting up in bed, with the sun shining in at the window.

"Of course you did," Mary said soothingly, "now you drink this and you'll feel much better."

"You sound like Alice in Wonderland." Susan drank it obediently and fell asleep. This time Father was angry with her. "*I told you not to talk to strange policemen,*" he said, "*you're just as bad as your mother.*"

She woke to find that it was dark. Her head ached steadily, the bedclothes were mountainous above her, the darkness was stifling. She was intolerably thirsty. Dry as the desert, dry as Sahara, Arabia, the Syrian plains . . . endless sand, endless loneliness and the hot sun above it all. But it *was* dark. When was it? Perhaps she had been ill for ever, for years . . . Then what had happened to David? She was too thirsty to think. Only the vast Sahara, the hot sun, the slow, unpitiful nights and days.

How many of them? When she next woke her head was clear. It was an effort to turn over in bed, and she lay still, wondering. The sun was still shining. Or was it, she wondered, shining again? She had no idea how long she had been asleep.

The door opened and Mary came in with a tray. "Hullo," Susan found she was very tired. "How long have I been asleep, Mary?"

Mary put down the tray. "Well, glory be to God. How do you feel? It does my heart good to see you awake at last. It's Sunday today. You've been asleep almost two days, and worrying the life out of us, too."

"I'm so sorry." It was all right. Only Sunday. David would not be back yet. He would not even know she was ill. How strange it seemed. Her eyes closed.

"For the love of goodness," Mary's voice roused her. "Don't tell me you're going to sleep again? At least you could eat a little soup first."

Susan pulled herself back from the threshold of her dreams and ate a few tasteless spoonfuls of soup before they closed in on her again. They were milder now. Instead of the hot Sahara she dreamed of the sea, coiling and uncoiling among the rocks at Pigeon's Cove. She was a sea anemone, a limpet, a crab . . . *"scuttling across the floors of silent seas . . ."*

When she woke it was afternoon and the doctor was there with Mrs Morton. "Very curious," he said. "Flu, of course, and it's bad this year, but I don't see why it should have affected her so badly. Has she been under any strain, Mrs Morton?"

"Of course not," Mrs Morton dismissed it. "What an absurd idea. She's a long way from home, of course, but I've been a regular grandmother to her, haven't I, Susan?"

Susan had inadverdantly opened her eyes. She smiled dimly up at them. "Why, yes," she said, "of course."

"There it is." The doctor closed his bag. "Rest, of course, and the medicine. I wouldn't let her get up for a week or so at least. And mind you don't frighten us like that again, young lady."

Later, Susan heard Mrs Morton talking to Mary in the hall. "Strain," she said, "I never heard anything so ridiculous. All the child's had to worry about has been her grades at Radcliffe . . . and that man in England, of course. It's funny, I always thought his name was Donald, but it must be David from the way she talked."

For four more days Susan lay dozing and dreaming. Even when she was awake, it was impossible to concentrate on anything. She did not want to read, or talk, or sit up. She just lay there placidly, staring at the ceiling and thinking vague thoughts about David, about the snow outside, about Julia so far away in Florida. The long hours were punctuated only by meals. Bringing the tray, Mary would pause for a minute to ask how she was, then hurry away to serve the family. The Horwoods were still there, so she saw little of Mrs Morton. Constant sounds of coming and going downstairs, cheerful voices, the banging of doors, made the house seem unlike its usual peaceful self. She was glad to be safe in her room. From time to time Olga would open her door and smile in at her: "How's it coming?" Out of her dream she would smile vaguely back: "Not so bad," and settle gratefully back into quietness.

But on Wednesday the Horwoods left and next morning Mrs Morton appeared in Susan's room with her solitaire board. "I'm ashamed at the way I've been neglecting you," she said, "but the doctor said you should rest, and I've been so busy with all my visitors. But now how about a little double dummy to pass the time?"

Susan's heart sank. "Why, now nice," she said, "but are you sure you have time?"

"Of course I have. It's high time I got some practice

169

for my bridge this afternoon, or the girls will make hay of me."

It was the chance Susan had been waiting for. "Goodness, is it really Thursday? I ought to do something about my tutorial tomorrow. I suppose I won't be able to go."

"I should think not indeed. We've had enough of a time with you as it is. I'm certainly not going to have you doing anything silly now. I'll call up and tell Professor Winter you can't come, though I'm sure he's the last person I want to talk to. I can tell you, Susan, I was really relieved when Julia Winter called up and said you had to come back. Eliza was quite shocked when she heard I'd let you go there for Christmas. I hope that dreadful wife of David Winter's wasn't there?"

"Oh, no," Susan said, "she wasn't there."

"That's one comfort. Though Eliza says she's heard some rather upsetting stories about David Winter himself. Of course one shouldn't believe everything one hears, but where there's smoke there's fire, you know. There must have been something odd about him, or he'd never have married that dreadful girl. But I told Eliza that a quiet little thing like you would never come to any harm." She settled the solitaire board across Susan's bed and cut the cards. "Your deal, Susan. Eliza's bringing Harriet Russell to my bridge this afternoon – dear Spencer's mother – she's staying with Eliza. Oh, you must have met her at the engagement party, of course, she came with Spencer and Olga."

"Oh? I thought Olga didn't come."

"Didn't come? What *are* you thinking of, Susan – to her own brother's engagement party? They got here," she paused. "Oh, it was just after you went to bed." She had been going to say something else. Of course, just after Roger and Mrs Merryweather left. Susan stared at her cards and remembered: "*Olga just phoned, Roger, she won't be home till late.*" It was practically the last thing she did remember from that confused

evening. Mrs Morton had been getting rid of Roger before
Olga arrived. "Two diamonds," she said. How difficult to
control one's voice.

"I've been meaning to speak to you about that night,
Susan." Mrs Morton's voice, too, had taken on a slight
edge. "I wasn't best pleased with the way you behaved. Of
course you weren't well, but I feel I ought to tell you; I'm
sure your mother would want me to . . . It wasn't quite the
thing, you know, going off with Roger like that. I know it
was difficult for you," she glanced down at her hand. "Two
hearts. I was sorry I hadn't been able to warn you, but when
you came flying home like that, what could I do?"

"Warn me?"

"About George's engagement."

"But why?"

"Well, really . . . It's your bid, Susan . . . I thought it would
be only kind after the way you . . ." She gave it up. "George
is such an attractive boy."

"Attractive? I'll pass."

Mrs Morton picked up her dummy. Something in Susan's
tone had puzzled her. "I must say you take it very well, Susan.
I only wish you hadn't been quite so obvious about it before
. . . But you English girls are so transparent . . ."

Transparent, Susan thought, *I must remember to tell David.*
Still, it was a useful misapprehension; maybe it would be a
mistake to disillusion Mrs Morton. "Oh, I'm all right," she
said vaguely.

"That's good – I'd have been miserable . . . It's your lead,
Susan, and mind you let me know just as soon as you
feel tired."

Ten games later the cards fell out of Susan's hand. "I'm
so sorry," she said, "I am a little sleepy."

Mrs Morton was in the middle of a story about Cousin
Jessamine's coming out party. "That's too bad. We'll just

171

finish the rubber and then you'd better have a little nap, and I'll go and call up Professor Winter."

Lying back exhausted – absurd to be so tired – Susan strained to hear Mrs Morton at the telephone in her room below. "May I speak to Professor Winter?" she was saying. "Oh, it is . . . This is Mrs Morton in Boston. I'm calling for Miss Monkton; I'm afraid she's not at all well; she won't be able to come to her tutorial tomorrow . . . Yes, she's a little better . . . Yes, flu; a very bad case, the doctor says . . . Yes, I'll tell her . . . I expect so . . . Goodbye."

What had he said? There had been a message: "*Yes, I'll tell her . . .*" Perhaps Mrs Morton would come up. She sat up in bed so as not to look as if she was asleep. But there was no sign of Mrs Morton, and presently she heard a car draw up outside and the front door bang. Of course, it was a taxi; Mrs Morton had gone to Elizabeth Arden. There was no hope of seeing her till the bridge afternoon was over. She was cut off, isolated, helpless. It was like being in prison. Suddenly despairing, she turned her face to the wall and fell asleep.

She had a letter from Julia next morning. Aunt Beatrice was still very ill indeed and Julia saw no hope of getting back to South Kingston till spring. '*I do hope you and David won't miss it too dreadfully,*' she wrote, '*but we'll make up for lost time one of these days.*'

One of these days. Time stretched interminably in front of her. How could she endure another whole week without David? She should have been seeing him this afternoon. If she could only call him up . . . Impossible.

The long day dragged. Mrs Morton had gone to a *Matin Musicale* at the Statler with Mrs Larraby and Mrs Russell: "Such a charming woman, and *so* intelligent." Susan had an appalling vision of all the old ladies of Boston gathered in their Sunday best to patronise the arts. Even imagining it, she was stifled. She wanted to shout, to scream for help, to escape ... In fact, she wanted to see David.

Somehow, dozing and waking, she got through the afternoon. The old clock struck four. She should be at the top of the little white flight of steps. He would be waiting for her at the window. The fire would be lit, the curtains drawn. What would he do without her? Reaching a long, tremulous arm to the bookcase she picked out T S Eliot's *Poems*. What was it he had said about *Ash Wednesday*? But she was too tired to read. She half dozed, dreaming about David.

When she woke up, Mrs Morton was standing in the doorway. "How are you feeling?"

"Better, thank you. How was your concert?"

"Delightful. A most masterly performance. His execution is quite amazing." She must be quoting the intelligent Mrs Russell. "I brought you your mail, Susan." She handed her a letter. "Posted in Cambridge, too."

"Probably Grace wondering what's happened to me," Susan said. David's writing was unmistakable.

"Go ahead and open it," Mrs Morton said, "don't mind me."

"Oh, well, there's no hurry." Susan stuck it in her book.

It was hours, it was centuries before Mrs Morton left her alone and she was free to open the letter. He was worried to death about her, he said. If only he could telephone her. If only he could come and see her. But he supposed she could not even write to him. Would she *please* (heavily underlined) write Julia at once and tell her how she was. Then at least Julia could write and tell him. He missed her all the time; she must get better as fast as possible. She felt better already. It was only another week. It would pass.

She asked Mary to post her letter to Julia Winter.

"Isn't it awful? I never wrote her a bread and butter letter."

"And I'm sure I don't see why you should," Mary said, "and her throwing you out like that."

Chapter Twelve

The long hours crept by. Slowly and reluctantly they built themselves into days while Susan lay cut off from the world, chafing and fretting and yet without the energy even to imagine herself out and on her way to Cambridge. After the momentary stimulus of David's letter, she flagged again. It would always be like this; lethargy and loneliness and David so near, just on the other side of the river, really, and yet so impossibly far away.

When the doctor came next she was still too weak to do more than sit up in bed, and both he and Mrs Morton were faintly impatient. "Just make an effort," the doctor said, "we have to do something for ourselves, you know."

Susan made the effort, but it was not much use; what energy she had was exhausted by long and conversational games of double dummy with Mrs Morton. It was not that she did not *want* to get better, she told herself one weary evening. She did desperately, but lying there wishing, she felt herself helpless. Normally healthy, she was baffled by this obstinacy of her body. She ought to get up and go out to Cambridge. *Why not?* She ought at least to get up. But the wish played helplessly on the inert refusal of her body. She had no control of it. It lay there, unresponsive, while she fumed and drank her medicine and thought how fast she would get well if she was only at South Kingston.

But perhaps if she really tried . . . Occasionally she would pause silently in the hall on her groping way to the bathroom and listen to the noises of the house. If she could only find a moment when Mrs Morton and Mary were out of earshot and get down to the telephone in Mrs Morton's room. David's voice would do her more good than any amount of medicine.

The second Tuesday her chance came. Mrs Morton had gone for a drive with Mrs Merryweather and now, as Susan stood shivering and holding on to the bannisters, she heard Mary bang the door on her way out. She felt absurdly weak as she rang for the elevator. It was a relief not to have to use the stairs, and she was glad to sit down by the telephone. Her hand shook as she dialled. He must be at home. He had no classes till five on Tuesday afternoon. She could hear his telephone ringing. Would he be sitting beside it in his armchair? No, it had rung too long for that. He must be upstairs or in the kitchen. The telephone rang and rang. It was no use. He was out. She had known it from the moment the telephone had started to ring.

Shivering with disappointment in her bed, she promised herself that she would try again in half an hour. He was probably still out to lunch. Soothed by the thought, she settled more comfortably in bed.

Mary woke her with a cup of tea at half past four. "Such a nice sleep. That'll do you all the good in the world."

She had lost her chance. Furious, she was convinced that he had got back just after she telephoned. Perhaps he had heard the phone ring and had not been able to get to it in time. She should have tried again immediately. *Idiot.* When would she get another chance? She *must* talk to him. It began to look as if she would not get to her next tutorial either. Time stopped.

Still, she was getting better. On Thursday afternoon she suggested hopefully to Mrs Morton that at least she was well enough to go down herself and telephone to apologise for missing another tutorial. But Mrs Morton was adamant, and again she had to lie furiously listening to the one-sided conversation and imagining David's feelings. He had not written again. '*I'd better not,*' he had said in his one letter. '*I can't even send you flowers, my darling, but don't forget how I'll be thinking of you.*' She knew the letter by heart already, and had written countless answers in her head as she lay staring at the dull ceiling.

On Sunday she was allowed to sit up in her dressing-gown. The sun was shining bleakly over the snow and Mrs Morton helped her settle by the big window in the spare room. "There," she said, "now at least you can watch the boats on the river, if anyone ventures out this cold day. I'm sure I wish I hadn't said I'd go driving with Martha. That car of hers is full of draughts and I'm tired of hearing her talk about Roger. I don't see why she doesn't make up her mind that that's all over. I believe I'll tell her I have to stay home and look after you, Susan. Mary's going out and I don't think you ought to be left all alone."

"Please don't bother about me," Susan protested, "I'll be quite all right, really I will. And I ought to do some work, you know. I'm sure I'll be well enough for my tutorial next Friday, and I'm frightfully behind."

"What a girl," Mrs Morton said. "Work, work, work. I'm sure that's what made you sick. But I suppose I ought to go. I don't want to hurt Martha's feelings."

Susan waited impatiently until she had heard the heavy front door close first behind the two old ladies and then behind Mary. Then she wrapped her dressing-gown more closely around her and went downstairs. It was the first time she had walked down; she would be able to tell David she was almost cured. Perhaps he would come and see her for a few minutes. Mrs Morton and Mary were safe away for two hours at least.

Her hand trembled and her finger slipped as she dialled so that she had to begin again. At last she heard the familiar buzz of his telephone. He must be at home. He was. The ringing stopped as the telephone at the other end was picked up. At last. But it was a woman's voice that said, "Hullo."

"I'm sorry." Susan's heart sank. "I must have got the wrong number. I wanted Trowbridge 2953."

"This is Trowbridge 2953," said the voice.

"Oh." Who on earth could it be? "Then could I speak to Professor Winter please?"

"I'm sorry, Mr Winter is out. Can I take a message?" It did not sound like a maid's voice. Besides, David only had a cleaning woman in the mornings. Anyway, she must not leave her name. There was a silence at the other end of the wire as the thoughts chased each other through her mind. "Oh, no," she said. "I'll call back, thank you very much. Goodbye."

"Goodbye." Was it her imagination, or did the voice sound faintly amused?

When she got back upstairs, Susan found that she was shivering convulsively. She wrapped herself in a rug and sat staring out of the window and wondering. It could not be a student. Not on Sunday afternoon, and anyway then David would have been there. Not a student, not a maid. Who could it have been? It was baffling, and, there was no getting away from it, disconcerting. Suddenly David seemed a stranger again; someone about whose life she really knew nothing at all. She drew the rug more closely around her. It was cold. Then, with a determined effort, she picked up her book and began to read. After she had turned over a few incomprehensible pages she put it down. It was growing dark outside and a star shone high up in a deep blue sky. Long ago, when she was young, she had wished on single

178

stars. Now, feeling very old, she whispered to herself, "Let it be all right, please."

The front door banged. It was hard to tell whether it seemed no time at all since Mrs Morton left, or centuries. Mrs Merryweather's voice echoed up the stairs. Good, Susan thought, at least no double dummy for a while.

The elevator groaned to a stop and Mrs Merryweather came in, taking off her coat as she came. She was so large that the slightest effort made her blow like a whale.

"Well, Susan," she panted, "how are you? I hear you've been having a horrid time."

"I'm better, thank you."

"I always say that a cold in January saves three in June." Mrs Merryweather sat down heavily.

"There, I wasn't gone long, was I?" Mrs Morton joined them. "It was so cold we decided not to stay out long. Did you get a great deal of work done?"

"Oh, yes," Susan said untruthfully.

"That reminds me," Mrs Morton settled on the chaise longue, "Martha's been telling me the most amazing story about that Professor Winter of yours."

Mrs Merryweather looked uncomfortable. "Really, Emmeline, I hardly think . . ."

"Nonsense, Martha. If the child's old enough to be away from home, she's old enough to hear about it. In fact, I think it's my duty to tell her." She had the gusto of one about to make the most of an unpleasant duty.

Clasped under the rug, Susan's hands were ice cold. "What is it?"

"It's probably nothing." Mrs Morton caught some of Mrs Merryweather's embarrassment. "But I'm glad you didn't stay on up there, I must say." She got up and moved across the room to draw the curtains. "How cold it looks out. Are you warm enough, Susan?"

179

"Plenty, thank you. But is there anything wrong with Professor Winter?" In her anxiety, she had nearly said 'David.'

"Oh . . . wrong," Mrs Morton paused. "Well, I don't know." She paused again, surveyed the subject, and began from a new angle. "The Winters' house is right across the road from Dunster House . . . but of course you know that, you've been there, haven't you?"

"Why, yes."

"I must say," Mrs Morton went off on a new tangent, "I've got a good mind to put my foot down about those tutorials altogether. I feel there must be someone more suitable. After all, I am responsible for Susan." She appealed to Mrs Merryweather. *Curious*, Susan thought, *it's made them friends again.* One touch of scandal . . . Because it was scandal; it must be by the way they licked their chops. But what? *Oh, David . . .*

Mrs Merryweather nodded portentously. "I suppose Radcliffe knows best, but one does rather wonder—"

It was too much for Susan. "But *why?*" Her voice was high. "What's happened?"

"I was telling you," Mrs Morton was sweetly patient. "Martha was at tea with her cousin yesterday . . . but why don't you tell her, Martha?" It was part embarrassment, part an honourable surrendering of a good story to its originator.

"Well," Mrs Merryweather picked it ponderously up. "My cousin Maud's a great friend of Mrs Lawrence – you know, the Master of Dunster House's wife?"

"Oh, yes." Absurdly, for no reason, the silly story about the Mistress of Bertram Hall flashed through Susan's mind . . . *but who is Bertram Hall?*

"Well, Freda Lawrence says," Mrs Merryweather was working up to her climax, "that several nights when she's come home late she's seen Professor Winter come out of his

180

house with a girl and drive away. Oh, quite late, she says she's seen them."

"And his arm around her," Mrs Morton put in, almost with glee.

"But that's not all," Mrs Merryweather took up the tale. "Yesterday, Mrs Lawrence saw the girl drive up bold as brass in a taxi-cab, with a whole pile of suitcases; and there she's been ever since. I never *heard* of such a thing! Unless it's really that wife of his." She had obviously made the suggestion before.

"Nonsense, Martha. You told me yourself that she left him months ago."

Susan had stopped listening. *Josephine*. Perhaps that was it. But if so, what did it mean? She must pay attention to what they were saying.

"I don't care what you say, Martha." It was Mrs Morton again. "I'm going to call up Dean Walsh tomorrow and complain. I won't have Susan going there any more; I can't think what her mother would say to me if she knew."

"Are you feeling all right, Susan?" Mrs Merryweather was looking at her. "Don't you think she looks rather white, Emmeline?"

"I am a little tired." Susan felt a thousand years old. "Maybe I ought to go back to bed."

"Maybe you should," Mrs Morton said. "And later on I'll have Mary bring you some nice hot soup. You'll stay for supper, won't you Martha? I told Mary she'd have to come back tonight; I can't possibly take care of an invalid all by myself."

When it came, the soup tasted of tears, reminding Susan of a glass of sherry, long, long ago, that had tasted the same. Better not think of that now. Better not think of anything. She must not let herself get upset; there must be a simple

181

explanation of it all. The thing to do was to get better, then she would find out. It would all be quite all right, of course. Her thoughts went round and round.

It must be Josephine. But she was in the Midwest with the vacuum cleaner man. The voice she had heard on his telephone sounded again in her ears, calm, competent and – had it been? – faintly amused. Not, at least, the voice of a student; not that of a maid. Ridiculous that she had thought it could be. It was the voice of someone in control; of someone – probably – in her own house.

Josephine's voice. Her thoughts were round again. *Josephine was in the Midwest.* She clung to the idea. She did not want Josephine to be real. As an abstraction, an unfortunate bit of David's past, she was easy to deal with, but not – no, not possibly as a figure driving up ("*Bold as brass,*" Mrs Merryweather had said), in a taxi to the house on McCarthy Road; a figure whose hands lifted David's telephone, whose voice asserted itself as in possession.

Where had she come from to answer the telephone? Had she been unpacking her suitcases in David's big bedroom? The idea was intolerable. But it was absurd. Josephine was miles away. She was working herself up into a perfect tantrum just because two old ladies gossiped. After all, she herself was the heroine of most of their story. With fleeting amusement she realised that in her agitation at its climax she had hardly paused to be grateful that the observant Mrs Lawrence had not identified *her*. Taking a firm hold of herself, she settled it: it was a cousin, or something. David might easily have dozens of female relatives about whom she knew nothing. Perhaps, even, it was Julia, back unexpectedly. If only it was. *If only . . .*

Chapter Thirteen

Susan woke next morning to find that the proportions of her world had shifted. It did not matter whether it really *had* been Josephine on the telephone the day before (it was, though), the mere fact of her thinking so had irrevocably made a reality of Josephine. She stood now, four-square in the way, no longer to be treated as a myth, no longer to be brushed aside as of no present importance.

In a way, Susan took a dry bite of toast, it was a relief. Because the reality of Josephine meant also, curiously enough, a new reality about David. Before, it had all had a peculiar quality of dream. Even at the time, the evenings at McCarthy Road, the walks in New Hampshire had had, somehow, the nature of mirage: unrelated with any past, they were incapable (there was the rub), of any future. That was why there had always been such bleak despair about her partings with David. Somehow, half-consciously, she had always felt that only by miraculous chance would she be able to dream the dream again.

Now (she put the tray on the floor), now at last, she was awake. David was real and she loved him. By real standards (Mrs Morton's, for instance), they had behaved scandalously. In the new light of Josephine's real existence she asked herself whether she regretted it. No, she was still sure she did not. And yet – how strange this new clarity was – now that the dream was broken, it seemed fantastic that it had ever been possible; certain that it never would, in just that way, ever be so again. Mrs Morton's world had her now, and there would be no more evenings in McCarthy Road; not till they were married. David would understand. As so often, she came back to the comfortable thought that David always understood. *"Only, for God's sake don't beat about the bush,"* he would say, *"evenings in McCarthy Road, indeed."*

She was smiling and blushing to herself when Mary appeared in the doorway. "Humph," she said, "all finished. I do believe you're really better. Your cheeks are almost pink. D'you have anything for the washing?"

"I don't believe so, thank you." Susan settled more comfortably on her back and stared at the ceiling. She knew so little about Josephine. After that first Sunday on Cape Ann she and David had hardly referred to her. Even when David had finally written from Julia's asking her to divorce him, there had been little discussion of the move. It had been tacitly assumed between the three of them that the whole thing had been David's tragedy for which, so far as possible, he should be consoled and compensated. Now, for the first time, Susan found herself wondering if it might not have been Josephine's tragedy, too.

But after all, it had been Josephine who had gone off with the vacuum cleaner man. (How odd, come to think of it; she did not even know his name.) *That*, Susan decided, *was crucial*. That settled it. Originally, perhaps, it might have been Josephine's tragedy; in retrospect Susan was even prepared to sympathise with her a little. But, however tragic, so far as Josephine was concerned, it was over. She had stepped out of the picture and that was that. To David she was nothing but an unhappy memory, so far away that he could even afford to be faintly sentimental about his adolescent feeling for her. That was why – Susan's thoughts settled comfortably into place –

that was why it was absurd to take her seriously as a current rival. As easily be rivalled by a ghost. She turned over and pulled the bedclothes up around her chin. It probably *was* Josephine. She had come, of course, to make arrangements for the divorce. Perhaps it would be all settled in a few days and David would be able to come and see her. Smiling to herself, she fell asleep.

"Well, what do you think?" Mrs Morton paused in the doorway at sight of Susan buried among the bedclothes. "Oh dear, did I wake you? What a shame. But Mary's just getting lunch, so you might as well wake up."

Susan sat up. "That was very quick."

"I just went to Stearns after all. It's so frightful underfoot I didn't feel up to doing any more. But guess who I met there?"

"I can't think. Mrs Merryweather?"

"Goodness, no. She'd never get in on a Monday morning. No, Freda Lawrence. They've got a party on tonight, so she'd just dropped everything to come to the hairdresser. Very sensible, I must say, though I can't say I approve of quite such a fair rinse. After all, she has got a grown-up son. But of course I told her it looked lovely."

"I didn't know you knew her." Susan was playing for time.

"I should say so. Her mother came to my coming-out party. I remember she had a purple taffeta dress; a great mistake with that hair. Freda's just her colouring. Anyway," Mrs Morton might wander this way and that, but she always came back to the main line of thought in the end, "I asked Freda whether she didn't think you ought to change tutors, and she said she didn't know what to think. She says she's talked and talked to her husband about it and all he says is that it's none of his business. Would you believe it, with it going on right under his nose? But at least after what happened the other day he's promised Freda that he'll ask Professor Winter about it at their party tonight. So I said I wouldn't do anything about it till I heard from her. After all, you won't be well enough to go this Friday, so we've lots of time."

It was suddenly too much for Susan. It was so complicated, so horrible, with everyone talking and talking about it, and yet nothing any clearer. She felt as if she were smothering in spider webs. She longed to tell Mrs Morton all about it: anything to have it all clearer. She had never before been so tempted to do so. But David had impressed upon her that she must *never* break down, however much she might want to. And he was right, she told herself, you had only to listen to Mrs Morton now to know how right.

"So Freda's coming to tea tomorrow," she concluded. "I told her I was afraid you might not want to change tutors, after all the work you've done for Professor Winter, and she said she'd come along and tell you just what her husband said. It's very nice of her, Susan." The dulcet voice reproached Susan for her failure to respond.

"Yes, of course." Would Mrs Lawrence recognise her? She had been close enough to see that David's arm was round her. Suppose she did, *what then*? Susan imagined the scene and shivered. But at least she would hear what David had said. Poor David. If only she could talk to him before he went to the party, and warn him. Perhaps there would be a chance to telephone him in the afternoon. What did it matter if Josephine was there?

But there was no chance. Mrs Morton sat with her all afternoon, to make up, she said, for neglecting her in the morning. There was hardly time even to think. It *must* have been Josephine. Of course David would stand no nonsense from Mr Lawrence. Why should he? It would all be settled in a day or so. They would be engaged. How long did divorces take? She had no idea; their discussions had never seemed to take that practical turn. Not long, surely, David always talked as if they would be married soon: Mr and Mrs David Winter.

The thoughts flitted in and out of her mind all afternoon, as she played her cards and listened to Mrs Morton, and hoped for a chance to telephone. She might write to him. But how to get it posted? Anyway, it would not get there till tomorrow morning; too late to warn him about the cross-examination tonight. Perhaps he would write to her. If something was wrong he would certainly write.

There was no letter next morning and she found encouragement in the fact. She had been making positive Andes out of Mrs Morton's molehills. If there had really been anything wrong, David would have written. Mrs Lawrence would report that her husband had been thoroughly put in his place. Susan imagined David doing it: the raised eyebrows, the look of distaste . . . Just the same, it would have been nice to talk to him.

Meanwhile, Freda Lawrence was coming to tea. Mrs Morton came up at lunchtime. "You'll come down for a little while and see Freda, won't you Susan?"

She had her answer ready. At all costs she must avoid meeting Mrs Lawrence. She was far too likely to recognise her as the heroine of her scandal. "Well, you know," she said, "I don't feel frightfully energetic today. I think maybe I'd better just stay in bed this afternoon. You could tell me what she says, couldn't you?"

Mrs Morton looked disappointed. "That's too bad. Freda was looking forward to meeting you, but of course if you don't feel like it . . ."

The afternoon dragged. Downstairs, the grandfather clock gathered itself together, hiccoughed and struck three. Another hour. Time stood still again. Susan had never felt so restless. *If she could only get up and walk about . . .* But she must preserve the fiction that she was feeling worse. She lay pleating the edge of her sheet and imagining what David would have said to Mr Lawrence. One of these days they would be together again, sitting over the fire at McCarthy Road, and he would tell her all about it. There would be so much to talk about, so much to tell him, so much to hear.

She never felt that anything had really quite happened these days until she had told David about it. And how amused – she smiled at the thought – how fearfully amused he would be when he heard how worked up she had got at the sound of that strange voice on his telephone. He would tease her to death for being jealous. She smiled again as she imagined his voice calling her an incorrigible witch and Julia's laugh as she came to her defence.

At last the clock struck four. Mrs Morton looked in. "You're sure you don't feel like coming down for just a little while?"

Susan shook her head. "I'm afraid I really don't; it would be so silly to go and have a relapse." It was absurdly simple, she thought, as the doorbell rang.

"That must be Freda now," Mrs Morton disappeared.

Susan heard their voices in the hall below, Mrs Morton's sweet as usual, Freda Lawrence's high and definite. "And how's the invalid?" Susan heard her ask.

"Not quite so well, I'm afraid," Mrs Morton's voice died away as they moved into the drawing room.

It was almost dark. Mary brought her a cup of tea and drew the curtains. "It's going to snow again," she said. "You can feel it in the air."

"Oh, dear," Susan propped herself up on her pillows. "Will it *ever* be spring, Mary?"

Mary laughed. "You feel it too, do you? The first winter I was over here I thought I'd go crazy for missing the grass and the greenness of things. But don't worry, you'll get used to it."

"Will I?" It was still strange to think that she was going to live the rest of her life in America with David.

Mary paused at the door. "Well, you would if you stayed. Though, mind you, nothing ever really makes up for the spring in the old country. Every year about March I get homesick all over again just the way I did when I was a girl. I'll go back there one of these days, whatever Mrs Morton says. Goodness me, and here I'm forgetting their hot water on them." She hurried away.

Susan drank her tea. David had promised to take her down to Cape Cod to see the arbutus as soon as it was spring. Mary was right, it was the greenness one missed. The snow was lovely at first, but what a bleak monotony of grey and white it settled into. The dull American woodcut, David called it. It was no use. On the surface she was thinking about spring, or arbutus, or snow, but underneath, her thoughts wheeled and circled round the room downstairs. *What were they saying? How long would Mrs Lawrence stay?* Mrs Morton would be on the sofa, with Mrs Lawrence in the chair Julia had sat in. The curtains would be drawn, and the room slightly dark as Mrs Morton liked to have it. They would have finished with the weather. Mrs Morton would be bolt upright among her quilts, her bright eyes watching Mrs Lawrence, her gentle voice ready with the most tactful of leading questions. But there Susan stuck. She could see the scene, but she could not hear the voices.

Absurd to be so tense. She had forgotten to eat her bread and butter and now she folded a piece together and bit into it resolutely. It tasted strong; Mary had made it at lunchtime and put it in the refrigerator. It was a habit of hers that made Mrs Morton furious. "The Irish are so feckless," she would say. "Just think of making orange juice the night before."

Susan ate another slice. Tomorrow she would get up. And she would write to her mother and tell her all about it. She felt a sudden wave of affection for her mother. How silly, really, to take it so for granted that Father had been the only one who understood her. Mother had been very nice about Donald – and quite right, she admitted now, smiling a little to herself. Mother would love David. She must send her the picture Julia had taken of the two of them at Thanksgiving, the one David said made her look such a complete American.

The murmur of voices downstairs became louder. Mrs Lawrence must be going.

"Just for a minute," said Mrs Morton's voice. The elevator door opened and closed, and the elevator began its usual creaking progress. But it was moving up not down. *They were coming to see her.* Lying there, trapped in her bed, Susan had a moment of pure panic. Then she pulled herself together. If she was going to be recognised, she was going to be, and there was nothing in the world she could do about it. *But poor David . . .* The elevator stopped at her floor.

"Here we are." The heavy elevator door creaked open. "Susan," Mrs Morton raised her voice, "I've brought you a visitor."

"I do hope you don't mind." Mrs Lawrence was tall and thin with very fair, very elaborate hair, "but I told Mrs Morton I felt so badly about poor David Winter that I really must come and see you myself."

By now Susan really did feel ill. "Oh?" she said.

"Yes, just think," Mrs Lawrence went in for rather impressive, sweeping gestures. "There was I telling Maud and everyone that he was entertaining all kinds of girls and all the time the poor boy was just making it up with his wife. I felt quite conscience stricken when Henry told me. He was almost angry, too," she appealed to Mrs Morton. "David Winter was dreadfully cross and Henry

190

seemed to think it was all my fault. But how was I to know?"

"Of course you couldn't." Absorbed in the point, they hardly noticed Susan. "After all, no one knew that man had left her. What a dreadful person he must be."

"Frightful." Mrs Lawrence remembered Susan. "He left her with no money at all out in Minneapolis," she explained. "The poor creature had to go to work in a cafeteria to earn her fare back. Henry says he thinks David Winter's behaving very well about it all," she was talking to Mrs Morton again. "He says we ought all to help him just as much as we can. I suppose we must, isn't it frightful? I must say I rather draw the line at having anything to do with that woman. Do you think I have to?"

Through all her own misery and confusion Susan was astonished to find herself sympathising with Josephine. This was the kind of thing she must have had to put up with. But there was no time to think.

"Well, anyway," Mrs Morton was saying, "I'm glad I didn't call up Dean Walsh. The poor boy's going to have a hard enough time as it is. Though I must say I don't much like the idea of Susan's going to the house with that woman there. I suppose if you feel you must do something for her, Freda, you must, but I don't see how we can be expected to associate with her. It was bad enough before, but *now . . .*" the pause was expressive.

"I must be running along." Mrs Lawrence pulled on purple gloves. "I'm very glad to have met you," for the first time she was really paying attention to Susan. "You know, it's a funny thing, but I feel as if I had seen you before somewhere."

"Really?" Susan was scarlet.

"Well, you probably have," Mrs Morton broke in. "After all, Susan's been up and down McCarthy Road going to her tutorials."

191

"That must be it. Well, get well soon, Susan. Please don't bother to see me out, Mrs Morton, I can find my way."

Mrs Morton saw her into the elevator and then came back to Susan's room. "Just think of that," she said, "how interested Martha will be. I think I must ring up and tell her. Do you need anything before I go down, Susan?" A sudden thought struck her. "For goodness sake, I quite forgot, there was a letter for you in the afternoon mail. Now, let me see, what did I do with it? I thought I had it in my purse . . ." she fumbled in the purse, "isn't that funny, I must have left it downstairs. How very tiresome . . . but Mary can bring it up with your supper. It's just from Grace, I think; it has a Cambridge postmark."

He had written. "Why don't I come and get it?" Susan began to throw off the bedclothes.

"I never heard of such an idea. You'll stay right where you are. Mary can bring it."

Once again, Susan was overwhelmed by a longing to shout the whole story out to Mrs Morton as she stood in the hall waiting for the elevator, but once again she restrained herself. She must not make things more difficult for David.

The letter would tell her all about it. How Josephine had appeared, what he had done to persuade her to agree to a divorce, what he was still going to do. Because of course, whatever Mrs Lawrence might say, it was impossible that he should have given in. She fingered her ring, safe on its chain around her neck. David belonged to her. Nothing Josephine did could change that. Perhaps it would take longer than they had expected – her vision of an engagement around arbutus time faded reluctantly – but it would be all right in the end. It was impossible that it should not.

As the future stretched more uncertainly before her, the worry that had gnawed furtively below the surface of her thoughts for the last few days came into consciousness, a declared toothache in her mind. *Perhaps they could not afford to wait.* "*Be careful with the boys,*" her mother had said. What would she say now? What would Mrs Morton say? But David would take care of her. *It would be all right.* How often she repeated the words these days. Besides, it was only a few days – she was probably being quite absurd. David had said she didn't have to worry. Poor David. The things he had had to tell her. "*Be careful with the boys.*"

She turned over in bed. Anyway, it was the least she could do not to make things harder for David. Even if she got the chance, she would not tell him about it. Not for a long time. Not till she was sure. And of course it was ridiculous. He had said it would be all right. She twisted his ring in her hands. Astonishing that one could love someone so much. He was everything and everyone; nothing else mattered. If Josephine was really being difficult, she must help him. Funny; that was what Mrs Lawrence planned to do. But what a different kind of help.

She heard Mary's voice downstairs. At last. She longed to call out and remind her about the letter, but she must not make a fuss about it. They thought it was from Grace. Mary had rung for the elevator. If he wanted to see her she would get up and go out, whatever Mrs Morton said. *How slowly it moved.* It was only because she was ill that she got so excited about things. He would laugh at her dreadfully when she told him about it.

The elevator door groaned open and Mary came heavily down the hall with Susan's tray. "I brought you your mail," she said, "someone in Cambridge loves you. I thought you said Grace was still out in Madison."

"Maybe she's back." *Yes, it was his writing.*

"And how's the invalid?" Mary settled the tray carefully across Susan's bed. "None the worse for your visitor, I hope?"

"Oh, no." If only she would go.

"That's good. We'll have you up and around in no time. Now, eat your soup while it's hot, there's a good girl."

"I certainly will, thank you, Mary." Thank goodness. Her hands were trembling. Ridiculous. It was a long letter.

'Susan, my darling,

"I don't see how I am going to be able to write this. I don't see how I can bear it. But you'll understand, won't you, and try and help me? You always will, won't you, Susan? Of course you will, you always have. But I don't think I can stand thinking about that now.

Josephine came back on Sunday. Herbert left her with no money in Minneapolis a month ago. She had been working for a month in a cafeteria to earn the fare back because she was afraid I wouldn't send it if she wired. She hadn't had my letter, the one I wrote her at Thanksgiving. She wanted to try again. I told her about you and she still wanted to. She said she was sure it had been all her fault before and it would be different this time. I said it was impossible. I thought she had made up her mind to it.

But yesterday, the children arrived. They had been staying with her mother. It was terrible. They look as if they hadn't had enough to eat for months and they use language I wouldn't want you to hear. And the oldest – David – is only six. She saw that I minded. How could I help it? They're my children, Susan. She says if I insist on a divorce she'll fight it and claim custody of them. And I think she might get it.

Of course, we should have been more careful, darling, and God knows it's my fault, but how could I make myself think you were something I had to hide?

Last night I went to a party at the Lawrences' – he's the Master of Dunster House – and halfway through the

194

evening he came puffing up to me – very unhappy – to say he'd been hearing some rather – well, awkward stories about me, and of course it was none of his business, but I would understand, he was sure, and he did so hope I could explain them away for him. He was sure there was nothing in it, but I could see, couldn't I? that it was – well – a little difficult. And so on, and so forth, all about women leaving my house in the middle of the night, and women driving up to it in taxis, and God knows what . . .

And, Susan, before I'd even thought about it – you know how sometimes your mind just seems to make itself up – I had told him that Josephine had come back and I thought I owed it to her to give her another chance.

As soon as I had said it, I wished I was dead. I mean that, Susan, and you must remember that I do. It's dying to let you go. But even now I don't see what else I could do. And there was old Lawrence puffing and blowing and saying it was very creditable, and he was so glad, and he was so sorry, and never even thinking that I hadn't begun to explain the stories he'd heard. But then, of course . . .'

The letter had fallen on the tray. A long time later Susan picked it up and finished it. He was desperately unhappy, that was clear in every word of it, but it was equally clear that he could not imagine doing anything else. *"After all, they are my children."* In one form or another the phrase kept reappearing.

Idiot. She had never thought of that. She had always thought of it as between herself and Josephine. What a child she had been. *I am paying for it now.* It was all over. It was unmistakable in his letter. There was nothing she could do. She might try to fight it; appeal to Julia, to Josephine even, but it would do no good. It would only make David unhappy, even, perhaps, angry, and that she could not bear. Life was bleak enough without having him angry with her.

What difference would it make if he was? She would not see him. Perhaps she would never see him again. How was she to disentangle herself from him? He was part of her thinking, the better part of her life. "*It is dying,*" he had said, and it was true. Better to die completely. But that, too, would make him unhappy.

He did not want to see her. "*I couldn't bear it, Susan. I don't even see how I'm to bear the places we've been together. Please help me . . .*"

It was an appeal that must be respected, even though in doing so she opened up new depths of despair for herself. It was impossible to believe that now, this minute, as she sat up in bed and the soup cooled on her tray, it was all over. How childish and frivolous her doubts and imaginings of the last few days seemed now, compared to this black reality.

Except the worry. It had retreated temporarily to the depths of her mind, but now it was back, the ache worse than ever. How did it fit in? Did she hold the winning card after all? But how could she put the same kind of pressure on David that Josephine had? Even if it was true and she did not turn out to be imagining things. What would he say if she told him? *But she was not to see him.* Anyway, it would make no difference. How could it? Josephine had three children.

She would have to go away. The kindest thing – poor David – would be not to tell him. Julia would help her. *If only Julia were here.* All of a sudden she was frightened. It was all too much. It must be a nightmare; life could not really be as bad as this.

"Well, I do declare," Mary's reproachful voice brought her back from the edge of chaos. "Look at your soup, cold in the bowl. How are we to get you well, Susan, if you won't eat your meals?"

"I'm so sorry, Mary. I clean forgot." Hurriedly, she took a spoonful of cold and tasteless fluid. "It's very good still, really."

Mary stood over her till she had finished. "Goodness knows," she said at last, picking up the tray, "you need as much looking after as a pack of children. Now, mind you go to sleep good and early. I don't like the look of you tonight. I wonder if I hadn't better take your temperature."

"Oh, don't bother, Mary," Susan's voice was tired. "I'm all right, really I am."

Chapter Fourteen

Curiously enough, she *was* better. The day after she got David's letter she sat up for half an hour, and two days later Grace came to see her and found her up and dressed.

"Have you heard?" Grace lost no time in getting to what was on her mind.

"Yes, I've heard." There did not seem much else to say.

Grace looked uncomfortable. "I'm most awfully sorry."

"Thank you. It's just one of those things, I suppose." Susan was amazed to find that she could talk about it without crying.

"They say at Radcliffe she threatened to do the most awful things if he didn't take her back; jump into the river and goodness knows what."

Oh, poor David. No wonder . . . He hated to see people cry. "I suppose there has been a lot of talk." She must keep Grace talking.

"Terrific. You've no idea. I'm certainly glad to find you looking so well, Susan. I've been worried silly about you."

Was there, Susan wondered, and reproached herself for doing so, a trace of disappointment in Grace's sympathy? Had she been looking forward to a tragic scene with herself in the role of comforter? Well, she was not to have one. For David's sake, if for no other reason, she must not let go. "It is grim," she said, "but I suppose I asked for it, really. It just goes to show how right you always were. And after all, I seem to be going to live." She was amazed at herself. *David would be proud of you . . .*

"I'm so glad. And after all, he was years older than you, Susan. I'm not sure it isn't just as well, you know. I always said—"

"I know you did." She could not stand any more; not now. "I hope you had a good holiday?"

To her relief, Grace took the hint and they talked about nothing in particular for the rest of the visit. Only when she got up to go she said, "I think you're amazing, Susan, I really do."

Again that faint note – was it? – of disappointment. "Oh, not really," Susan managed – even at the time she was proud of it – to keep her voice light. "Come and see me again soon. Mrs Morton's acting dragon and won't let me out of the house. I'm getting bored to death."

She was alone with her thoughts. Nothing would change them; nothing would change the loneliness. She was condemned for life. But at least she had now the slight, the almost ridiculous consolation, that at this first and hardest interview she had managed to keep her head. There had been no violent breakdown to make Grace suspect how much deeper and further it had all gone than she had ever realised.

Somewhat to her own, and clearly to Grace's surprise, she managed to preserve this calm tone through Grace's frequent visits. But even if she could have persuaded herself that she wanted to, there was nothing she could do to stop Grace bringing her all the latest gossip about David. He looked tired; he looked sick; he looked much better. He was making jokes in his lectures again. He had been seen at the Sanders Theatre Symphony with his wife. Grace reported it all in all innocence, convinced by now that Susan had been much less involved than she had supposed. *If she only knew*, Susan thought, turning the sword in the wound. But she did not, and never would.

Recovering slowly but steadily, Susan took her mid-year exams in a daze. It was, Mary said, a real mercy that she was well enough to take them, "After all your studying, too." It was a mercy, Susan privately thought, that they happened when they did. By the time she was well enough to go out, lectures were over for the term and there was no question of tutorials. Besides, they had provided her with a perfect pretext for shutting herself up in her room, as she said, to work.

And, rather to her own surprise, she *had* worked. There had been thoughts of David to urge her on: "*You've got to do me credit,*" he had said, and she would, even if no one was ever to know it. She had given up trying not to think about him; she could not help it, she could not even regret it. It seemed as if she was to live the rest of her life doubly: both for herself and him; and, if so, how much she had really gained. She was lonely, desperately lonely; she missed him every minute of the day. Everything she did reminded her of him. Combing her hair, walking downstairs, reading in her room; how could she help thinking of him? But this was nothing like the earlier loneliness at Brimmer Street, because now she had someone to miss. His voice was always with her, she thought his thoughts at the same time as her own. No, really, it was not loneliness.

There had been a strange moment that was part incredible relief, part bitter disappointment, when she knew that the worry had been groundless: she was *not* going to have his child. Without realising it, she had clung to that as a hope, a possibility . . . There had been dreams; how could she help it? She had retreated to the house at South Kingston; Julia was looking after her; one day David suddenly appeared: "*Susan, why didn't you tell me?*" But now the dreams

201

were over and her loneliness was bitterer for the memory of them.

She went in terror of seeing him. If she did, and wherever she did, she knew she would cry, all at once, the tears she had refused to let fall. But here, too, her sickness had been a great help. Grace had brought her books and she had worked at home shut up in her room, with the tired grey snow outside. Gazing out at it, she thought that she would never announce her engagement and see the astonished faces: Mrs Morton and George, Roger and Olga. Curious that it had been daydream, after all.

The exams seemed easy. It was only by thinking of David that she could bring herself to care about them at all, but she did her best and felt that at least he would not be embarrassed. Probably, she told herself in one of her moments of despair, he would not even know how she had done. It was horrible to feel the bond of common knowledge between them gradually slackening. Now that lectures were over for the term, she could not tell herself at five o'clock on Tuesday that now, this minute, he was giving his drama lecture, or, on a Saturday, that now he was hurrying to his nine o'clock. Josephine would have changed all his habits at home (intolerable to think of it); already it seemed as if she knew nothing about his life.

She had tried, when she answered his letter, to make him as little unhappy as possible. There had been nothing – there had been everything to say, and for days after she had posted the letter, she had been haunted by agonising second thoughts as to what she should have said. It had been easier writing to Julia. To her she had been able to say the things that David must be spared and that Grace would not understand, She felt, these days, a generation older than Grace.

So, from day to day she improvised. She could not plan, she did not even want to try. David was going to arrange for her to have tutorials with someone else. She did not even wonder what excuse he would give. All that was so unimportant.

Increasingly she found herself wondering, those sad, grey days when it seemed that the sun would never shine again, exactly what *was* important. None of the old things were anymore. There had been so many things: examination results; the future; people – Donald, for instance . . . Now, they were all lost in the same grey fog of unreality.

Nothing was interesting. She did not want to read; she did not want to think. Once her exams were over she was glad to throw herself into the preoccupations of Mrs Morton's life. She had certainly never imagined in the fall that she might find herself grateful for the nightly sessions at the bridge table, but now, in this new strange state, she found herself looking forward to the evening as a time of refuge from the grim monotony of her thoughts.

"I must say, Susan," Mrs Morton said one stormy night as Susan dealt for their second game, "your bridge has improved beyond recognition. You do me credit these days. I only wish we could make up a four sometime so that you'd have a real chance to practise your bidding. Maybe Eliza'll be too busy to come on Thursday and you can take her place. She finally decided to have George and Betty's party this Saturday, you know."

"Did she? I thought she'd decided to wait till spring."

"So did I. It's really most inconsiderate of her to change her mind like this. Madame can't possibly have my dress done in time, and I'm not at all sure that Olga'll be able to come up. It's very tiresome."

"That's a shame. What kind of a party is it going to be, finally?"

"Just cocktails. Oh, and that reminds me, Eliza said you must be sure to come. Very thoughtful of her, I must say."

"How nice." There was a time when the thought of a party would have been exciting.

The Larrabys' house was large and formal. Looking at the banked chrysanthemums, the highly polished furniture and the equally highly starched maids who were serving the drinks and emptying ashtrays, Susan wondered what sort of mental comparisons Mrs Morton would be making with her own party at Christmas. Odd to think that this was the first time she had seen Mrs Morton in any house but her own. Away from the security of her quilts and sofa she looked smaller and, confronted with Eliza Larraby, who was stately in black taffeta, somehow diminished. Susan suddenly felt full of affection for her. "Wouldn't you like to come and sit on the sofa?" she asked. "You've been doing an awful lot of standing."

"Aren't you a thoughtful girl," Mrs Morton was touched. "But I'm very happy as I am. Why, goodness me, there's Olga."

There indeed she was, with her fur coat thrown over her shoulders as she evaded a hovering parlourmaid to make her entry.

"I do hope you don't mind my crashing your party like this, Mrs Larraby?" She had the poise of a young princess, whose intrusion could be nothing but an honour. "I got deathly homesick for Boston when I thought of you all celebrating up here, so I just hopped on a plane and here I am. Hullo, Gran, d'you think Mary'll kill the fatted calf for me?"

For Mrs Morton, the success of the evening was assured. Even Eliza Larraby, politely acknowledging Olga's apologies, was inevitably aware that from now on the evening was only partly her family's. Beside Olga's dark metropolitan charm, Betty Jane faded to blonde insignificance. Olga was as clearly aware of it as anyone. She stood for a moment in the corner talking to her grandmother, a careless shoulder turned to the party and its glances of admiration and recognition. "Who is she?", "There she is!" You could almost feel the party catch its breath.

Standing near, Susan heard Mrs Morton say something about Spencer Russell. Of course, where was he? After all, he was Betty Jane's first cousin.

"Oh, him," Olga said. "I had dinner with him the other night. I suppose he may be coming . . . I can't say I care much. I'm so tired of his literary stories I could *scream*."

Something had happened. For once, Olga's poise was achieved by an effort. *The lady doth protest too much*, Susan thought. She could feel the restlessness in Olga and, sensitive on her own account (how often she had thought she saw David in a crowd), noticed her quick, almost furtive glances towards the door. She's actually feeling insecure, Susan thought, what can have happened?

Mrs Morton noticed nothing. "What's become of that nephew of yours?" She spoke to Mrs Larraby, who was drifting by on some hospitable errand.

"Spencer? I know, isn't he naughty? He never will come to my parties . . . I expect Olga could tell us where he is, though." She looked archly at Olga, who flushed almost imperceptibly. Inwardly, Susan felt, she was seething.

"I haven't the slightest idea." Again, Susan was sure she was the only one who noticed that the casualness was too studied. Olga turned, stood poised for a moment, and then, with what Susan felt as a violent effort, plunged into the party. Its tide closed around her, and Susan, established as usual in a corner, watched with amusement as, vaguely drifting on one pretext or another – "More drinks?" "Let me get you a cigarette," – more and more of the men who had surrounded Betty Jane gravitated towards Olga. Soon her smooth black head was lost among them, and Susan turned to see how Betty Jane was taking it.

She did not seem to be taking it at all. She and George were impregnable in the security that surrounds a newly-engaged couple. They had withdrawn into a bay window and were talking eagerly. As Susan watched, Betty Jane put one hand lightly on George's shoulder as if to press her point. A devastating wave of self pity swept over Susan and she looked away. Doing so, she noticed that Olga was looking at George and Betty, too. Suddenly, she knew that Olga was even more to be pitied than she was. *Why?* She had everything. *Yes*, Susan watched her turn back to her circle and reassume her charm, *everything but security*. There was something desperate about her today. She seemed lost, searching . . . She was, it came to Susan, far more lonely than her. Even if it was only in her memories of him, she had David. She could never be alone as Olga was, standing there glittering among her crowd of casual admirers, with under it all some unfathomed and, to Susan, unfathomable depth of private desperation.

"A penny for your thoughts."

She looked up. "Hullo, Roger, when did you get here?"

"Just this minute. How are you? I haven't seen you for ages. Are you really better?"

"Oh, yes, thank you very much." There was a short silence. "Olga's here."

"Is she?" He made no movement. "I didn't know she was coming up. But I asked you a question."

"A question? Oh, you mean my thoughts. Not very interesting, I'm afraid. I was thinking about loneliness."

Roger felt in his pocket. "Rather discouraging for a party," he said, "but here's your penny. Mind you don't spend it on riotous living."

She laughed. "I won't."

Roger collected two Manhattans from a passing maid. "It

looks as if you're going to have to break out of your sherry habits tonight," he handed her one. "Here's to you, and may you never be lonely at parties."

"Thank you." They drank to it.

Looking over her glass Susan noticed that the crowd around Olga had broken up, suddenly centrifugal. Breaking from it, Olga came across to them, flinging, as she came, a last over-the-shoulder remark into the circle. "Hullo, Roger," she joined them, "surprised to see me?"

"Yes," he said.

It was not quite what she had expected. "And delighted, I hope?"

"Naturally." The word fell dead between them.

"I got homesick," she felt it necessary to explain. "Besides, it's high time someone led you astray a bit for your own good. Roger's going scholarly on us," she turned to Susan, "and I think it's the least we can do to see that his arteries don't harden too fast. Isn't it, Roger?"

"It's very thoughtful of you." Again his voice was dry. "I was sorry not to see more of you at Christmas."

"Wasn't it a bore?" She finished her drink. "Does anyone want my cherry? But that's what comes of the cloistered life. You can't expect to see anyone if you work all the time. Can he, Susan?"

"If it isn't one thing it's another," Roger said. "My cloistered life, as you call it, or your social one . . ." he let the sentence drop.

But Olga had a clue. "I do believe he's sulking because I went out with someone else at Christmas. How ridiculous. What right have you to object, anyway?"

"None," he said. "Let me get you another drink. Finish up, Susan, it won't hurt you." He took their glasses and vanished into the increasingly strident crowd.

Olga was silent for a minute, then, "I don't know what's got into Roger today," she said. "He's really quite disagreeable. Oh, good, there's Gran."

Mrs Morton had her fur coat on and her face looked old and tired under its professional finish. "Here are my girls," she said. "What are your plans, Olga? I thought I'd be getting along home. All this excitement makes my poor old head ache."

While she spoke Roger had reappeared with the drinks and silently handed them to Olga and Susan. "Tell you what," Olga took a long pull at hers, "why don't we all take you home? Mary could dream up some supper for us, couldn't she, Gran?"

"Why, I think that would be lovely." Mrs Morton looked surprised.

"Good," Olga could be very executive when she chose. "Roger, be a lamb and get me my fur coat. I dumped it on the chair by the door. You'll come, won't you?"

Roger looked at Mrs Morton. "If you're sure it's all right?"

"Of course." She was definite, if not enthusiastic.

"Then I'd love to. Can I get your coat, Susan?"

"No, thank you," she put down her drink untasted, "I left it upstairs."

The upstairs hall was deeply carpeted and hung with sporting prints. From this range, the sound of the party was considerably less than human. Susan paused with her hand on the bedroom door. The words, "Poor Olga," had come out to her. Inside, Betty Jane and her sister were powdering their noses. They paused, somewhat consciously, at sight of Susan.

"Are you going already?" Betty Jane asked. "The party's just getting warmed up."

"I'm afraid so." Susan dabbed powder on her nose. "Mrs Morton's a bit tired, so we're going to take her home."

"We?"

"Olga and Roger and I." Susan moved away to look for her coat.

"*Really*?" Betty Jane looked amused. "What did I tell you?" she spoke to her sister.

Priscilla laughed. "You're too clever, that's what's the matter with you."

How disgusting Boston was, Susan thought, silent beside Mrs Morton in Roger's car. Nothing but gossip and slander; whispers in ladies' rooms, whispers behind hands; voices on the stairs, on the street corner; over drinks, over tea, over coffee . . . Voices comparing notes, starting possibilities, hoping always for the worst . . . She hated the place; it had not occurred to her before; she hated it not only on her own account, but on Olga's. What had Betty Jane told Priscilla? Something about Spencer? Something about Roger? Something true? Probably not, but what difference did that make? . . . *The story was started.*

Chapter Fifteen

Mary was delighted at the unexpected party and grumbled even more than usual as a result. "Flying about in planes at this time of year," she said to Olga as they sat down to supper. "If I were your mother, I'd beat some sense into you. Don't you think she needs it, Roger?"

Thus directly appealed to, Roger laughed. "Why should we grumble, Mary, when we're the gainers by it?"

Across the table, Olga's secret, superior smile was back. *That's better*, she seemed to be saying to herself. Susan was quiet at her end of the table. It was a relief to have Mrs Morton fully occupied for once and to be able to withdraw a little into her own thoughts. These days she sometimes found herself almost resenting anything that distracted her from her inner talk with David. The noise and interplay of the party, Roger's conversation, and Olga's, had all seemed unreal when set against the deep, reverberating music of her thoughts. Strange that now, when she had lost him, her mind should be brimming over as never before with David; stranger still, that with so much sorrow there should be so little bitterness.

"Susan's dreaming again," Roger's voice roused her. "What is it this time, Sue?"

She smiled. (But how treacherously near she always was, these days, to tears.) "I was just thinking . . ." she left it vague.

Roger laughed. "Not very flattering to your company, I'm afraid."

"Poor Susan can't help it if she's too highbrow for us," there was an edge in Olga's voice. *She must be unhappy*, Susan thought, *that's not like her*. "Talking about highbrows, Gran," she went on, "were those tickets for tonight's Symphony that Mrs Larraby gave you?"

"Gracious me, yes. I'd forgotten all about them. I'm afraid your poor old Gran's losing her memory, Olga. I don't think my wretched head would stand another outing today, though. Why don't you and Roger go? A quiet evening would be more the thing for a couple of invalids like Susan and me. But if you're going, you'd better be getting started; it's quite late."

"So it is," Olga stood up. "Roger, you're all ready, aren't you? I'll just run up and powder my nose. It's a gorgeous programme: Haydn and Mozart; you're an angel to let us use the tickets, Gran."

So far Roger had not said a word, but as Olga disappeared he crumbled a slice of bread on his plate. "It's very nice of you, Mrs Morton, but I really ought to be getting home. Wouldn't Susan like to go?"

"Don't be absurd, Roger. It would be far too late for Susan to be out." Susan smiled to herself: *Olga at the Symphony with another girl; outrageous*.

"But some music might do her good," Roger persisted. "How about it, Susan? Wouldn't you like to?"

"Of course I'd love it, but I don't think I ought to go out tonight, thank you very much." Susan stifled a pang. The idea of an evening of music and peacefulness was beyond anything attractive. But Olga had decided: of course Roger must go. Even Mrs Morton – resigned for once – realised that.

Olga reappeared. "There, never say I can't manage a quick change when I want to." She had changed her black suit for a brilliant crimson dress and looked, if possible, handsomer and more highly polished than ever. "Come on, Roger, we're going to be late by the time you've got the car parked. It's fierce round Symphony Hall."

Roger made a last effort. "You're *sure* you don't want to, Susan?"

"*Susan* go?" Olga dismissed it. "What an absurd idea. Goodnight, Gran. Enjoy yourself, Susan."

As the front door banged behind them the telephone rang. "Ah," Mrs Morton said. "Martha, I expect. Hullo . . . Yes . . . Just a minute, please. It's for you, Susan – a man." She sounded surprised.

David. And to think she might have been out. She had even been feeling disappointed at not going. *David.* Her hand trembled. "Hullo," she said.

"Is that Miss Monkton?" It was not his voice. She had never really felt despair till now.

"Yes," she said.

"Well, Susan, what a time I have had getting hold of you. This is Bud Dennison, by the way."

"How are you?" she said mechanically.

"Never better. But I'm sorry to hear you've been poorly. I hope you're okay again by now; I called up to ask if you'd come to the Symphony tonight. I'm sorry about the short notice, but you know how it is with press seats . . ."

"Oh," she hesitated, "it's awfully nice of you, but—"

"Now, then," he interrupted, "no 'buts'. You can't let the old South down, mind. And if you're worrying about the weather, don't. I'll pick you up in a cab and not a flake of snow shall touch your head. We Southerners . . ."

Without thinking, she interrupted him. "I know, the age of chivalry is not dead. I'd love to come, Bud, thank you very much."

She rang off, explained about Merton Dennison to an

213

astonished Mrs Morton, and hurried upstairs for her coat. She was still quivering from the disappointment of hearing Dennison's voice when she expected David's. After that, a domestic evening with Mrs Morton and all the memories of other days when the secret that kept her company was a happy one would have been too much to bear. She must get out, and a concert – even with Merton Dennison – would be a blessed relief from the leering memories that lurked in the big Brimmer Street drawing room.

Dennison arrived with surprising speed, and blinking and shaking hands with Mrs Morton, explained that he had been dining on Beacon Hill. With his usual over-courtesy he apologised for depriving Mrs Morton of her charming companion: "Gross selfishness, I'm afraid. But we'd best be moving," he said to Susan, "or we'll miss the *Surprise*. Wrap up well, it's snowing like mad."

"Is it?" Susan tied a black scarf Julia had given her over her hair. "It makes you look like your Madonna," David had said. She bit her lip. How near the tears were.

"There," Merton Dennison held open the taxi door, "I said I'd take good care of you."

He had been very busy, he said, doing a long article on Christmas in New England for the Texas *Evening Journal*, but he had not forgotten their date. "We Southerners never forget." Then there had been mid-years; they managed, he implied, these things better in Texas. And then he had heard (from one of his sources of information, of course), that she had been sick. "But looking very beautiful on it. Quite the Madonna in that scarf." She was better now? Good. And back at work, he hoped. Which reminded him: she must tell him all about Professor Winter. What a business; naturally she would know all about it. Did she think . . .

To Susan's intense relief the taxi drew up outside Symphony Hall. The last stragglers were hurrying up the steps and into

the Hall. They were just in time, and in the flurry it was easy
to ignore the question. As they found their seats, which were,
as he pointed out, good ones in the first row of the balcony,
the audience burst into applause. Koussevitsky had entered.
"Ah, the maestro," whispered Merton Dennison, "I'd heard
he was sick." Silence was creeping through the audience;
passing over them, it laid a subduing finger on Dennison.
Susan settled more comfortably in her seat.

The lights were low, though not, she thought, quite low
enough. But even so, a great sense of peace and privacy came
over her as she drifted away with the music, her own unhap-
piness forming a sombre counterpoint to its gaiety. When it
was over she came back as from a great distance and clapped
mechanically, reluctant to break the quiet of her mood.
Beside her, Merton Dennison was applauding vehemently;
tempted, she suspected, to shout "bravo". "Magnificent," he
said instead, "superb. Particularly the last movement; such
mastery, such style. Didn't you think so, Susan?"

Doubtful whether he was referring to the composition
or the performance, Susan temporised with a vague, "Yes,
indeed."

"A great man, Haydn," he went on, "a very great man.
A little superficial perhaps, but very fine so far as he
goes. I confess I'm a Wagner man myself, I like my music
significant."

"And noisy?"

"I can see you're a heretic, but never mind, I'll convert you."
He plunged into a lecture on Wagner, which was interrupted
by the dimming of the lights. "Stravinsky," he said. "Hmmm.
I suppose it's very high-minded of Koussy, but I don't mind
telling you that I get tired of all these moderns." Again the
wave of silence engulfed him.

Reluctant though she was to agree with him, Susan had to
admit to herself that the Stravinsky meant little or nothing

215

to her. She sat, half listening, half dreaming back over the day and all the other days. Time seemed to flow around her; there had been so many days, there would be so many, many more. It was idle, really, to be unhappy; her misery, like her happiness, would wash away down the stream and all that would remain would be the succession of days; fine days and rainy ones, sunshine and flurries of snow out under the stars. When the applause broke out again she was farther away than ever, watching, far out by the milky way, the slow ebb and flow of time.

"Well, that wasn't so bad after all," his voice broke in on her. "Shall we go downstairs and stretch our legs?" He got up.

He knew an amazing number of people and stopped to exchange a sentence or two with each of them. After they had passed, he would turn to Susan. "Fascinating man; walked across the Sahara with nothing to eat but sugar candy," or, "You must have heard of her, the author of *Alone I Suffer*?" The fact that Susan had heard of none of them put the crown on his delight in imparting information.

They ran (Susan had been wondering what would happen if they did) straight into Roger and Olga in the lobby. Olga, Susan saw, was restless again. Had her capture of Roger been less satisfactory than she expected?

"Well, look who's here," Olga was the first to speak. "I thought you were at home with your books, Susan?"

"So did I," Susan said. "This is Merton Dennison. Olga Horwood. Roger Merryweather." Detached, she watched her own competence with amusement. How impossible the introduction would once have seemed.

They all shook hands (Merton Dennison could be relied on to exact the last formality from any occasion), and stood, uneasily, in the first pause of strangers who know of no common ground. Merton Dennison took charge of the situation. "Not, surely, one of the Salem Horwoods?"

"Oh, yes," Olga was bored, "originally." Susan noticed that, as at the party, she kept glancing quickly, nervously around. She was clearly looking for someone.

"But then you must have seen the Hawthorne manuscript?" Merton Dennison's voice was reverent.

"Oh, that. No, I never have. My great uncle keeps it up at Salem and I never could remember to make him show it to me."

As Merton Dennison began to exclaim over the uniqueness of this manuscript of the *Scarlet Letter* which had unflattering comments by Herman Melville in the margin, Roger caught Susan's eye. "I'm so glad you got here after all. I knew you really wanted to."

"Yes, I did rather." No point in denying it. "I haven't been to a concert for ages, and I do love Haydn and Mozart. I sometimes think they're my favourites, but of course it's silly to have favourites really, and anyway I don't know anything about it."

"You mean you refuse to be one of the 'I don't know much about it, but I know what I like' school?"

"I try not to be, but it's frightfully difficult."

The warning bell was ringing. By now Olga and Merton Dennison were deep in conversation. "Oh, yes," he was saying, "I know Mark well. But of course he's so busy with the Hasty Pudding show these days . . ."

Olga turned to Roger and Susan. "Well, children, time to get back. I'm very glad to have met you," she said to Merton Dennison. Then (if Susan had not known her she would really have thought the idea had only that moment struck her), "But why don't you and I change places, Sue? The Larrabys' are beautiful seats; you can see everything."

She really is looking for someone, Susan thought. Spencer

217

Russell? She followed them with her eyes: Olga, tall and elegant, her fur coat thrown over her shoulders, with Merton Dennison pink and overwhelmed beside her. The last Susan saw of them, Merton Dennison was standing gallantly aside to let Olga go through the entrance first. His lips were moving. "*The age of chivalry,*" he was undoubtedly saying, "*is not dead.*"

"Well, this is very nice, Susan." Roger settled her coat on the back of her seat.

She had been feeling, as so often, rather sorry for him, and cheered up immediately. "I'm glad . . ." A wave of applause as Koussevitsky came in ended her sentence for her.

The Mozart was David's favourite symphony. Since she never knew symphonies by their numbers, Susan had not realised it until the first quiet notes rang their clarion call in her heart. Julia had given him the recording of it for Christmas and he had played it over and over again during the few days she was there. There had been a point at the end of the second movement where the record changer always stuck and David would go into an elaborate mime of fury while Julia, quiet and competent as always, got up and released the record.

As the movement ended, Susan found she was crying. There seemed to be nothing she could do about it. The tears rolled one after another down her cheeks, not painfully, but easily and with relief. If only the lights were lower. Fortunately, Roger was tilting his programme this way and that in an effort to read it. Susan fumbled in her bag and found a small and ragged piece of Kleenex. Surreptitiously, she mopped at her eyes. It was no use; the tears still flowed, the Kleenex was sodden. Desperately, she felt along the bottom of her bag, dislodged her powder compact, caught a nail on her comb and finally pricked herself with an open safety-pin. It was in vain: there was nothing at the bottom of the bag but a little dust. A tear fell in her lap. As Koussevitsky raised his baton, Roger quietly passed her his handkerchief. Muttering an embarrassed 'thank you', she mopped at her eyes. What a blessing, though, that it was Roger, not Merton Dennison.

He turned to her as Koussevitsky was taking his last bows. "You don't really want to go on for a drink, do you?"

She was feeling for the sleeve of her coat. "But I don't want to spoil the party . . ."

"Here," he guided her hand into the sleeve. "It won't spoil it. We'll tell them you're not feeling well and I'll take you home. I'm sure Olga won't mind if you don't."

They found Olga looking haughtily bored and Merton Dennison paler and pinker than ever. But Roger wasted no time. "I'm afraid Susan's not feeling too well," he said. "I think I'd better take her home and leave you two to go have that drink."

"But," Merton Dennison began, but Olga was too quick for him. "That's too bad, Susan, but if you must . . . I know; we two will go on to the Ritz and you can drop Susan and join us there, Roger. There's no sense in our all trailing round there on a foul night like this."

The snow was falling faster and thicker than ever and a chilly crowd stood on the steps of Symphony Hall whistling hopefully at unresponsive taxis. Susan shivered in her light English tweed.

"Oh, lord," Olga said, "this looks pretty hopeless. Roger, you'd better go get the car and we'll all go round by Brimmer Street and drop Susan. What a bore." She pulled her fur coat more closely round her. Susan had never seen her so bad-tempered. Poor Olga . . .

But Roger had made a dash into the middle of the road and now returned, triumphant, on the running board of a taxi. He opened the door. "In you get, Susan." He handed his car keys to Olga. "You know where the car is, Olga. You two had better collect her and go on over to the Ritz. This is no night for an invalid to be out." Before Olga could answer he had got in after Susan and closed the door.

"Roger, she'll be furious," Susan protested belatedly.

"I can't help it." He leaned forward. "Thirty-five Brimmer Street, please. I'm not going to have you catching pneumonia, and Olga's strong as a horse. I've taken her to enough football games to know. Are you feeling better now?"

"Oh, yes, thank you. I'm really frightfully sorry."

"Don't be ridiculous. Besides, I'm grateful for the excuse. I don't feel a bit like going out again."

"But you'll go on, won't you? They're expecting you." The taxi stopped.

He leaned forward to look at the meter. "I certainly shall not. I know Olga told me I would and I didn't contradict her, but after all, she's got my car and your escort. What more does she want?" He paid the driver. "As a matter of fact," he went on as she unlocked the door, "I'm coming in to see you get a hot drink before you go to bed."

"And have some yourself?"

"Naturally. I never pretended to be a pure philanthropist. Don't look so worried, Susan. It's high time Olga learned she can't dictate to everybody all the time. She's got away with it longer than is good for her as it is." He led the way to the kitchen. "It's my fault, really. I've been lying down and letting her trample on me for years; but I'm on strike now. Let me see," he opened the refrigerator, "hot milk, I think. What shall we put in it? Coffee? No, that'll keep you awake. D'you know where Mary keeps the cocoa?"

"Over here, I think." Susan found it in a tin marked cinnamon.

"Thank you. Now you sit down and relax. I make delicious cocoa, though I do say so."

Susan was glad to do as she was told. The wicker chair creaked as she sat down and the orange cat woke up in his box by the stove, cocked an inquisitive ear at them and then got sedately up and came and sat on her lap.

"That looks comfortable," Roger said. "I often think this is the nicest room in the house."

"It is nice," Susan agreed. Under Mary's cheerful influence it had lost the antiseptic quality of so many American kitchens. The white table and refrigerator were more than counterbalanced by the straggling plants on the window-sill, the cat's red rug and the brightly coloured religious pictures on the walls. It looked a human room, one where real food was made, where cooking was not a mere matter of flans and fricassees, but you could expect the good, rich smell of baking bread and might even catch a predatory child in the act of stealing the fresh crust from the loaf.

"There, the milk's boiling." Roger mixed cocoa and sugar with a little cold milk. "Cocoa's one of my specialities." He added the hot milk. "We used to make it with condensed milk at camp and it was wonderful. Greedy little pigs, we were. The secret of success, of course, is to let it boil long enough. I hope you aren't dying of starvation?" He put the saucepan on the side of the stove for a minute and fetched the cookie jar. "Good old Mary," he brought out a sample handful, "ginger snaps and toll house cookies."

"Do you think we should?"

"Of course. She'll be delighted. She adores you. She told me the other day that you were the only person who was nice to poor old Ginger."

"Well, he is rather a disreputable old thing, isn't he?" She tickled him behind the ears and he purred ecstatically and stretched out in abandoned bliss on her lap.

"No," Roger said, "he wouldn't go very well on a good black dress, would he? Poor Olga." The connection was obvious.

"*Poor?*" It was what she had thought at the party.

221

"Yes. She makes life so tough for herself. You should have known her when she was younger. We used all to go up to Vermont in the summer, you know, and we had a wonderful time. Olga always did everything better than any of us. She wasn't a bit good-looking then – pigtails, and bands on her teeth and all – and she didn't give a damn. She used to go in swimming in the mill stream in April – my God it was cold – and she climbed every tree in miles . . ." The cocoa started to boil over and he took it off. "Those were the days. Old Mrs Morton was in despair about her – even I could see that. She's happy now, at any rate. There," he brought the two cups and the cookie jar over to Susan, "I shall sit at your feet. I expect Olga'll get over it in time, but if she doesn't, heaven help the man she marries. Heaven help her, for that matter. I hope they're having a good time at the Ritz."

Susan sipped the hot cocoa. "So do I. Are you sure you oughtn't to go? They may wait and wait."

"Let them. I'm far too comfortable where I am." He stared into his cup. "I'm sorry you're so miserable, Susan."

"Me? It's just because I've been sick."

"Is it?" They were silent for a few minutes. "Look, Susan," Roger said at last, "you're going to think I'm a brute either way, but I can't help it. You see I do think you're miserable. I've got some friends in South Kingston . . ."

Susan listened to the silence and said nothing. She was remembering. People she and David had met on their walks . . . *What had they seen? What had they said?* Not that it mattered, somehow, at this point. Nothing mattered. She was tired out, beyond caring, almost beyond remembering. But of course that was why Roger had been so kind the night she got back from South Kingston after Christmas. *He had known all the time – or for how long?* Nothing was ever secret; how had she imagined it could be?

"I'm awfully sorry, Susan," he went on. "I do hope you

don't mind. Of course I haven't said anything; people can be so unattractive. It's wretched for you, the whole business . . . I took English 'A' with him; I liked him a lot."

"Thank you." Susan did not quite know what she was thanking him for, but it seemed somehow the right thing to say.

"I wouldn't have told you," he went on, "only I thought you might like to have someone you could talk to. I do hope you'll believe I didn't mean to poke and pry."

"Of course not."

"Because, you see . . ." he stopped, then went on with a visible effort. "You see, Susan, I suppose I'd always really planned to marry Olga. You know, the way you take it for granted that some day something or other will just happen? I think we all rather took that for granted. But it won't do, you know." He had been staring at the floor, but now he looked up at her as if for reassurance. "It really won't do. We'd both be miserable, even if she'd have me, which she wouldn't. There's Mrs Morton for one thing." *He almost hates her*, Susan thought. "I'm going to teach," he went on, "that's settled. I've even got a job, I think, at Middlesex. I'm damned lucky to get it. But it's no good thinking Olga would stand for being a schoolmaster's wife; an ambassador would be more in her and Mrs Morton's line these days."

He got up and fetched the saucepan. "There's a dividend; here." He filled up their cups. "I'm doing this frightfully badly, Sue, I hope you'll forgive me. Olga's quite right, I'm no good at this kind of thing. But you see, it is so difficult. It's not the slightest use my trying to pretend . . . I mean, we both of us know . . ." He gave up in despair, then started again in a rush. "Look, Susan, I think you're about the nicest person I've ever met, and I'd be very happy indeed if you'd marry me."

"Why, *Roger!*" She felt as surprised as a Victorian heroine and, if possible, more helpless.

223

Now that it was out he talked more easily. "Don't say anything yet. You see that's why I wanted you to know I knew all about you and David Winter." *Not all, surely*, she thought. What should she do? "I know you're unhappy now," he went on, "and you know I've been having a bit of a time with Olga – though I'm over that, of course – so why couldn't we, well, kind of share it? I'd try to make you happy, I really would, Susan."

"I'm sure you would." The cat stirred on her lap and stretched luxuriously in its sleep. "I can't, Roger," she said at last, "it's terribly nice of you, but I really can't."

"Please think it over, Susan, There's lots of time."

There was indeed; it stretched before her, grey and interminable. She stroked the cat with long, regular movements. If she could only say, yes. It would be an end to loneliness . . . But it was impossible, now and for always. "It's no use, Roger. Really and truly I wish I could, but I can't. It wouldn't be fair to you to say I'd think about it. Nothing's going to make any difference, ever."

"But, Susan, you can't . . . Nothing goes on for ever. It just doesn't happen. You'll get over it, really you will. Look at me and Olga."

"But are you over it, Roger, really? I don't think you are, you know."

"Of course I am, don't be absurd." The very certainty of his voice betrayed a doubt. "You'd love it at Middlesex, Susan. Concord's a beautiful place. Have you ever been there?"

Had she been there? The first time, David had told her about Sir Christopher Wren designing the first Cape Cod house. She had always meant to ask him if it was really true or if he had just been teasing her. She would never know. The cat stirred on her lap, the mouse of his dreams evading him. "I wish you wouldn't, Roger. It's no good, I tell you." Her voice was higher than she expected.

224

"I'm sorry, Susan. Isn't there anything I can do?" He got up moved restlessly over to the sink, and stood there staring out the window into the darkness.

Nothing, nothing at all. "You can lend me your handkerchief again."

"But, Susan," he had said it before, "nothing goes on for ever."

"This does." It was final, and he recognised it as such.

"I'm sorry, Susan. It would have been so good."

"No, it wouldn't, Roger," she was clear about it now. "You and Olga . . ."

"Talk of the angels!" Olga's voice came from the doorway. "What about Roger and me? I thought you were coming on to the Ritz, Roger?"

"I'm sorry." Roger did not try to explain. The silence stretched out, tense and precarious.

Olga broke it at last. "Cocoa," she said. "I haven't had it for years. Do you remember how we used to make it in Vermont, Roger? It always tasted different with condensed milk. Make me a cup, like a lamb, I'm starved. That's a very exhausting friend of yours, Susan."

Susan, who had expected a storm, looked up and smiled. "He is rather, isn't he? Did he tell you about his autograph collection?"

"Did he not! Roger, I'll mix it and you can watch the milk. I must say this is far nicer than the Ritz; it was so crowded you couldn't hear yourself think. How wise you two were. But you still haven't explained about me and Roger, Susan. Don't think you can get out of it so easily."

In the new silence Roger's spoon scraped on the bottom of the saucepan. Susan looked at him helplessly. "Oh, well," he made up his mind, "as a matter of fact, I was asking Susan to marry me, and she won't."

225

"Oh," Olga said, and then, "My condolences. I'm so sorry if I interrupted."

"But you didn't," suddenly Susan felt that she had control of the situation. "I was just telling Roger it was absurd to ask me to marry him when it's *you* he's in love with." She put down the cat and stood up. "And now, if you'll excuse me, I think I'll go to bed. After all, I am supposed to be an invalid. Thank you for everything, Roger. Goodnight."

"*Well*," she heard Olga draw her breath as she closed the door. She climbed the stairs feeling extraordinarily light-hearted. It was an appalling thing to have done. Where on earth had she got the courage? David had always said she was braver than she knew; perhaps he was right. What would they be saying now? She smiled to herself. Funny that Olga had talked about Vermont, too. She was nice under it all; silly not to have realised sooner. Roger had given himself away all the time: "Olga's quite right; I'm no good at this kind of thing . . ." Had he asked her before? Would it really work now? What fun if it did . . . Poor Mrs Morton . . .

Poor Susan. So many engagements . . . Mr and Mrs David Winter. The second Mrs Winter. "You've got to do me credit, darling." Oh, David . . . Her thoughts were softening and loosening into dreams of him when she was roused by a knock at the door.

"May I come in?" Olga asked. "I hope I didn't wake you?"

"Not seriously." Susan switched on the light.

Olga's hair was untidy and her face looked alive as Susan had never seen it. The mask was gone. "I just wanted to say thank you," she said, "and get you to congratulate me. After all, you really should be the first. Roger said he was sure you wouldn't mind."

"Mind? Of course I don't. I think it's lovely."

Olga sat down on the bed. "I'm so grateful to you," she

said. "You know it's a funny thing, I never realised I was in love with him till I saw him with you. I must have been for ages really. Isn't it silly? How could I waste so much time? Did you see Spencer at the concert tonight?"

"No, was he there?"

"Yes, with Priscilla Larraby." She was going to say something else, but she paused, changed her mind and was silent for a minute, picking at the edge of Susan's bedspread. *I'll never know what really happened*, Susan thought. Something in New York? At dinner that night? "He's really a perishing bore," Olga went on. "I can't think how I managed to think he was so wonderful. Of course it was Gran, partly. D'you think she'll be furious, Susan?"

"I expect so. Does it matter?"

"Not in the slightest." Olga curled her feet up under her on the bed. "Roger's got a job at Middlesex – I expect he told you," she grinned at Susan. *We're friends*, Susan thought, *how odd*. "If he does all right (and of course he will), we'll be married next spring. Isn't it wonderful? It's all over. I feel as if I was me again, somehow. D'you know what I mean?" She leaned towards Susan, searching for words to make her meaning clear even to herself. "All this time I haven't been, really; I've been so busy rushing about with people like Spencer Russell, being afraid of things . . . Roger says the beauty about being engaged is that you never need be lonely at parties – or anywhere else, I suppose. It's true, you know. Susan, I'm so happy; you've no idea."

"I think I can guess," Susan said.

Chapter Sixteen

Mrs Morton was not pleased, and all that Sunday battle raged in Brimmer Street. It was, Susan saw from the first, a losing battle on Mrs Morton's part, but it was equally clear that she would not admit it till the last tear had been shed and the last heart attack unavailingly threatened.

The twins came to lunch, so an amnesty was tacitly declared for its duration and Mrs Morton contented herself with sighing over her duck and sending her ice-cream away in untasted dissolution on her plate. Ralph and Randall, however, were absorbed as usual in the serious business of food and noticed nothing, somewhat, Susan suspected, to the disappointment of their grandmother, whose sighs became more and more portentous as the meal wore on and no explanation of them was demanded. But, primed in turns by Olga and Susan, Ralph and Randall kept up their innocent prattle about the pleasures and pains of life at Harvard until Mrs Morton arose with the most enormous sigh of all and announced that she must go and lie down. "Your poor old grandmother's feeling her age today."

"That's too bad, Grannie," said Ralph.

"You're looking so well," said Randall.

It was the last straw, and Mrs Morton retired. Olga caught Susan's eye as she followed. "I'd better let her get it off her mind. I told Roger not to come till tea-time."

Susan smiled sympathetically and pressed more coffee and peanut brittle on the twins.

Mrs Morton and Olga were still closeted upstairs and Susan was alone in the drawing room when Roger arrived. He greeted her rather sheepishly and was obviously relieved by her ready congratulations. It was, however, a difficult subject and they were both glad to change it for the ready alternative of Mrs Morton's reaction.

"Has it been very bad?" he asked.

"You've no idea."

"Poor Susan. And you'll be left with it. It does seem unfair."

"I know, there's no justice. I shall expect you to provide me with lots of moral support."

"I certainly will. God knows, it's the least I can do. You are a marvel, Susan, you really are."

"I don't know why."

The exchange of courtesies was interrupted by the appearance of Mrs Morton and Olga. Mrs Morton had changed into a black dress that accentuated the pallor of her cheeks. It was not the first time that Susan had wondered whether she normally used rouge.

"Well, Roger," she settled wearily on her sofa, "I congratulate you. You're a lucky boy. At least I suppose you are. I'm too old to pretend, so I won't say I'm pleased. I'm just a poor disappointed old woman and you must let me have my say. I've told Olga before and I'll tell her again that I think she's throwing herself away and you're making a great mistake. She's no more cut out for a schoolmaster's wife than I am. Now, if it was Susan, there'd be some sense to it." The three of them exchanged glances and Susan blushed. "But there it is, and I only hope you won't both of you live to regret it. I know it's taken years off my life already, not that anyone cares about that, of course. I had such hopes for you, Olga."

"I know you did, Gran," Olga's voice was still patient, "but you see they didn't suit me, really. And after all, I am old enough to make up my own mind."

The very kindness of her voice seemed to finish Mrs Morton. Anger she could have met with anger, and scenes with scenes, but before Olga's tolerance she wilted visibly. "Well, I've said my say and done my best and all I ask is that you don't ever say I didn't warn you. Now, I suppose we'd better have some tea. Not that I could possibly eat anything. My poor head aches frightfully. Susan, dear child, fetch me my medicine."

It was a strange meal. Mrs Morton drank tea with a martyr's grace while Olga and Roger, opposite her, exchanged glances and, visibly, glowed.

"I suppose your grandmother's delighted?" Mrs Morton poured her third cup of tea.

"Yes, I think she's pleased," Roger had been very quiet so far. "She thought you would be," he went on more boldly.

"I know; we used to talk a lot of nonsense, she and I, and I suppose this is a judgement on me. But what's the use of talking? I can see you children are bound to break my heart. And Olga might have done anything. I always thought she'd marry an ambassador."

Roger caught Susan's eye. "So did I. I do know how lucky I am, really I do, Mrs Morton." He looked at his watch. "If you're going to catch the six o'clock, we'd better get going, Olga."

"Yes, darling." Mrs Morton flinched as Olga got up obediently. "My things are all downstairs. Goodbye, Gran," she bent and kissed her, "I'm dreadfully sorry you feel this way, but this is right, really it is. Goodbye, Sue, and thanks for everything."

*   *   *

231

They were gone, and the cold shadow of a New England Sunday evening fell over the house. "What was Olga thanking you for?" Mrs Morton was still drinking tea.

"Oh, nothing in particular," Susan was vague. The story of the night before belonged only to the three of them, and, so belonging, it seemed to give her a share in the happiness of the other two. The knowledge of this had been warm inside her all day and now stood her in good stead as she faced the querulous evening.

It was beginning already. "If I'd known what was going to come of it," Mrs Morton said, "I'd have sent you to the Symphony with Roger last night. How Olga can throw herself away like that is a mystery to me. Why, there was Spencer Russell just crazy for her at Christmas. If only he'd been at the party last night. But Eliza *did* say he was going to the Symphony; I thought . . . But perhaps it'll all work out right in the end. I must write to her mother. Susan, my dear, would you pass me the cake; I believe a little something to eat might do my poor head good. I don't know how Olga can be so inconsiderate when she knows how delicate my health is." She was temporarily silenced by a large mouthful of chocolate cake.

"They do seem so happy," Susan ventured to say.

"Happy." Mrs Morton snorted. "Happiness. Where will that get them? Five years from now Roger will still be an under-master correcting term papers all day with Olga in a little house in a back street smelling of diapers. She'll lose her looks . . . Oh, I've no patience with her. And she might have married *anyone*." It was almost a cry. "Would you cut me a tiny piece more of that cake, Susan?" The telephone rang. "I suppose that'll be Martha calling up to gloat. I don't see how I can bear it."

Susan picked up the receiver. "Yes," she said, "it's Mrs Merryweather." She brought the telephone over to Mrs Morton's sofa.

"Hullo," Mrs Morton said. "Yes, Martha, it's me . . .
Lovely? . . . I'm glad you think so." Her voice was faint and
tired; she seemed to shrink back into her quilts as she talked.
"Yes, I'm feeling a little tired. It's all been a great shock. I
haven't been able to eat anything all day and my head aches
frightfully . . . Expected it? I should say not. Oh, I know we
used to talk back in Vermont . . . No, I won't deceive you,
Martha, I'm dreadfully disappointed . . . of course he's a nice
boy, but . . ."

The conversation was obviously going to go on indefinitely
and Susan began to collect the tea things. An imperious
gesture from Mrs Morton directed her to leave the chocolate
cake beside her, and the last thing she heard as she left the
room with the tray was Mrs Morton's voice, fainter than
ever: "I'm too old for these disappointments, Martha, I'm
too old . . ."

She believes herself, too, Susan thought, running hot water
over the dishes, while the cat made hungry figures-of-eight
round her ankles. If asked, she would say that she was making
this fuss entirely for Olga's own good. *This hurts me*, Susan
told herself, *more than it does you.* She put the tea things
away on the pantry shelves and went into the kitchen to
see what Mary had left for their supper. The cat followed,
tail in air.

"Oh," Susan said. "So you're hungry, are you? You're as
bad as Mrs Morton." She opened the refrigerator. "Here,"
she got out his dish. "Not many cats get liver on Sunday
night."

He purred and stood on his hind legs with two hopeful
paws on her knee. She put down the dish and stood smiling,
as, purr turning to a delighted growl, he fell on the liver. As
she stood there, it occurred to her that she was happy or, at
least, she modified it, content. It was astonishing. Nothing
goes on for ever, Roger had said. Could he have been right?

The thought was dreadful to her. She did not want to lose David, and to stop remembering him would be to lose him all over again.

And yet for a few minutes she had been happy; she had forgotten. It was not worth it. As the memories flooded back on her, she welcomed them as familiar and irreplaceable sorrows. What would he be doing now? Did Josephine like to eat supper by the fire? Did he cut up her apples for her? All the questions were swallowed up in the one overriding one: Would she ever see him again? Roger was wrong; her memories would always be the same, would always be her secret strength, her certainty. Better to have loved and lost . . .

Mrs Morton opened the door. "There you are. I was beginning to think you'd deserted me, too. I suppose we really ought to do something about supper." She was carrying the empty cake plate.

Chapter Seventeen

Cold February blew itself out into wet March, and March into treacherous April, while Susan worked and ate and slept her way through the wintry days, almost grateful for their monotony. Preoccupied with her memories of David, she did not want new thoughts or feelings; she had enough. As the cold days grew slowly and reluctantly warmer and the streets around Radcliffe grew daily more treacherous with slush, she went about her trivial affairs in a strange numbness that was very near to content.

There was, after all, enough to distract her. Mrs Morton still bewailed Olga's engagement nightly over the bridge table, while Susan did her unsuccessful best to reconcile her to the inevitable. It was no use, and Mrs Morton's constant lamentations had at last worn out even Mrs Merryweather's almost inexhaustible patience.

"Well, Emmeline," she said one day as they finished a gloomy tea, "if that's the way you feel about Roger, I suppose there's no more to be said, but I think you're making a great mistake." She stood up, large, red-faced and surprisingly dignified. "I think it's time I was going." She left and did not return.

It was a real deprivation to Mrs Morton, who had depended more, Susan suspected, than she herself realised, on their frequent drives into the country and the sociable, scandalous teas afterwards. But it merely confirmed her in her antipathy to Roger and at last even Susan almost gave up trying to defend him.

She made no secret, however, of the fact that she herself saw him fairly frequently. He had kept his promise of moral support and by now they had a standing engagement for Monday lunch. Often he would be just back from spending the weekend with Olga in New York and full of their plans. Despite Mrs Morton's angry letters, Mrs Horwood had been easily won over to Olga's side. A gentle creature, she had the habit of being bullied too thoroughly implanted from her own childhood to be able to stand up against her determined daughter.

"Mrs Morton'll give in in the end," Susan told Roger one bright April Monday. "Don't you worry. She's fearfully fond of Olga, you know, poor old dear."

"Then I wish she'd hurry up about it," he said. "She's managing to make everyone so miserable."

"I know," Susan said, "specially herself. It does seem too bad. Oh goodness, Roger, I've got to go. I told Merton Dennison I'd go to the movies with him."

"I didn't know you still saw him."

"I don't really," she laughed. "But from time to time he gets free seats for something and calls up and tells me the age of chivalry is not dead and asks me to go. He's very nice, really." She had a qualm of conscience.

"And do you call him Bud?" They stood up.

"Believe it or not, I do. Thank you so much for the lunch, Roger. I think it's a scandal." They had had the argument many times.

"It's nothing of the kind." As always, Roger was firm. "You're the oldest friend of the family, aren't you? You wait till you start coping with your responsibilities as a godparent."

"Aren't you a little ahead of yourself?"

They parted, laughing, outside St Clair's. "I won't ask you to give my love to Mrs Morton; it wouldn't be kind."

"But I shall tell her I've had lunch with you. I think it's good for her."

Now that she was used to him, Susan enjoyed her occasional outings with Merton Dennison. He was, she thought over sherry at the Statler, no trouble at all. He could be relied on to carry the conversation indefinitely, and, more charming still, to treat any contribution she made to it as the quintessence of wisdom.

"Here's to the great paper," he raised his glass, "how's it coming?"

"Not so bad."

"And you still don't regret being so independent about it?" He had been astonished to hear that she had had no tutorials this term.

"Oh, no." It was a bitter lie. She thought of her tutorials: David with his arm around her quoting Marlowe, David laughing at her for a feminist, *David* . . .

"I hope you're going to let me see it before you turn it in," he was saying.

"I don't know about that." Nobody should see it before David did. It would be the last communication between them. It must be good. If hard work could make it so, it would be. She remembered an old daydream of hers: he was to have been so impressed by it that he asked her to collaborate with him on his book. Oh, those daydreams . . .

"Yes, wasn't it good?" She answered a question she had hardly heard. "I thought Groucho was marvellous. It was awfully nice of you to take me, Bud."

"It was a delight and a pleasure. I hope I'll see you again soon."

"I hope so." She smiled vaguely at him as they parted. How easy people were if you didn't get bothered about them.

She walked home across the Public Gardens where the grass was turning green and the swan boats were being painted by the pond. Spring. The arbutus would be out by now. Would David be finding it for Josephine?

Mrs Morton was sitting by the window of her room. *She looks much older*, Susan thought, *she's wearing herself out*.

"There you are," she was delighted to see Susan. "I thought you'd never get home. What have you been doing all day?"

It was pathetic, Susan thought, what an interest Mrs Morton took in her activities these days. "Oh, I went to class. Grace had been in Vermont for the weekend. She says it was frightfully cold."

"I remember one year Olga went in swimming in April," Mrs Morton said. "I was sure she'd catch pneumonia. But Olga was always strong-willed." She sighed.

"I had lunch with Roger." The chance was too good to be missed.

"Did you?" Mrs Morton tried not to sound interested.

"He was down in New York for the weekend. Olga's very well, he says."

"I'm glad to hear it." Mrs Morton's tone implied that it was more than Olga deserved.

Susan did not have the heart to pursue the subject. "And then I went and saw the Marx Brothers with Merton Dennison. They were wonderful."

"How nice. I haven't been to the movies since I can remember. George used to take me sometimes when he lived here, but of course nobody remembers a poor old woman these days. Why should they think of a useless old thing like me?"

Susan felt angry with George; he really neglected his grandmother horribly. "I tell you what; why don't you and I go?"

Mrs Morton brightened up. "What a nice idea. But we've

no car and I wouldn't venture my poor heart in taxis these days."

"Oh dear." Susan was temporarily baffled. Then she had an idea. "I'm sure Roger would love to take us."

"Roger? What an extraordinary idea." Then she wavered. "It would be nice to go."

Susan said no more, resolved to put the idea to Roger next time she saw him. Poor Mrs Morton; it had been a dreadfully dull winter for her.

"I clean forgot." Mrs Morton interrupted her thoughts. "Julia Winter called up. She's staying the night in Boston and wants you to call her back. The number's on the back of the telephone book. Capitol something or other."

After a long and frustrating search, Susan found the number on the back of a letter Mrs Morton had had that afternoon. She is getting old, she thought, her memory's really bad now, not just an excuse.

It was no use waiting to be alone. She probably would not be all evening. As she dialled she tried to keep down the irrepressible hopes in her heart.

Julia answered. "Hullo, Susan, it's very nice to hear you. How are you?"

"Very well." There was so much to say.

"I'm glad. I've been miserable about letting you down so."

"But you couldn't help it." Susan was aware of Mrs Morton behind her.

"I suppose you can't talk?"

How quick Julia was. "No, not really."

"Well, look. What I called up for was to see if you could come up to South Kingston this weekend. I'll be all alone and I'd love to see you."

"Oh, Julia . . ." she paused. Could she face it?

"Do come," Julia said. "It'll be lovely up there now. And

it'll do you good, really it will. Besides, I want to hear all your news."

All her news. All her nothingness. "Well, thank you very much," she said at last. "I'd love to."

"That's good." Julia was comfortably definite, as always. "I'll meet you on the five o'clock on Friday."

"Well," said Mrs Morton, "what did she want?"

"She wants me to go up for the weekend," Susan said, "and I think I will. It ought to be lovely in the country now."

Mrs Morton's face fell. "This weekend? Oh dear, what shall I do without you?" Another thought struck her. "That disreputable brother of hers won't be there, I hope?"

Susan controlled sudden fury. "No," she said, "it'll be just the two of us."

The week was full of ghosts. Several times, Susan's courage failed her and she almost telephoned Julia to say she could not come. But it would be outrageous cowardice. The ghosts must be faced sooner or later, and, she told herself over and over again, it would be nice to see Julia. Besides, there was a secret voice within her that would keep hinting that now, at last, she would have news of David. If the memories she had to face had been twice as formidable, she could not have stayed away.

Julia was standing tall and calm on the platform when Susan's train pulled in. She kissed her. "It's lovely to see you."

"It's nice to be here," Susan said. "Mostly."

"It's brave of you to come." Julia always understood. "But it's the best thing. I can't tell you how sorry I am, Susan."

"Thank you." Susan stared out of the car window. There was so little, after all, to say.

The house was the same as ever. Susan was surprised. Somehow she had expected it to be changed. But the living room was still full of the peace she and David had liked; the view from her bedroom window was only changed by the new greenness of the countryside. It was heartless, she thought, the way things did not change. She put her hat on a chair, combed her hair and went quickly downstairs.

Julia was waiting for her in the living room. "I thought a fire and some sherry would be cheerful," she said. "How well you're looking, Susan. Prettier than ever."

"Pretty?" Susan was amused.

"Yes, pretty. I wish you'd do yourself justice, Susan. You've got so much, you know."

So much. Susan stared into the fire. There was a question she had to ask. The longer she put it off, the harder it was. She looked up. "How is he?"

"Quite well." Julia seemed relieved to have the subject started. "But not happy, Susan. I went out there to dinner on Wednesday. It's a strange business. Poor Josephine's really trying so hard; it's pathetic. It's hard on her, too." She picked her words with care.

"Oh dear." But it was impossible not to be glad.

"He sent you his love," Julia went on. "And told me to ask how the paper was going."

"Oh." Susan said again. Impossible, too, not to hope. But she must not. "And the children?"

"They're little darlings." Julia was on firmer ground. "I don't often lose my heart to children, but I certainly did to them."

"Really? David said they were so frightful when they first came." It was a major triumph to have got his name out.

"I know, but that was Josephine's mother. She's a terror. Josephine's very good with them, and of course they adore David."

Folly and madness to hope. "So that's that."

"Susan, dear, I'm afraid so. I'm so glad you're being so

241

brave about it, because I think it's the only thing. David says there's no hope of a divorce. It's much harder for him than for you, you know."

"He has the children." Susan was surprised at the bitterness in her voice.

"Yes," Julia agreed, "he has the children, but it's about all he has got. It isn't easy for him, Susan. He's too fine a person to compromise, and his life's one long compromise these days, poor David. It makes me miserable just to see him . . . That's why I hope you'll do everything you can to help him."

"Haven't I?"

Julia reached over and patted her hand. "You've been wonderful. All I ask is that you go on. After all, you'll get over it, Susan, you're young. It's been an unhappy business all round, but you must forget all about it, and us, and forgive us if you can."

"Oh, forgive," Susan said, "there isn't anything . . . But I won't forget, Julia, how could I? Anyway, I don't want to."

"Susan, you must. You're young." Julia repeated it. *Young*, Susan thought. "You'll go back to England and it'll all seem some kind of dream; that'll be all."

"I'm not sure I'm going back to England."

"Not going? Julia asked. "But why not?"

"I like it here." The Atlantic was too wide, too final. England was too far away.

"Oh, Susan, don't make me feel any worse. You mustn't let it do this to you."

Susan got up and walked to the window. "Do what?" she stared out into the gathering dusk. "I'm perfectly happy. I'm not expecting anything, or hoping for anything. It's very comfortable, really."

"But Susan, you're *young!*" Julia wailed.

"What's that got to do with it?" Susan silenced her.

Staring out of her bedroom window at the moonlit contour of the hills, Susan thought again of her sudden announcement that she might stay in America. If it had surprised Julia, it had surprised her just as much. But, after all, why should she go home? Mother would not really care particularly one way or another (was that fair? she asked herself, and did not wait for an answer); Mrs Morton was already bewailing the lonely prospect of the following winter. She would be delighted to have her stay. She could get a job. What kind? There was plenty of time to worry about that. A great deal might happen in the course of the summer. She got into bed without cross-examining herself as to what, exactly, the great deal covered.

Julia returned to the attack at breakfast next morning. "I hope you won't think I'm an interfering old busybody, Susan," she began, and Susan made a deprecatory exclamation, "but I do hope you weren't serious about staying in America. I do think it would be a mistake, you know."

"Do you?" Susan finished her coffee. "Oh, well, I haven't decided yet. I'll think about it, I promise."

"Good." Julia was obviously not satisfied, but Susan avoided all conversational leads towards the subject and the rest of the weekend passed on a purely superficial level. If Susan's heart jumped every time the telephone rang, there was no reason for Julia to know it, particularly as she had even managed not to ask the question that hung so constantly in her mind: Did David know she was there?

"It's been lovely, Julia," they were at the station again, "thank you so much."

"It's been lovely having you. Come up again any time you want to. Just call up the night before and I'll tell you if it's all right."

She doesn't want me to meet him. "Thank you so much." There was a new distance between them. *I shan't come again,*

243

she thought, as her train snarled its way into the station and made conversation impossible. *Never again. Not unless . . .* Smiling down at Julia from the platform of the train, she left the thought unfinished.

She found Mrs Morton sitting forlorn in the big drawing room. She used less light than ever these days and Susan suspected that she must have crept round one night putting twenty-five watt bulbs furtively into all the lamps. At any rate, the shadows that had always lurked in the house had advanced from the corners of the room till they lay close around her. Faintly illuminated by the one reading lamp behind the sofa the old face looked pale and ghostly. She's an enchantress, Susan thought, a wicked fairy whose spells won't work. *Poor old thing . . .*

"Ah, there you are." Susan's heart reproached her at the genuine pleasure in her voice. "Did you have a good time?"

"Yes, indeed. And how about you?"

"Oh, me." Mrs Morton sighed. "Who cares about me? I amused my old self as best I could. The twins came to lunch today, but aside from them and Mary I don't believe I've spoken to a soul since you left. Would you pass me my medicine, like a dear child? My head is quite frightful tonight."

The medicine no longer lived upstairs in Mrs Morton's own room, but was concealed behind the everlastings on the mantelpiece.

There was no doubt about it, Susan thought, walking through the Square on her way to lunch with Roger next day, Mrs Morton would make herself ill if something didn't happen to cheer her up. At her age it was unsafe to carry an imaginary malady to such a pitch. But what should she do? Write to Mrs Horwood? Interference again; not that she didn't seem to make a practice of it these days. She smiled to herself.

244

Roger had got a booth. "You're looking well."

"I was away for the weekend." She sat down.

"Oh?"

"At South Kingston with Julia Winter. She's just back from Florida." It was a great comfort that Roger knew about it.

"How was it?" he asked sympathetically.

"Not too bad." Had it been? It was hard to say. "I'm glad it's over, though."

"Poor Susan."

They ordered their lunch. "Look," Susan said when the menus were safely disposed of, "are you doing anything tonight?"

"No. Why?"

"I'm worried about Mrs Morton. She's going to fret herself sick soon. I was wondering if you'd drive in and take us to the movies."

"Good Lord, wouldn't that be rather rash?"

"I don't think so." The more she thought about it, the surer she was. "I suspect she's dying to make it up and doesn't know how to begin, poor old dear. Do take a chance on it."

"Goodness knows it'd be wonderful if it worked." He hesitated. "It's wretched enough as it is. All right, Susan, you're the doctor. What d'you want to see and what time shall I come?"

They decided that Deanna Durbin should cheer Mrs Morton up. "She's a marvellous sentimentalist under the grumbling, bless her old heart," Roger said, "let's hope she bursts into floods of tears and gives me her blessing on the spot. Remember, I'm relying on you to protect me if anything goes wrong."

"Oh, yes," they were in the street, "and I'll call you up if she has fits at the very idea."

Susan got home early and found Mrs Morton gazing sadly out of her window. She spent more and more time, these days, doing nothing at all.

245

"I've got an invitation for you," she plunged straight in.

"For me?" The old face brightened.

"Yes, for both of us. Roger wants to know if we'll go to the movies with him tonight. Deanna Durbin's on at Keith's and he says he'd love to drive us over."

"Well, I declare." Mrs Morton suspended judgement while Susan held her breath. Then she smiled. "He's really a very thoughtful boy," she said, "don't you think we should ask him to supper, Susan?"

"What a nice idea. Shall I call him up?"

"Yes, do. Goodness knows what he'll get to eat, though. Mary's been cross all day."

"I'll take care of Mary." Susan was dialling.

Taking care of Mary was easy. Susan found her sitting gloomily in the wicker chair with Ginger on her lap. Mrs Morton's depression had communicated itself to her and even her cooking had lately lost its old cheerful abandon. They had not had lemon meringue pie for weeks.

She looked up as Susan came in. "What does she want now?"

"It's me," Susan said. "I've gone and got Roger invited to supper. Can you possibly manage one more, Mary?"

Mary looked at the big kitchen clock. "Six o'clock," she said. "Fine goings on, guests at this time of night." She smiled at Susan. "Roger, is it? I suppose maybe if I put my mind on it . . . Down you get, Ginger." She opened the refrigerator. "D'you think he's too proud to eat chicken croquettes?"

"Roger?" Susan asked. "What do you think?"

"I think he's going to."

When Susan got back upstairs she found Mrs Morton settled in her quilts in the drawing room. "That's all right," she told her, "Mary's delighted."

"Good." Mrs Morton had changed her dress. "Do you think maybe it would be nice if we opened a bottle of sherry?"

246

It was a cheerful evening. Roger completed his victory by arriving with a large bunch of daffodils for Mrs Morton and by the time they had been arranged and Mrs Morton had had her second glass of sherry, Mary came wandering up to greet Roger like a long lost son and announce that supper was ready. The chicken croquettes were followed by a magnificent lemon meringue pie – "I'm sorry if it's still warm," she set it proudly in front of Mrs Morton."

Mrs Morton had a second helping and Roger and Susan ensured the success of Mary's evening by finishing it between them. Even the film turned out exactly according to specifications, and Susan was pleased to notice Mrs Morton shedding a surreptitious tear when Deanna's fortunes reached their lowest ebb. The feud was over.

"I had a lovely evening," Mrs Morton said as Roger drove them home. "It was sweet of you children to arrange it. When are you going to New York next, Roger?"

"Next weekend, actually." Roger stopped the car outside the house.

"Well, tell that girl of mine it's high time she came up to see me. I won't bite her. I'm a cantankerous old woman, I know, but I'm not as bad as you think."

Roger laughed nervously. "I'll tell her."

When Susan got back from class next day Mary greeted her in the hall. "Guess who's here?"

Mrs Morton and Mrs Merryweather were sitting in full gossip over tea and cake. Whatever awkwardness there might have been at first, it was entirely over by now and they were deep in discussion of George's forthcoming marriage.

"There's nothing like a June wedding," Mrs Merryweather noticed Susan. "Well, Susan, how are you? And how's the bridge?"

"Coming along, thank you," Susan accepted a cup of tea

from Mrs Morton. "Only Mrs Morton's still disgusted with my bidding. I do hope you can come on Thursday?"

The depth of the breach between the two old ladies had been measured by the fact that since their final scene, Mrs Merryweather had found one excuse after another to avoid the Thursday bridge. Susan had been pressed into service to take her place, so that she had a personal interest in the reconciliation.

"Why, yes," Mrs Merryweather helped herself to more cake. "I believe I could manage it this Thursday, if you'll have me, Emmeline?"

"I should say so. D'you know, Martha, it must be forty years since you and I had our first Thursday."

"I suppose it must. Well, Emmeline, we're not getting any younger; it's no good pretending about it; we're getting old, you and I. What delicious cakes Mary does make; I really must have another tiny slice. Oh, and that reminds me, Maud says she hears little Marjorie is engaged."

"Is she really? Who to?"

Susan smiled and left them to it.

Chapter Eighteen

Olga came up two weeks later and the reconciliation was complete. It was celebrated by an unusually well-attended Sunday dinner, with George and Betty, Roger and Olga, the twins and Susan. As usual, the guests vanished almost immediately after coffee, Mrs Morton went happily off to lie down (she was looking better already, Susan noticed with pleasure), and Susan helped Mary with the dishes.

"Quite like old times it is," Mary said. "And isn't Olga's ring a beauty? Isn't it time you were getting yourself engaged, Susan? What's that boy of yours doing over there anyway?"

"Donald? Goodness knows. I expect I'll be an old maid."

"Don't you do it," Mary said. "I never heard such nonsense. If I had my time over again you wouldn't see me taking any chances. Don't you do it, Susan."

Susan laughed. "Oh well, time will show, no doubt, though goodness knows what, come to think of it. Is that all, Mary? It's too nice to stay in; I think I'll go for a walk."

The Sunday crowds were out in full strength by the river and she walked quickly through them, thinking, as she so often did these days, about nothing at all, or rather about a series of trifles so inconsiderable as to weigh out at less than nothing. She ought to let down her blue skirt . . . Should she accept Olga's invitation for a weekend in New York? . . . David had wanted to show her Radio City . . . She would

249

have to fix the skirt before she went . . . It was very nice of Olga . . . Funny how she had disliked her at first.

A car drew up beside her. "You look as if the devil was after you. Can I give you a lift?"

"David."

"Nothing but 'David'?"

He looked older, his face tired in the bright sunshine. "How are you?" The formal phrase sounded ridiculous. She stood staring at him helplessly.

"Let me give you a lift. Please."

"I shouldn't, David, should I?" The question betrayed her and he opened the door.

She was beside him and the car was moving forward. "Oh, David, I shouldn't have. Suppose someone sees us?"

"Suppose they do." He was even firmer than she remembered him. "It's a poor world if I can't give my favourite student a ride. How are you, Susan?"

"I'm very well." How often she had dreamed of this conversation, and now – now there was nothing to say.

He seemed to feel it too. "I've been having lunch with Aunt Beatrice," he said. "She's been scolding me just the way she had last time I met you here. Remember?"

"Of course I do."

There was another silence. "She's much better," he said presently. "She says Julia's a marvellous nurse."

"I'm sure she is." They were crossing the river.

"I hear you were up at South Kingston. I hope you had a good time."

"Yes, lovely. David, you'd better drop me here." In a minute they would say goodbye. She would not think about it; she did not dare.

"I shall do nothing of the kind," he said. "You've been kidnapped, my girl, and you might as well make up your mind to it."

250

"Oh, but David, we *mustn't*."

He had turned up Brattle Street. "We not only must, we're going to. I've been desperate to talk to you, Susan; don't think I'm going to lose this chance. Besides, I want to see if our apple tree survived the winter."

"David, not there."

"Yes, there. Where else, Susan? How's your paper coming?"

"Pretty well. I've got the first draft done, but I can't seem to get Beaumont and Fletcher fitted in." How natural it all seemed, after all.

"They always did give you trouble, didn't they? What seems to be the difficulty now?"

"Just that I've written the whole paper without mentioning them."

"Tut." How familiar it was, and how strange, to have him teasing her again. "I don't think your tutor would approve of that. I should think it would mean at least half a grade's difference, and you've got to get an A-plus, that's always been settled. Of course you could put them in a footnote, but I don't think it would be quite fair."

"No," she found herself falling into his tone, "it really wouldn't."

"Well, let's think," he said, "what are the general lines of the paper these days? I suppose it's changed beyond recognition since we last talked about it?"

"It's changed quite a bit. You see . . ."

He kept her talking about the Elizabethans all the way to. Concord, and, absorbed in the strange tutorial, she had no time to think, no time to remember, or to wonder what it was that he had wanted so desperately to say to her.

Thought and recollection came flooding back upon her when he stopped the car. She sat without moving as he got out. "David," she said again, "I wish you wouldn't."

"Please." She had never been able to resist his pleading voice. "I *do* want to talk to you, and," his tone became bitter, "I can't very well invite you to McCarthy Road."

Almost unconsciously, she got out and followed him. "Is it very awful, David?" She referred more to his tone than to anything he had said.

"It's not pleasant, Susan, it's no use pretending it is." He was leading the way along the bank. "Even if I didn't miss you with every breath I take, I couldn't be happy with Josephine. Oh, she's trying this time, for what it's worth. It's pathetic, I suppose. But it's hopeless, Susan, hopeless."

"I am so sorry." Unseeingly, she brushed aside a bramble.

"I shouldn't have let her stay a minute," he said. "I can't think what made me do it. It was lunacy."

"But you had to, David." How odd to find herself trying to console him. "The children . . . How are they?" It was, somehow, a triumph to have got the question out.

"They're wonderful, Susan. You must meet them."

Meet them . . . But how? They had got to the clearing. Half consciously, she noticed that the trees and bushes were covered with the very faintest of spring green. She would never meet them.

"Watch out for poison ivy," David said. "It's death in the spring, and with that skin of yours . . ."

Once again, as when he had drawn up beside her, Susan had the dream feeling that it had all happened before. Soon she would wake . . . If only she could. If only it was last autumn. But the poison ivy had been scarlet then; now its shoots were palest coral. The apple tree was not in leaf yet. Standing beside it and fingering a budded twig, Susan looked up at David. Now that he had got her here, he seemed not to know how to begin.

"Susan," he had picked up a stick as they walked along,

and now he scraped away the dead leaves from around a violet plant, "have you missed me?"

"David, you know I have." The question was almost an insult.

He realised it. "Of course I do, but I'm so desperate, Susan, I don't feel as if I could be sure of anything these days."

"You can be sure of that. Always." It was worth having come to have been able to say it.

"I'm glad." He was silent again. Then at last he spoke in a rush. "Susan, you know I love you, don't you? Nothing's changed that; nothing ever will. It can't."

"No, it can't." Again it was blessed comfort to agree.

"Then, please, listen to what I've got to say."

She looked at him, surprised. "Of course."

"You see," he went on, "I've talked and talked to Josephine and it's hopeless, she'll never agree to a divorce. She knows by now I wouldn't have a chance of divorcing her, specially after letting her come back like this, and she says if I try she'll do everything she can to drag you into it. Oh, she says it quite nicely; we don't quarrel any more; we're past that; but she says it, and she means it. And she'll never divorce me. Aside from her family and the business of being a Catholic, she knows when she's onto a good thing." His voice was bitter as she had never heard it before. Poor David, what a time he must have been having to make him like this.

"So there I am, Susan, settled for life, God help me." He was silent for a minute.

"David," she said, "I am so sorry. I hoped . . ." But had she? Had she not really hoped he would be unhappy? Her conscience accused her. She had not realised it would be like this, or do this to him. Poor David . . .

He dropped the stick and took her hand. "You still love me, Susan?" It was statement as much as question.

"Yes." What was the use of pretending?

Gently he pulled her towards him. "Then stay in America with me, Susan."

As gently, she resisted. "With you?"

"Yes, with me. I can't ask you to marry me, Susan, but God knows I can promise to love you, always. I couldn't help it if I tried. I'd take care of you, Susan."

Still she held away from him. Gently, but somehow she herself knew, ruthlessly, she asked, "What do you mean, David?"

Again he pulled her towards him. "Susan, help me. You know what I mean. You could live in Boston. We could go up to South Kingston. I'd see you every day."

And this was David who used to tease her for not calling a spade a spade. She leaned back against the trunk of the apple tree and looked up at him through a threat of tears. It was comforting to feel the rough bark against her back. "Oh, David," she said. She would *not* cry. It was bad enough without that. "David, I'll always love you." Why was it that now, of all times, she should feel a faint quiver of doubt? "But I can't, you know I can't." Before he could speak, she went on. "It was all right, before. I don't quite understand why, but it was. But not this, David. You know we couldn't."

"Why not, Susan? Why's it different?" He would not try to understand.

She traced a ridge of bark with her finger. "It wouldn't be right for either of us, you know it wouldn't." Again she appealed to him, and again he refused to respond. "Think of Julia." Maybe this way she could make him see. "We couldn't go to South Kingston, you know. It would all be hiding and horrible, and in the end we'd get angry with each other. Please, David, don't spoil it all. Say you understand."

"It's you who don't understand, Susan. You don't realise what my life's like. I don't see how I can go on without you.

If I could only escape sometimes . . . If you were there . . . You used to love me, Susan."

"I still do." The words sounded strange and austere.

"How can you, if you'll leave me like this? You don't think I'm really married to Josephine, do you? It's nothing but a misery and a sham and it never will be. Why should I lose the best part of my life, because of an obstinate, bigoted—"

"*David!*" Her shocked voice forestalled the noun. "You *married* her."

"Yes, God help me." Again she was appalled by the bitterness of his voice. But he was gathering himself for another appeal; she must anticipate it; anything more would be too much to bear. Already, she could feel cold premonitions of the wave of desolation that would swamp her when the crisis was over. At all costs she must end it before her strength failed her. There would be time later for all the agonies and vain regrets; now, she must finish it.

"Look, David," she said, "I know you're older than I am and know more about things, but you must believe me when I say this wouldn't do. Not for either of us. When you think about it some more, you'll see I'm right and be grateful to me. Really you will." She ignored his protest. "It would spoil everything." She was pleading as if for her life. "And it *was* good, David, too good to spoil."

He had let go of her hand. "Yes," he said, "it was good. I never thought you'd forget so soon. I thought I could count on you."

"David, you *can*, always. That's just why . . ." It was too much. She was going to cry. "Please," she said, "let's go. I can't stand it." She turned and walked slowly towards the road.

He followed her. "I'm sorry, Susan. I shouldn't have said that. Won't you kiss me goodbye?"

She looked up at him through a mist of tears. "*Please*," she protested.

But he put his arms around her and kissed her; and for a moment she was lost, her courage and conviction a shadow and a mockery.

He felt it. "Susan."

"No, David."

This time he knew it was final. They walked in silence to the car, and as silently drove back to Boston. Still she was not thinking; still she did not dare.

"The old corner?" he asked as they crossed the Charles Street bridge.

"Yes, please." She should have been thinking what to say. There was so much. There was nothing at all.

"Here you are." The car stopped.

She turned and looked at him. "Goodbye, David. I'm sorry . . ."

"Goodbye, Susan." Nothing more. He drove away.

This was despair. She had lost everything. Before, she had still had David, had her memories, her certainty of him. Now, there was nothing. She walked blindly to a bench and sat down. Perhaps he would come back. But what if he did? She would only have to send him away again. There was nothing; nothing at all . . .

She was sitting on a bench by the river, right under the windows of Mrs Morton's house and crying as if her heart would break. As if it hadn't already. *You asked for it*, she told herself, *and you got it. Now, pull yourself together*. She blew her nose. That was better. She looked at the river. The yachts were turning to their moorings. She looked at her watch. It was almost six. Her eyes were focusing again. Roger and Olga had taken Mrs Morton out to tea at the Merryweathers'; they would all three be back for supper. She had promised Mrs Morton she would get things started on the stove.

She went home and washed her face in cold water. It looked as if she had been crying for years. She went downstairs and lit the oven. When the front door banged, the casserole of chicken was heating up and the canned peas were boiling merrily.

A flood of cheerfulness and conversation came in with Roger and Olga. What was there for supper? They were famished. Roger whistled as he laid the table; Olga came and helped Susan make toast.

"What a heavenly weekend," she said, scraping a burnt piece. "You're an angel, Susan."

"Me?"

"You fixed it, didn't you? Roger says you upped and did a miracle on Gran practically under his nose."

"Oh, that. She was dying for an excuse. I didn't do anything." It was still difficult to keep her voice steady.

Olga looked at her. "Are you all right?"

"Why, yes." But she was almost in tears.

"Hi, Roger," Olga opened the dining room door. "How about some sherry for us cooks?"

"Fine idea." He brought the bottle. "And I'll take Mrs Morton some."

"Yes, do. Drink up, Sue," Olga went on as he went upstairs. "It'll do you good. Oh, lord, there goes my toast again." They finished the preparations in a sociable silence that Susan found extraordinarily comforting.

She did not know whether Roger had noticed her state or whether Olga had managed to signal it to him, but between the two of them they managed to keep Mrs Morton safely distracted all through supper. After they had finished, she retired to bed: "All this excitement will be too much for my poor old heart, if I'm not careful. Have a good time, children, and don't miss your train, Olga."

"Don't worry, Gran, I haven't missed a midnight yet. And

257

thank you for a heavenly weekend." They kissed each other. The quarrel was over.

"You know what," Olga said, when the last dish had been rather silently dried and put on its shelf, "I believe I'll stay over. I've only got French tomorrow morning and Madame Dobrée never notices. Roger, be a lamb and call and cancel my sleeper."

"But what about your family?"

"They won't know, bless their hearts. I was going straight back to college. Think what a shock it'll be for Gran when she finds me at breakfast tomorrow morning. And if you ask me nicely you can come in and take me to the train, Roger." He went off obediently to telephone the station. "There," she went on, "now what would you like to do this evening, Sue?"

"*Me*?" Belatedly, it dawned on Susan that the change of plan had been on her account. "Olga, you shouldn't . . ."

"Why not? It's pure self interest, I swear. I know; let's make Roger take us for a drive. It's too fine a night to stay indoors."

They drove down to Duxbury and threw stones into the moonlit sea. Sitting silently between Roger and Olga on the way back, Susan felt a slow, reluctant warmth steal through her from the hot buttered rum they had made her drink. ("Purely for medicinal purposes," as Olga had explained.) As the outlying lights of the city began to flash past, first singly and then in constellations, she felt herself slowly relaxing into an exhausted peace. It was all over. She had lost him. Could it really be that what she was feeling was relief?

Olga sent Roger straight home from Brimmer Street: "High time we girls were in bed."

Later, when Susan was sitting up in bed brushing her hair and trying not to think, Olga knocked at the door and came in. "D'you want to talk about it?" she asked. "I'm not a bad shoulder, as such things go. People have

258

been crying on me for years. But throw me out if you'd rather."

"No, do come in." Susan was surprised to find that she *did* want to talk about it, still more surprised, a quarter of an hour later, to find herself almost literally crying on Olga's shoulder as she told her the whole story.

And what a relief it was. Olga did not seem to be either shocked or surprised. "I thought something was going on," she said at last, "and I'm most awfully sorry, Susan, but honestly, don't you think you're well out of it?"

Susan looked up from her wet pillow. "That's the frightful thing; I almost do."

"Frightful?"

"Yes, frightful. I've really lost him now. And it makes it all seem so awful, somehow."

"Well, you mustn't think about it, that's all. Anyway, the main thing is that now you really will get over it. Though actually, don't you think you're a bit more over it already than you've been admitting to yourself? One does do the oddest things, you know. I mean, there I was at Christmas breaking my heart like anything about Spencer Russell, and all the time it was Roger. You can imagine all kinds of things."

This was rather too much for Susan. "But I love him, Olga."

"Of course you do." Olga was soothing. "You're bound to. It would be worse if you didn't. But now you know it's over, you'll get over it."

It was what Roger and Julia had both said, but this time she realised that it was true. "Yes, I suppose I will. But poor David." She cried again and Olga let her have it out.

"But you'll be surprised, really," she said at last. "It will be easy now. Specially when you go back to England."

Of course, she must do something about her passage. *In*

two months she would be home. Too late for the spring, but home for the roses. "Olga, you're an angel," she said, "thank you so much."

"Don't mention it, any time. After all, I owe you quite a packet, you know." She switched out the light.

Chapter Nineteen

Home for the roses, Susan told herself next day, filling out forms at the shipping office. For the high midsummer pomps: meadowsweet and foxglove and Canterbury bell; Sweet William and wallflower heavy-scented in the wind, and small, rich roses everywhere. How had she managed not to realise how homesick she was? There would be long, light evenings in the garden; the sudden rain that beat upon the roses and made them almost violently sweet; early mornings when the dew shone silver in grass glimmering with gossamer and moon-daisies. Insanity that she had thought of staying another year.

Insanity? She left the office with an armful of leaflets and a passage for the first possible date after the end of term. Insanity, perhaps, but there had been happiness in it. All very well to solace herself with imaginary and future roses, but what of the solitary present? What of today?

Well, she shook herself mentally; today, having cut all her morning classes, she would go and have lunch with Roger – dear Roger – and tell him all about it. No, not all about it. It had been enough to tell Olga; there was no need of further confessional. She was free. There was no getting away from it, she might be lonely again, today, as she faced the new green of the common and the spring sociability of people in the streets, but she was free.

Free, she wondered, pressing her dime into its slot, free

261

from what? From David, or from her imaginings of him? And poor David, what would he do to himself with this new ingrowing bitterness of his? What – it was horrible and cold-blooded even to wonder it – would he have done to her? *Am I a monster*? she asked herself, staring out the window as her train crossed the Charles.

"D'you think I'm a cold-blooded brute, Roger?" she asked as they settled in their booth at St Clair's.

"You, Susan? Good, Lord, no. Why?"

"I was just wondering." The restaurant felt cool and calm after her hurried morning. "I saw David yesterday." She approached it from another angle.

"Oh. We thought something had happened."

"You were darlings. I'm terribly grateful." She paused.

"Did that make you think you were a cold-blooded brute?"

"Yes, it did, actually." No, really, she would not betray David to Roger. "You see," she took it up again. "I don't seem to feel so badly today as I thought I would."

"Oh, poor Susan! So you think you're heartless?"

"Well, I do rather."

"You do make me feel so grandfatherly, Susan. Do you by any chance remember a famous occasion when I told you nothing lasted for ever?"

"Yes?"

"Well? May I say I told you so?"

She could not help laughing. "If you like. Just so long as you don't mind my reminding you that your own logical position wasn't too strong on that particular and, as you say, famous occasion." How strange, how entertaining and how good that she could laugh over that evening with him now.

He was equal to it. "Remind away to your heart's content. I'm far too happy to mind having made a fool of myself. So long as you've forgiven me, Susan."

"Of course." It had long ago been tacitly settled between them.

"That's why I so want you to be happy," he went on. "I do recommend it, you know."

"Do you now?" Her voice had nearly been bitter.

He recognised it. "Yes, I do. And I won't have you taking that tragic line either, Susan. By your own admission, you're over it, or as near as dammit, and you'd be much better off if, instead of worrying about yourself, you'd just settle down and enjoy life a bit. Stop having crises, for God's sake."

No one but David (and, long ago, Father), had ever spoken to her so firmly. For a moment she was angry. What business was it of Roger's? Then she laughed. "Have I really been carrying on like a tragedy queen?"

He was merciful. "Good lord, not as bad as that. But you do tend to take life a little hard, don't you?"

She paused, thought, drank some water, and admitted it. "Oh dear, I suppose you're right. What a frightful bore I must have been."

"Oh, never that." She caught his eye and they laughed.

"Well, anyway," she said, finishing her salad, "I never pined away and refused my food."

"No? What about all that flu at Christmas?"

"*Roger*; it's you who's the brute!"

"I'm sorry, Sue. I was only pulling your leg."

"Oh, no, you weren't. And the awful thing is I suppose you're right. What a farce I am!"

"No, you're not, but I must say you're incorrigible." He left her to take his point.

"You mean, here I am at it again? Have a heart, Roger, it's hard work being so deflated."

"I am a brute," he said, "and I'm luckier than I deserve that you aren't throwing things. Are you furious with me?"

"No. As a matter of fact I'm rather grateful. I booked my

passage home this morning." It was not altogether a change of subject.

"Did you? That was a good idea, wasn't it?"

"Very. They tell me there's no place like home."

"It has its advantages. Ice-cream?"

"Yes, please. Coffee with butterscotch sauce. I'm going to miss you frightfully, Roger."

He gave their order. "I hope you will. We'll miss you, too. Have you told Mrs Morton? She's going to be devastated."

"No I haven't. I feel rather badly about her. I'm afraid I've kind of let her take it for granted I'd stay on."

"You really meant to?"

"Yes."

"Why?"

She blushed. "Oh, I don't know. Just general stupidity, I expect."

She told Mrs Morton at supper that night. "I booked my passage home today." The words sounded cold and final. It was all over.

The old face across the table had drawn itself up tight. "But I thought you were going to stay another winter. What'll I do without you, Susan? A poor lonely old woman like me, too old to make friends. You don't really want to go, do you? I thought it was all settled that you would get a job and keep me company. Besides," a new idea struck her, "there really is going to be a war, George says. You don't want to get into all that."

"I can't believe there'll really be one," Susan said (but David had been very gloomy, as long ago as Christmas). "But if there is, all the more reason for me to get home. Mother's not strong, you know; I ought to be there." Curious that it had never occurred to her before that her mother might need her.

"Don't be ridiculous. Your mother would far rather have you safe over here, I'm sure. And what's to become of me?" Mary appeared with the dessert. "Just think, Mary," Mrs Morton appealed to her, "Susan tells me that she's booked a passage home; she's deserting us."

"Is she now?" Mary put a tremulous jelly down in front of Mrs Morton. "Well, I'll not say I won't miss her, but there's no place like home. You're a sensible girl, Susan, and it's not for the first time I'm telling you so. Oh dear," she paused in her favourite attitude against the kitchen door, "maybe one of these fine days I'll be going myself. Will you be home for the bluebells?"

"I'm afraid not, but I'll be there for the roses."

"But, Mary," Mrs Morton's voice was sharp (*She's old,* Susan thought, *poor dear, she's really old*), "what's to become of us all alone here next winter?"

"We'll get along," Mary said. "There've been winters before this and we've always managed . . . In time for the roses, Susan? Maybe I'll come with you."

"Oh, get along with you, Mary," Mrs Morton lost her temper. "You'll never go home and you know it."

"I suppose I won't, not really, but I'll go on thinking about it just the same. And don't you forget, Susan, you're a sensible girl."

Sensible, Susan thought after Mrs Morton had grumbled her way to bed, sensible? Was it sensible to have congratulated herself all day on being free from David and now to long so desperately to telephone him? Free of him. She laughed at herself. How could she be free? Things didn't end; they grew into one. She had been right when she thought that David would always be a part of her. But then (her room was too small for her tonight), perhaps that was how to get free of him; to absorb him. You sound like an ant-eater, or something, she told herself, prowling

265

again across the room. *David*, she thought, *I'm going; it's all over.*

She must stop thinking about him. Firmly, she turned her thoughts to Roger. A tragedy queen, he had called her, and quite right too. And what was the other thing he had said? He was too happy to mind making a fool of himself. How wonderful it sounded. But how did one set about being happy?

One way, she soon discovered, was to be thoroughly busy. As the leaves came out on the trees, and the magnolias burst into extravagant blossom on Commonwealth Avenue, day seemed to swallow day with increasing and formidable rapidity. Mrs Morton was getting ready to go to Maine for the summer and the spare room was full of her renovated summer clothes, the evenings preoccupied with problems of trimmings and the deplorable shortness of skirts. Mary was to go with her. "Though I never see the Atlantic," she said, "but I'm so homesick I'd gladly lie down and die. War or no war, you're a lucky girl, Susan."

Susan supposed she was. There had been real pleasure in her mother's answer to her announcement of her sailing date. '*I'm afraid things don't look too good over here,*' she had written, '*but if I've got you safe home I won't feel so badly.*'

Susan surprised herself by crying a little over the letter and was then still more surprised to realise how little she thought about Father these days. Poor Father. She looked at his picture on the bureau. He looked as understanding as ever, but – he was dead. *Let the dead past bury its dead.* Poor Father. Poor David. She opened the desk, took out the big envelope that held Donald's picture and added Father's to it. Then, remembering, she picked her handbag off the bed, took out the wallet, removed a picture of David, and tucked it, too, gently into the envelope.

She had lunch with Julia next day. The barrier that she

had felt between them when she last left South Kingston was gone and she felt that they were old, tried friends.

"Will you write me sometimes, Julia?" she asked over dessert. "I would like to hear."

"Of course I will."

So far they had talked about trivialities: Susan's preparations, the weather, the garden at South Kingston; now the plunge must be taken. "How is he?" There was no need to be more specific.

"I don't really know," Julia said. She looked at Susan. "I'm a bit worried about him, to tell you the truth."

"I'm sorry."

"Poor David; it's so hard for him. But there it is; there's nothing to be done . . ."

"If only there was something I could do," Susan's protest was against the whole waste of it.

"But there is," Julia said, "and you're doing it. He'll be much better when you're safe in England, he really will. A sea's a great healer, you know."

"Well, it's a great division at any rate. Let me know how he is, Julia. Don't tell him you are if you don't want to."

"Shall you see him before you go?"

"Oh, goodness." The whole complex temptation was back upon her. Would it never be over? "I don't think so, Julia." The words came slow as drops of blood. "Unless you think it would help him."

"Oh, no." Julia was quick, relieved.

"Then what's the use?" She stood up. "Goodbye, Julia. Thank you so much. Give him my love."

Nothing but goodbyes. Her paper was in by now. David would be reading it. She knew, at least, that it was good. He would recognise the fruit of the suggestions he had made that last afternoon, though she would never understand how she had been able to bear to act on them. For the rest of her

267

life, Beaumont and Fletcher would mean the bitter taste of tears. But the paper was good. He would not be ashamed. Would she ever really stop thinking in terms of him? How had she managed to think she was free?

And yet there were moments . . . Coming out of the last exam with Grace, the June sunshine hot in their faces: "Just think, Grace, three weeks, and I'll be home."

"Isn't it wonderful?" For the last time they turned into their drugstore and Susan ordered her soup and sandwich. "I'm starved. Exams certainly are hungry work. Which questions did you do?"

They compared notes for a while. "Susan," Grace said at last, "I've always meant to ask you: did you ever see him again?"

"David Winter?"

"Yes."

"Once."

"Oh?"

Susan looked at Grace, so kind, so friendly, so inquisitive. It was not fair to part on that monosyllable. "Yes," she amplified, "we met by accident. He drove me out the way we went that first time. It was awful. We said goodbye." She was remembering it for Grace's benefit. The misery of that moment when she stood feeling the bark of his apple tree with her cold hand came back to her out of the past, bitter and strange as the taste of yesterday's tears.

"And that was all?"

"Yes." She had said enough.

"Oh, well," Grace was brisk, "I'm certainly glad you're over it. They say he's frightful to that poor wife of his."

"Do they?" Susan did not want to hear. "Look, Grace, it's awful but I've got to go. You're really going tonight, are you?"

"I should say I am," she was her old emphatic self. "See

me staying in this prison a second longer than I have to. No more *Beowulf*. It's amazing!"

"It is. I hope you'll be very happy, Grace."

"Thank you. Will you write to me sometimes?"

After they had parted Susan stood for a while watching the people come and go in Brattle Square. She felt full of affection for them; for the Cambridge women with their sensible clothes and too-individual faces, for the busy undergraduates who had once seemed so heartless, for Grace, whose letters she knew even now would never be answered.

"Well, as I live and breathe, if it isn't my little English Susan. And there I was planning to call you up this very night." Merton Dennison swept down on her and took her arm. "And how's my English rose? Still set on quitting us and breaking our hearts?"

"That's right."

"The heartlessness of women. Ah well, I'm going home on Thursday myself. I start with the *Journal* next week."

"Good for you." She was impressed. "I'm awfully glad, Bud."

"Thank you." He took it as his due. "I'm looking forward to it, I must say."

"How are the autographs?" Susan asked as they crossed Harvard Square with the usual hazard of life and limb.

"Accruing. I got MacLeish's when he was here. And that reminds me," (*Here it comes*, thought Susan), "there *was* something I've been meaning to ask you. You remember that charming friend of yours we met at Symphony Hall one night?"

"You mean Olga Horwood?" Susan helped him.

"Yes, that's it. Well, she very kindly promised to see if her uncle had any Hawthorne signatures he could spare. I wonder . . ."

They were pausing at the top of the subway steps. "Oh,

269

goodness," Susan said, "I don't know. She's going to be up next weekend, though; I'll ask her then. And that reminds me," (how deeply buried the subject must have been; she had never remembered it till now), "I never did ask Professor Winter about Emerson. I am so sorry."

"Don't give it another thought," he smiled at her palely and patronisingly as ever. "I asked him myself. I told him I was a friend of yours. I hope you don't mind? It worked like a charm anyway; he gave me an unpublished poem of Emerson's. I meant to thank you."

"Oh. When was this?"

"Just a week or so ago. He said you were the best student he ever had. Must you really go? Do we part like this?"

"Yes," Susan said. "Goodbye. I'll let you know about the Hawthorne."

Her first reaction, standing staring across the subway lines at an advertisement for a modern funeral home, was fury. What business had Merton Dennison to go asking favours of David on her account? What must David have thought? *What did it matter what he thought?* But of course, it did. Should she call him up and apologise? The temptation was strong. Or she could write to him. The sentences began to form themselves in her mind. Still debating it, she got into the train and was carried, brooding, into Boston.

She would do nothing about it, of course. She walked down the steps from the Charles Street station. After all, David had given Merton Dennison what he wanted. He could not have been too angry. Besides, if she could not rely on him to realise that Merton Dennison had asked him without consulting her, what *could* she rely on? To assume that he would not understand would be the last breach of the confidence there had been between them. Anything, rather than that. Thin and fine drawn though it had been since their last interview, she liked to feel that the bond still held between them. *David would understand.*

She had turned and walked down to the river. Now, leaning against the parapet, she stared down into the water and twisted at the ring she still wore on its chain around her neck. She had never thought of giving it back. It was her remembrance of him. She wondered if he guessed she still wore it. Probably. After all, he did tend to understand.

She was singing as she walked up Brimmer Street; her confidence in David over this trifle had re-established something between them. The final scene in the woods at Concord was dimmer in her mind; theme for pity, not recrimination; while all the old times were newly clear. Ridiculous that for a while she had thought that last scene cancelled all the previous ones.

Mrs Morton met her in the hall. "Here's a letter for you from Olga. I had one, too. Such lovely news: she wants to come and spend next winter here."

Of course. Why had she not thought of it before? Roger would be teaching at Middlesex; Olga would want to be as near him as possible. "How lovely," she said, "so you'll have company after all." Just as well she had not planned to stay. Between Olga and her there would have been no question of a choice.

She opened her letter. Olga described the plan. She was to take a domestic science course – Susan smiled – and see Roger at weekends. Then she turned to Susan's own plans; since she was sailing from New York she must plan to stay with them for a night or so beforehand. The Horwoods would be up for George's wedding just before. Maybe Roger could drive Olga and Susan down; he was due for a visit in New York? *"We'll give you a real send-off."*

Susan wrote an enthusiastic acceptance. Time was whirling

271

by her now. There were days of shopping with Mrs Morton; brief extravagances of her own; a visit to Radcliffe to get her grades: all various shades of A, with A-plus for the paper; David must have been pleased. Then the paper itself came back to her through the mail with a note from David. '*I thought you wouldn't want to come and get this,*' he said. '*Of course it's excellent. I'm proud of you. Good luck, Susan.*' And the old, highly stylised signature, '*David.*' Nothing more.

It hurt at first, but soon she decided that it had been a final piece of consideration on his part. He did not want, now, at this last hour, to reopen the old wounds. She put the note carefully away with his photograph.

Cambridge was beginning to look deserted. Only a few figures hurried across Harvard Yard, and up at Radcliffe the lawns were no longer criss-crossed by chattering, brightly clad figures. Grace was at home and glad to be there, as she had announced on a gleeful postcard. Merton Dennison must by now have started work on the Texas *Evening Journal*, fortified by a Hawthorne autograph for which he had written an enthusiastic note of thanks: '*I'll see you in England,*' it had ended; he already had a future cut out for himself as a war correspondent. ('*Of course there'll be a war.*')

How sad endings were, Susan thought on her last Sunday morning, as she stood looking out the drawing room window at the river where only a few white-sailed boats still hurried to and fro. They were all scattering, all separating; there would never be quite the same good times again. Already the old, everyday things were bathed in a rosy nostalgic haze: lunches with Grace at their drugstore; her troubles with Anglo-Saxon; Merton Dennison, kind and irrepressible; David . . .

A key grated in the lock. Mrs Morton was home from church. The familiar rhythm played itself out for the last time: Mary took the ice-cream ("Coffee and peppermint stick," said Mrs Morton), and Mrs Morton came creaking up in the elevator and joined Susan in the drawing room. "Nobody here yet? Really, George is the most unpunctual boy, but I'm surprised at Roger and the twins. They aren't usually late for their old Gran."

Roger is completely a member of the family now, Susan thought as the front door bell rang. First the twins, apologising in chorus, then Roger, breathless, and finally George and Betty Larraby, too full of wedding plans to notice that they were late. Roger opened the sherry bottle. Conversation flowed more easily. Next week Mrs Morton would be in Maine; George and Betty on their honeymoon; Susan on the Atlantic.

As the plans were bandied to and fro, Susan felt already excluded. Mrs Morton had jumped ahead to the coming winter. She and Olga would do this, do that; they would go for drives, go out to visit Roger . . . "How we shall miss you, Susan," she said once in perfunctory tribute, and passed on instantly to more plans. *It is time to go home*, Susan thought, they were forgetting her already. Besides, she was forgetting them, her thoughts vagrant and preoccupied on the other side of the Atlantic. Incredible that she had ever thought of staying. And yet, now, when she realised this, she also realised for the first time that she had strangely, unexpectedly, incredibly been happy here. But it was all over, all in the past tense.

Ralph and Randall were staying on to go to their cousin's wedding. "The first I've ever been to," said Ralph.

"Me, too," said Randall.

Mary leaned against the kitchen door to hear all about it: Betty Jane in cream coloured satin and her grandmother's veil . . .

"Dearie me," said Mrs Morton, "how it does take me

back . . ." Coffee was served before the tide of reminiscence ebbed.

"How about a drive?" Roger asked Susan as he helped her dry the dishes. "I've got to be back to meet Olga at six, but that leaves us lots of time."

"What a nice idea. Of course I've got dozens of things to do, but I expect they can wait."

The trees were green beside the turnpike, and in Concord the air was heavy with the scent of syringa. Roger slowed down. "Would you mind if I just dashed into School for a second? I've been meaning to call up, but this would be better."

"Of course not."

Roger parked the car outside the school gates and Susan sat dreamily gazing at the Sunday stream of cars. Suddenly she stiffened. Surely that was David's car that was approaching so slowly? But David never drove slowly. Or only when his arm was round her. There was time for the memory to overwhelm her: "At least a modicum of caution," she remembered his laugh.

The car was David's and David was driving it. Beside him, close beside him, with her face tilted up towards him, was a dark, laughing girl. His head was bent to hers, his eyes half-turned from the road and only one hand (they were past, but Susan was sure of it), only one hand on the wheel.

She sat on, staring at the cars that passed. *Josephine*, said a refrain in her head, *Josephine is fair and thirty*. The dark girl? Twenty; perhaps a year or so more. "*I'm worried about him*," Julia had said. "*Good luck, Susan*," his letter: such a quick, a casual farewell. The scent of syringa filled the car. A thrush was singing on a telegraph pole nearby. *Josephine is fair and thirty*, answered the refrain in her heart. *Poor Josephine.*

Roger found her sitting staring at vacancy. "I'm awfully sorry to keep you so long," he started the car. "I got involved."

"That's all right," Susan said. "I really didn't notice."

Chapter Twenty

The organ burst into '*Here comes the bride*', and Betty Jane Larraby appeared, cream satin, veil and all. The church was full of roses. Tomorrow, the drive to New York; next day, the sea. It was all a kaleidoscope now: the happiness, the misery; Concord and South Kingston; David teasing her; plans for how they would announce their engagement; her own white satin, fully-fashioned in her imagination. All of it now, memory and fancy alike, had the same quality of dream.

The congregation subsided with a rustle of summer dresses. The service had begun. It was odd not to have his chain and ring around her neck. Mechanically, she rose for the prayer. Just the same, she was glad she had not given in to her first impulse and sent them back to him. Besides, what could she have said? Thank goodness she would not be seeing Julia again. Poor Julia. Did she know?

In bridesmaid's taffeta, Olga looked even more handsome than usual. Bad luck on Betty Jane, really. Olga was always eclipsing her: first at her engagement party, and now . . . But could one really be eclipsed at one's own wedding? For a minute, the old vision had life and she saw herself standing beside David at the altar. Then it faded for the last time. *And I'm not going to cry either*, she thought, sliding forward to kneel, *what a blessing*.

After that, there was only the sensation of time. It was

strung into moments; they slipped past, hesitated for an instant, then vanished for ever. There was the wedding reception at the Larrabys': the parlourmaids more starched than ever; Roger and Olga plying her with champagne. How nice they were to her. Illuminated and released by her second glass, she told them so, and they laughed and told her it was because they were fond of her. "The oldest friend of the family," said Roger with portentous and alcoholic solemnity.

The morning swallowed itself and was gone. All that remained were a headache and a bit of confetti in her shoe. Coming in to help her pack, Olga confessed that she had a headache, too. "A pretty state of affairs for your last day. What would you like to do, Susan?"

Susan looked at the pile of clothes on her bed. "Finish packing, to begin with."

Olga laughed and kneeled down by the trunk. "Here, pass them along."

Despite the headaches, it was a light-hearted business. "You're glad to be going really, aren't you?" Olga said as they sat, side by side, on the trunk to lock it.

"Yes. It's odd, but I am."

"It isn't odd at all. Ah, there's Roger." The doorbell had rung. "Am I as dirty as you are?"

They washed their faces and went downstairs. Mrs Morton was in a state of plaintive reaction from the wedding.

"Everyone's getting married and going away," she said, "and I'll be left high and dry in this great house all by myself."

They cheered her with coffee and cookies and talk of plans for the winter until she agreed that Susan should be taken for a drive as it was her last afternoon.

"Besides," she said, "my poor old head aches frightfully and I think a little nap will do me good."

Roger's car was outside. "Well, where's it to be?" he asked as they got in. "Any preferences, Susan?"

She had been thinking. "Could we go up to Cape Ann? I've got a ghost to lay."

"Of course. Lay as many as you like."

Fruit blossom was in its glory in the gardens they passed. They watched it silently, sleepy with champagne and sunshine. "Just wake me if you see me going off," Roger said. "You're a lucky girl, Susan, to have eight days to sleep on the boat."

When they turned onto the cliff road beyond Gloucester he turned to Susan. "Does this ghost inhabit any particular bit?"

"Yes," Susan said. "A place called Pigeon's Cove."

"Shows good taste, anyway," remarked Olga.

Pigeon's Cove was deserted. The sea was high and blue, the sky cloudless. Susan looked around. She had really expected to find David and the dark girl there. But there was no one, there was not even a ghost. Or if there was, it was only her own that waited there, still looking out at a grey sea, still murmuring, perplexed and miserable, "I don't know."

Did she know now? Did the blue summer sea hold answers that the autumn one had withheld? Was she sorry it had all happened? She looked from sea to sky and from sky to sea. What was the use of being sorry? It had happened. It was over. Anyway, she was not sorry; not for herself, at any rate.

Olga and Roger had lingered by the car. Now they joined her. "Well," Roger asked after a quick look at her, "how are the ghosts?"

"Laid, thank you," she said. "And it's positively my last appearance as tragedy queen, Roger. Isn't it a comfort? Just think," she pointed. "England's over there."

The road back flickered and was gone. Afterwards, she remembered a late tea when they all discovered they were extremely hungry, and much merriment over the English muffins. Then, supper, with Mary leaning against the kitchen door and remembering Ireland, until Mrs Morton scolded her into the kitchen for more rolls, or water, or the lemon meringue pie ("Your favourite dessert, Susan").

Mrs Morton pronounced the evening's epitaph: "I expect it'll be a long time before I have such a nice bridge four again. Susan, it's high time you were in bed."

And in bed she was, tossing, ghost-ridden and, she was sure, set for a sleepless night; but, no, it was morning. There was only breakfast – fish, because it was Friday – the sun shining for the last time on the dust of the old dining room . . . Then Roger had the car at the door; there were goodbyes: Mrs Morton, a stammering attempt at thanks, a hearty kiss (what an old dear she was); Mary, who had taken out her feelings in an enormous picnic lunch; Ginger, unconcerned in his basket.

"Come on," said Roger. "I hate to be brutal, but we ought to get going."

She loved it all: the red brick of Beacon Hill, the golden dome of the Capitol, the gleaming river . . . And on the other side was Harvard; Dunster House, red and white in the sunshine . . . But it all went too fast; there was no time to think or to feel anything but a general dazzlement. She found herself almost grudging while she was grateful for the speed of it.

There were more roses: crimson and white and golden in Connecticut gardens; scarlet ramblers all along the banks of the Merritt Parkway . . . Then chicken for lunch (the inevitable Brimmer Street chicken), with a bottle of Chianti that Roger had brought; and a sudden pang as she remembered another bottle and a winter picnic with David and Julia. *But that's over*. She passed the bottle to Roger. "What time do you think we'll get there?"

"Oh, lots of time to show you the sights of the town. Do you think the Rainbow Room, Olga?"

So they were drinking Scarlet O'Haras and Susan was remembering again. Impossible not to remember. David had wanted to show her Radio City. "You'd love it, Susan." What a darling he had been. He *had* loved her, too. Nothing that happened, nothing he did now could affect that. That was why it was all right. But poor David. What would happen to him?

An enormous regret washed through her. She turned to Olga. "If only," she began, then stopped. What was the use?

"If only?"

"Oh, nothing." She finished her drink.

Olga looked at Roger. "Come on and look at the view."

Susan stood almost breathless looking far down at the lights of the city. The dark patch was Central Park. Across it, fairy strings of lights. Then again, the irregular pattern of lighted buildings. All over the island people were sitting and talking in drawing rooms; children muttering in their sleep; mothers pausing for a minute in doorways ("Is he asleep at last?"); lovers turning towards each other in the darkness. It was late . . .

Susan sighed. "Goodness, I'm glad I came."

"Good," said Roger.

"To America, d'you mean?" Olga asked. "Or to New York?"

"Oh, both," Susan said. "All of it."

"I'm glad you've liked it."

Roger laughed. "You sound like a hostess, Olga, thanking her guest for thanking her."

"I feel like one. After all, Susan did loathe it at first, didn't you?"

"Oh, yes, like anything," Susan remembered.

"Well," said Olga, "there you are. So long as you don't regret any of it."

281

Susan looked again at the shining strings of light below. "Heavens, no," she said, "I don't regret a thing."

Not a thing, she repeated to herself next day as the ship moved down the river and she watched the skyscrapers march and countermarch in the morning sunshine, not a single thing. Even Olga and Roger, who had waved from the pier till the last minute, were shadows now, belonging to a bygone world, but neither they, nor any of its company of shadows, were to be forgotten or regretted. Only, she smiled down at a loaded ferry ahead, they were the past.

Looking up, she caught the eye of the tall young man who stood beside her at the rail. He smiled at her: "You look happy."

She smiled back. "Why, yes," she said, "I suppose I am."